WHEN THE KING
COMES HOME

TOR BOOKS BY CAROLINE STEVERMER

A COLLEGE OF MAGICS

WHEN THE KING COMES HOME

Caroline
Stevermer

TOR®

A TOM DOHERTY ASSOCIATES BOOK
New York

WHEN THE KING COMES HOME

Copyright © 2000 by Caroline Stevermer

This book is printed on acid-free paper.

Edited by Delia Sherman

A Tor Book
Published by Tom Doherty Associates, LLC
175 Fifth Avenue
New York, NY 10010

www.tor.com

Tor® is a registered trademark of Tom Doherty
Associates, LLC.

Library of Congress Cataloging-in-Publication Data

Stevermer, Caroline.
    When the king comes home / Caroline Stevermer. 1st ed.
        p. cm.
    "A Tom Doherty Associates book."
    ISBN 0-312-87214-3 (acid-free paper)
    1. Artists Fiction. I. Title.

PS3569.T4575 W49 2000
813'.54 dc21   00-031683

First Edition: November 2000

Printed in the United States of America

0 9 8 7 6 5 4 3 2 1

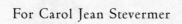

For Carol Jean Stevermer

ACKNOWLEDGMENTS

So many people helped me with this book, I fear an attempt at acknowledgment will only embarrass me, as I'm sure to forget someone crucial. This took so long to write and required so much grumbling (from me) and encouragement (from my friends) that I feel sheepish. How fortunate I am no stranger to that sensation. Even the erudition, wisdom, and fortitude of these people could not protect me from my mistakes, although they tried their level best. My deepest gratitude, therefore, to Barbara T. Ashkar, Charlotte Boynton, Mary and Jerry Dahlstrom-Salic, Pamela Dean, E. Ryan Edmonds, Beth Friedman, Greer Gilman, Mark Gorman, Theresa Gurney, Beth Hillemann, Ellen Kushner, Alex McKenzie, Janet Myers, Leslie Schultz, Delia Sherman, Eve Sweetser, Jody Tanji, Betty G. Uzman, Betty T. Uzman, Erica Winston, Angela Wrapson, and Patricia Wrede. I am, for a wide variety of reasons, forever in your debt.

WHEN THE KING COMES HOME

ONE

(In which I am born into a family of wool merchants.)

I was born on the coldest day of the year. When the midwife handed me to my father, he said, "Hail the newcomer! Hardy the traveler who ventures forth on such a day."

After four sons, my family was pleased to have a daughter at last. My father persuaded my mother that I should be named Hail, to commemorate the welcome I'd been given. My name is a greeting, dignified and sober, not a form of bad weather.

My family is in the wool trade and are as hardworking as they are prosperous. My earliest memory is of chasing my brothers through the wool market, a maze of bundles and bales, a mob of people haggling. Fleece in every shade from purest white to dusty black, in every stage, from unwashed and full of burrs to neat bales ready to be shipped downriver—all were there in plenty, for Neven was a busy place in those days, the most prosperous town in northwestern Galazon.

I am not too old to travel home to Neven, even yet. That day will come, but I could still make a journey of moderate length, given a proper escort and sufficient preparation. I don't choose to visit there, though I have no doubt my brothers' families would welcome me. I'd rather remember it as it was, a clean and quiet town. My memories range beyond the town itself, from the heights where the flocks spent the summer in wild and open country above the forests that filled the crooked valleys below. Stands of the great old trees were cut even in my youth, sent down the river tied in rafts to feed the shipwrights of

Shene. Since then, I'm told, the forests have been much reduced. (I don't wish to see it now.) Neven was always a sleepy place, and I prefer the city. Aravis itself can seem sadly quiet to me now.

There are benefits to a quiet life. I have more work to do than there are hours of daylight, but the nights are long. The time has come to write down what I've learned. I've studied the notebooks and treatises written by the masters who have gone before me. It is my turn to set down what I have learned and to explain how I learned it. May this work please those with the wit to read it and instruct those with the wish to learn. I have only the ordinary skill at writing, but if I do not at least attempt to set down my experiences, all will go to waste when I am dead.

Waste was something my family could never abide. My parents expected all their children to work, and to work hard, boy and girl alike. To allow us to neglect our wits through insufficient education was folly, and so we were all set to study with Master Nicholas, a schoolmaster engaged to teach the children of the members of the wool merchants guild.

In addition to our hours at school with Master Nicholas, my brothers and I learned everything about the family business, from tending a flock to keeping the accounts. I was not permitted to do any of these things unaccompanied, at any rate not for long, but by the time I was thirteen I had a full understanding of what we Rosamers did for a living and of just how many of us there were. With so many brothers ahead of me to choose the tasks they liked the best, I had to work hard at each thing to learn the work and earn praise for my skill. At that age, it was not yet clear to me what my role would be.

Some families might have stinted a fifth child, boy or girl, but mine was determined to make the best use of each of us, just as our family made a point of making the best use of each part of every sheep, from a hank of fleece to the toughest mutton chop. My mother held me to an even higher standard than my brothers, for in addition to my schooling and my work in our family trade, I was taught how to keep household accounts. I learned what was needed to make sure that we had sufficient food, shelter, and clothing. Aside from the size of the numbers in the ledger, it was not very different from learning the business. Smaller sums, but the work was just as hard.

For the first few years of my life, I displayed no more genius than any child does, though I liked to make pictures with bits of charcoal or chalk or anything else of that nature which came my way. My brothers delighted in teasing me for this, but I learned soon enough that there was an element of envy in their merriment.

Each year at Twelfth Night, my brothers helped Father's apprentices with the revels, sometimes devising masques or plays. When I was fourteen, I began to help with the costumes. This gave my mother false hope. She was well versed in the arts of needlework and would have taught me much had I shown the slightest interest. But I had no use for practicality. To set a sleeve into a gaudy doublet, that it might adorn the Master of the Revels, was worth squinting over for hours. To hem a petticoat, for no better reason than to adorn myself, I considered a waste of time.

This is folly, and one common to young artists. For the same apprentice who will work hours, days, and weeks to design and cast a frippery cloak pin will scorn the pains it takes to make a simple pewter spoon. Look well to the spoons, the tankards, and the porringers, for in the old simplicity is found greater art than in the new style. More art and use in that honest petticoat hem than in a dozen such doublets, run up in haste for holiday attire.

By the time I was a gawky girl of fifteen I had used up the schoolmaster's patience. Master Nicholas presented my parents with an ultimatum. I must either pretend to pay attention to his lessons or find some other use for my time. In any case, I was to stop drawing caricatures on my slate. It distracted the other girls and boys. He suggested I be put to some honest labor. As my brothers were all deeply interested in the family business, there was no need for me to manage accounts. But perhaps, with time and application, I might manage to make a competent shepherdess. With a qualified dog to help me, of course.

There was some merit in this suggestion of his, for I had a strong back and long legs. Many other families would have considered my sturdy frame qualification enough for the outdoor life.

Fortunately, my parents were in no particular hurry to see their youngest out the door. Since he had seen a good many of my caricatures, my father thought Master Nicholas was merely offended by my latest effort at portraying him.

My mother found worth in what Master Nicholas said, however, and the pair of them spent a merry quarter of an hour suggesting trades for me. The thought of me as a nun made them laugh the hardest. I didn't see what was so funny, but I was of an age that seldom saw humor where people of my parents' advanced years did.

When he had wiped his eyes and rested his ribs, Master Nicholas looked across the table at my mother and said, "Hail will be a nun when the king comes home. But I was at school with Angelica Carriera. She has an atelier in Aravis. Shall I write her to see if she has room for another apprentice?"

I gaped at him. Even I had heard of Angelica Carriera. She was a famous painter. The old king himself had paid her to capture his likeness. Her paintings hung in palaces and Master Nicholas knew her? To write to? Why do people never tell one the important things? I made it clear to everyone that this was the most brilliant idea Master Nicholas had ever had.

Mother glanced at Father, who was pretending to poke the fire. "It's too soon."

"Aravis?" Father looked at me. "It's too far."

"It's just down the river," I protested. "You go there every year with the woolpack and the timber."

"Only once a year. You're much too young to live in the city all alone."

"Most apprenticeships begin at fourteen," said Master Nicholas. "Though Hail does sometimes seem quite young for her age. She would hardly be alone in a studio like Angelica's."

"Madame Carriera may not wish to have another apprentice," said Mother.

"If she is as prosperous as people say, she must keep several apprentices busy just cleaning her brushes," said Father. "I suppose it does no harm to inquire."

*   *   *

Master Nicholas sent his letter a few days later, and in a month the reply came back. Provisionally, I was acceptable. I was to travel down-river with the next shipment of wool. In Aravis, I might be chosen to join the apprentices who helped clean Madame Carriera's brushes. If I applied myself, and if I behaved myself, well, Madame Carriera would see what she could make of me.

It was a very brief letter, considering how much I read into it. I had an entire filigree of meaning embroidered around each line. To me it all seemed clear beyond possibility of error. My opportunity at Madame Carriera's was a promise of success, for surely there would be no limit to my hard work. I would live in Aravis, the center of the world, and I would learn everything Madame Carriera had to teach me. I would learn all her techniques. I would invent new forms of art. Fortune was assured, and fame would surely follow. Undying admiration would be mine, deservedly, and any student of art would learn my name along with the greatest of painters.

There are no slower days in life than those between the promise and the performance of one's release into the world. I am better at waiting than I was then (not saying much), but I would not relive those impatient days before my departure for the great world of art. I couldn't survive it now. The strain would kill me. What I wanted, now that I knew at last what it was I wanted, I wanted with every fiber. What I knew, I wished the whole world to know. What I wondered, and in my impatience I wondered about almost everything, I wondered ceaselessly.

I am surprised my family did not disown me during those fretful weeks. Certainly they must have been as glad to see me go as I was to take my leave.

The way to Aravis was a familiar one to my father. The wool trade took him there every year. From Neven, the water route ran down the Ruger to the broader current of the Lida. The Lida, made stronger yet by its union with the sleepy Celle at Ardres, passed between the Folliard Hills to the east and the higher, bleaker Howlet Fells to the west. I had studied the maps at school without interest. From the river, I found every mile exciting.

First there was the woolpack to load. The fleeces were baled and stacked on a raft of logs from the forests around Neven. There was an art to lashing the logs together and a greater art to stacking the bales of fleece. Too high was dangerous, as was too low, and too heavy. Anything else was not economical. With one trip downriver a year, waste was unthinkable. By the time we set out we had the best possible raft with the safest arrangement of bales. My father and his men were responsible for navigating the river. I was not permitted to help. Sitting quietly on the cargo was my job.

My mother and my brothers came to wave us off. I didn't cry. There was nothing to cry about, after all. I was setting forth to seek my fortune, a joyous occasion. It bothered me that my mother wiped her eyes with her white handkerchief more than she waved us on with it. I understand that better now, but I still remember my impatience at her sentiment.

The Ruger is a narrow river. In places it is deep. I had all I could do keeping still, such was my excitement as our craft was shepherded past the difficulties of the current. At the end of the third day, the Ruger flowed into the Lida, and it seemed our pace eased. The river does not run more slowly; it is that the water is wider. As the banks fall back, the world seems to withdraw. Broad water reflects the sky as the horizon drops. Half the world is air. After the hills of Galazon, it seemed flat as a table to me; for the weather was bad, lowering clouds shutting the distance out.

In three more days we came to the great tooth of Ardres, jutting up at the confluence of the Lida and the Arcel. The castle on the rock guarded the whole valley, stone wall within stone wall, rising to slate-roofed towers only a shade darker than the sky.

There was a storm that night. We traveled on despite it. Delays ashore could be as bad as any river snag. By morning, the weather had cleared, so we could see the green waves of the Folliard Hills to our east and the raking bleakness of the Howlet Fells off in the heights to our west. The river ran colder, it seemed to me, the farther from home we traveled. There were waterfowl in plenty, the familiar ducks and geese and heron of home, and new kinds, birds I couldn't name. They were the birds of the sea. I marveled at the variety of them, the differences in wing and head, markings and mode of flight. What else might the world hold, if it could hold so many things so new to me?

The seagulls were my first sign of the world waiting for me in Aravis. By the time we tied up at the wharf in Shene, I was almost used to them. There was too much more to notice. I couldn't keep still any longer. The very air smelled different, a compound of fish and sweat, for even in the little town of Shene there were more people than I had even seen before. I could hardly keep to my father's heels as we found our way through the crowds toward Aravis, so often were we jostled.

Maps at school meant nothing to me. In Aravis, I longed for one. I was glad to follow my father, but I didn't like not knowing what streets we were on. Our few possessions were left at an inn where Father often stayed when he was in Aravis. How would I ever find my way back there if we were separated? I could probably follow my nose back to the wharf easily enough, but I had no interest in Shene. All my heart was set on finding Madame Carriera.

My father knew the way. Through streets packed with houses as tightly as our raft was packed with wool, he led me past more people than I'd ever dreamed could fit into one place. The noise, the smells, the half steps and haltings all conspired to confuse me, yet only my body was lost. My mind was fixed as a needle toward a lodestone, focused on our destination. The rest was mere detail.

Madame Carriera's house seemed large and high ceilinged to me that first day. There was a distinctive scent to the place, a combination of familiar household smells, lavender and beeswax, but with a sharp overlay I could not identify—until I boiled my first batch of sheep parchment into liquid and combined it with chalk to make gesso. After the bustle of the streets outside, the house was quiet. A girl with red hair showed us the way into Madame Carriera's salon and left us there. After a short wait, the great painter joined us.

At that time Madame Carriera was probably in her middle forties. To me she seemed prodigiously old. She was tiny, and as finely made, as tightly laced, as any lady of fashion, but no one could ever mistake her for an ordinary person. Her eyes were keen, almost piercing. Her merest glance had force, and her hands were a revelation. I was vain of my own hands, which were slender and fairly well shaped. I had recently come to fancy they were proof of my artistic nature. But Madame Carriera's hands rid me of any such foolish notion. Madame Carriera's hands were as swift and sure as a hawk's flight, as elegant as ivory.

My father was a tall man, but well knit and graceful for his size. He loomed over Madame Carriera, who was the picture of courtly grace in black velvet and boned lace, wearing pearls worth our whole season's woolpack.

She looked him up and down, glanced dismissively at me, and demanded, "Where is my earth of cullen?" At our blank expressions, she frowned. "My umber. Nick promised to send some with you. It lies about on the ground where you come from. Or so he claimed in his letter."

"Master Nicholas did entrust me with a parcel for you, Madame Carriera," said Father. He caught himself slouching a little to meet her eyes and drew himself up straight. "But he said it was pigment. Cologne brown. It is with our gear at the Sheepcrook. I will send for it now if you wish. I didn't think city folk went about with parcels when they paid calls."

"It looks like dirt," I said, "and it is very heavy."

She hardly spared me a glance. "The parcel can wait," she said to Father. "I see you brought a baggage with you." She smiled at him then, and the stiffness went out of his shoulders as he smiled back. "Nick can be such a pedant. Thank you, then, for troubling to bring me my Cologne brown. Earth of cullen is its common name." She turned to me then. "I may teach you to grind my colors for me, girl. And more, if you pay attention. What's your name again? Nick put it in his letter, but my memory grows worse by the day."

"Hail Rosamer."

"Good heavens." She looked at Father. "What were you thinking? Why not give her a sensible name, like Daisy? Or even Maud. She can't help growing up a virago with an extraordinary name like that."

"She's an extraordinary person. She will be a great artist."

I felt my eyes sting with love and pride and embarrassment. I had always known my parents loved me, yet to hear Father speak so to Madame Carriera herself nearly choked me. I treasure the memory now, but when I was fifteen the embarrassment of it nearly killed me.

Madame Carriera sniffed. "Nick thinks she can draw."

"She can do whatever she sets her mind to."

"We'll soon see about that. Here, girl." She tossed me a stub of chalk as if it were a sweetmeat and I a dog. "Draw me a circle."

I caught the chalk. Then I looked around the room. Madame Carriera's salon was very elegantly furnished, but there was no sign of artistic activity to be seen. Not so much as a scrap of paper. "Where, ma'am?"

"Anywhere. But I just had the walls done last summer, so leave them alone. The floor is slate. That will do."

If there is one thing every artist's apprentice learns, it is that the hardest shape to draw is a perfect circle. But I was not an apprentice yet. I had no training, and so I did not know enough to worry about my circle. I was an ignorant girl, rawboned and ill-mannered, face hot with embarrassment over my father's pride in me.

So I knew no better than to sit cross-legged at Madame Carriera's feet. I found a spot that looked right to me, and I drew a chalk circle about nine inches in diameter on the well-scrubbed slate tiles.

She inspected the circle in silence. When she spoke at last, she sounded so gloomy that I looked up, fearful that I had done something irretrievably wrong. "It isn't a perfect circle."

I tilted my head and studied it from a fresh angle. "No? But it looks perfect."

"Draw me another."

Her gloom had shaken my confidence, and my second circle wobbled. "Would you like me to try again?"

"No." She helped me to my feet. "That will do. You are willing to serve your apprenticeship with me? It is seven years, Hail."

"You still want me? Even though the second circle was crooked?"

"It is only on the strength of your second circle that I am willing to take you at all. If all your circles were like your first, you'd have nothing to learn from the likes of me."

"But even the first one wasn't perfect."

"Perfection abides in heaven, child. It looked perfect, that's what matters. Reason tells us there must be some flaw, though our eyes cannot perceive it. What is reason but a rumor? It is our eyes we trust." To Father, she said, "If she applies herself, and if she behaves herself, I will instruct her for seven years. And then we shall see."

Two

(In which I begin to work in the atelier of Madame Carriera.)

When first I learned to grind pigment for Madame Carriera, I fretted to make the brilliant colors. Vermilion, orpiment, ultramarine—to me the very sound of their names held magic. But her old-fashioned methods won out. Long before I ground my first sinopia, I understood that all colors, be they never so exotic, fall far below the king and queen of pigments: black and white.

Eventually I learned to find merit in the subtler colors—ocher, umber, staniel—and perhaps because I had brought it with me all the way from home, and because it was the first pigment I learned to grind, I grew to like earth of cullen best of all.

On my first day in Madame Carriera's service, I asked her why it was not earth of Neven, since the pigment came from Neven, not from Cologne.

Madame Carriera fixed me with a keen glance. "When you are famous for your use of it, you may call it earth of Neven, if you wish. You may call it Rosamer brown, if you wish. You may even call it ultramarine, if the whim strikes you and you think anyone will pay attention. Not yet a while though, girl."

"But it's from Neven."

"So are you. Yet you are living in Aravis now. While you are in my service, under my roof, you will call it earth of cullen. Is that clear?"

"You give it the wrong name, and you don't use my name at all, just 'girl' or 'child,' like you were calling a dog. I am in your service, and very grateful to be so, yet I'm not the only girl here. How will I know you are addressing me if you don't call me by my proper name?"

" 'Hail' can hardly be considered a proper name. What was your father thinking of, naming you so?"

"He was glad to see me, when I was born. So was Mother. It's my name, and if you keep calling me 'girl,' I'm not going to answer."

"I shall call you what I please, baggage. If you don't like it, you can go home."

"My parents want you to instruct me. If I am to use the wrong words for things just because you tell me so, I think they'd rather I went home."

Madame Carriera studied me, eyes hooded. "Ocher."

I thought it over. "Yes, Madame. Ocher."

"You've plenty of the stuff left to grind."

"Yes, Madame."

"Get back to work, then. Girl."

"Yes . . . Madame."

"That will do. Finish that, and I'll show you the proper way to clean my brushes."

"Yes, *Madame*."

There were three apprentices in Madame Carriera's workshop when I joined: Gabriel, Saskia, and Piers. As long as we worked well together, we did not have to get along. Yet often we did.

Gabriel was the most advanced apprentice, glad to be able to lord his own ability over us. He and his friends often modeled for each other. If you have ever seen a pouting Dionysus languish doe-eyed, his dark curls as rich and glossy as the grapes he holds, you have seen Gabriel. If he wasn't the actual model, he might as well have been. He was nearly as beautiful as he thought he was.

Saskia was next in age and ability—well able to size a panel or stretch a canvas. She preferred to work in metal. Luckily, Madame

Carriera was an old-fashioned taskmistress. She believed that we must learn all the skills proper to an artist, and that included metal smithing. Saskia had profited by her training so well that she could not only paint portraits but craft the settings. Her particular delight was in medallion portraiture, such as one sees on classical coins. Her taste was for things severe and aquiline, very refined. Except for her red hair (and the temper that so often accompanies it), she looked more like a cherub than anyone I have ever known, very rosy and cozy and round. Most deceptive.

Piers, a year younger than I, came next. He had the temperament which ought to have accompanied Saskia's cherubic looks. I had often wished for a younger brother, and Piers would have thus suited me admirably. He had sparkly eyes and rough brown hair, with a tuft that stuck up at the crown of his head like a little handle. At first I thought I was the only one who sometimes had the urge to yank that lock of hair. As I grew to know Madame Carriera and her apprentices better, I realized almost everyone had that urge. No wonder Piers was so nimble. He had to be.

It was lucky that Piers was good-natured, because it made it hard to be envious of him for long. Everyone had to envy him at least once a day, because Piers had art—high, true, unequivocal art—born in him. People sometimes speak kindly of my line. Well they may, for I have worked hard at my line and at times I produce works that nearly please me. Yet my line is nothing in comparison with Piers's, and his line was the least of his virtues.

Gabriel, Saskia, and Piers could all copy Madame Carriera's style without difficulty. I was ordered to learn the same, but it seemed strange to me.

"I haven't perfected my own style yet," I explained to Piers and the others. "How can I learn someone else's without influencing my own?" I was careful not to utter such heresy in Madame Carriera's hearing.

"You don't have a style," Saskia said. "You're not supposed to. You're here to help Madame Carriera. It's her style that matters."

"Are there many trees in Neven?" Piers asked solicitously.

Piers had never cared for my stories of home and family before. His abrupt interest made me wary. "Yes, lots. Why?"

"I thought there must be. If your style's been influenced, that's probably where the influence came from—all that wood."

It was inevitable that the other apprentices would tease me. I was a newcomer; I expected it. Indeed, with four older brothers, I was well prepared. For the first few days, Piers and Saskia had busied themselves sewing my pillow and my sheet together. They soon wearied of these mild entertainments. Gabriel preferred pranks that interrupted my studies, such as putting sand into my ocher. It was tiresome, but I held my peace.

After grinding pigment, the next task I learned was pouncing. A pounce bag is a soft cloth sack filled with charcoal ground to the finest powder. Pat the pounce bag on any surface, the result is a puff of charcoal.

The patterns our workshop used were made of stiff paper, each line of the drawing pricked out with a needle until it was a string of little holes, which, once vigorously pounced, left a delicate line of charcoal dots upon the surface beneath. Pin, say, a pattern for the Magdelene's draperies, or St. John the Baptist's feet, against the laboriously prepared ground of a fresh panel, pounce until the arm wearies, and remove the pattern. The essential line, whether of draperies or of feet, is there on the panel, waiting for the more detailed drawing to begin.

The pattern should then be shaken and brushed to recover as much charcoal dust as possible and the sheet folded away until the next Magdelene or John the Baptist is required. When the drawing on the panel is finished, all but the lightest trace of charcoal must be brushed away, lest it spoil the pigment to come. Pick out the traces in ink, let the last of the charcoal be removed, and you are ready for an ink wash to be laid down, the first truly irrevocable step in the painting.

The more detailed the drawing, the more experienced the apprentice who worked on the panel. Madame Carriera would sometimes do the most demanding under-drawing herself, removing lines she did not like with a flick of a crow's feather, putting in halftones and darker shadows with a stick of charcoal rubbed to a fine point with sandpaper.

I pounced too hard at first and made the air thick with charcoal dust. I pounced too lightly after that, until Piers showed me better. I pounced very well for a short time, until Gabriel took the bag away from me and pushed it down the back of my gown. Saskia helped me extricate it, then hurled it at Gabriel as he made for the door. The mark it left on his best shirt, square between his shoulder blades, was a tribute to the keenness of Saskia's eye and the strength of her arm.

It was as well the paper pattern had not yet been unpinned and that it was there to protect the surface of the panel, for quite a lot of things in the room were pounced before order was restored.

It took devoted study and much trial and error, but in a year's time I had mastered all the elementary tasks of the workshop. I could grind pigment into the characteristic colors of Madame Carriera's palette and lay those colors in the proper order on an immaculately prepared palette in the shades and shadows she preferred. Years it had taken her to learn the techniques that she had mastered, to use them to bring her ideas and vision to the blank perfection of the panel.

"Who were you apprenticed to?" I asked her once, when I was bored with cleaning brushes. "Who taught you?"

"My father trained me." Madame Carriera's sharp eyes softened. "In his apprenticeship, he served Troilus of Vienna, who was a great deal more demanding of his apprentices than I am. You're allowed to grind pigment from the apothecary. Father and the other children in Troilus's atelier had to learn the very stones of the earth to find the proper ingredients for their colors."

"I know earth of cullen," I reminded her. "I don't see the point, though. Why go digging in the dirt, looking for shades of brown, when the apothecaries have material from all over the world? It's much faster to find the whole palette at the apothecary shops."

"There's more to craft than making haste. Clean the big hog bristle brush again—do it slowly this time, and perhaps I won't make you repeat the process."

"I suppose they had to make their own brushes too."

"No, but that's a good idea. Make yourself a hog bristle brush like that one, good and big. I'll give you a week before I ask to see it."

"Of course it would be a big hog bristle brush I'm ordered to make."

"Don't mutter. Hog bristle is easy to come by. I could have been stern and ordered you to make a brush of miniver—you could buy a herd of pigs for what that would cost you."

Of all the lessons Madame Carriera set me, I found imitating her style to be the hardest of all. Grinding pigments, blending the colors with oil to make paints and glazes, even binding hog bristles, stiff as wire, into a brush, I managed. To see as Madame Carriera saw, to yield my line to hers, that was difficult.

It was like learning a language for which I had no aptitude. I had to give up my way of thinking, order my sense of line and shape to another kind of vision.

It was that long space after trying in earnest to learn that was the hardest, a long cold empty time of fearing I was unable to muster such skills, of feeling shame at my ineptitude, my ignorance. Some birds can sing, some birds cannot. I feared that my skill was limited and that I had come near to the end of it.

Saskia encouraged me. Piers gave me all the help he could. Even Gabriel showed pity, forbearing to tease me for long weeks as I ruined panel and paper, reduced to scratching on a slate to keep from wasting materials for no reason. I grew sad and seemed always to have a sniffle, if not a complete cold. I parted my hair in the center and pulled it back into a braid so tight it made my eyebrows look surprised. I prayed and lit candles and gave up dancing. It was like a never-ending Lenten season, all striving and no assurance of Easter.

Then one day I held my wrist a different way, made some invisible adjustment to the way my charcoal met the slate. The line I drew looked more like Madame Carriera's than my own. The next attempt was better, the third better still. In a few days, I was back at ink washes, and this time I could see the shades of gray as she might see them, shape them in her manner. Long and long it took, before I could see her colors as I saw her monotones. I had patience for the struggle. I had learned a few words of her visual language. I could structure them as she did. I knew, at least, I could learn. The joy that knowledge gave me made my confidence soar. If I could learn a little, I could learn it all.

The days, which had seemed so burdensome and long, grew too short to contain all I wished to do. I combed out my hair and let it float in a dark unruly cloud down my back. Piers pulled it now and then, repaying me for the times I couldn't resist a tug at his. I felt taller and stronger, and I never caught cold. The world widened around me, no longer confined to the workshop or the garret.

Madame Carriera's house was in the oldest part of the city, at the end of Giltspur Street. The house had once belonged to a goldsmith who kept a shop on the ground floor. She had made few changes to the place.

The level above the shop contained the salon, where Madame Carriera received callers, and her private quarters. The level above that, which was high enough that the windows actually let in enough light to work by, contained Madame's studio and workrooms. Above that, at the very top of the house, were the slant-ceilinged garret rooms.

Gabriel and Piers had a small room at the front of the house, while Saskia and I shared an even smaller room at the back. The light would have been excellent, had the windows not been painted shut and then encrusted on the outside with years of dust and grime. In the summer, the heat was cruel; in the winter, the cold a constant source of misery. When we complained, Madame Carriera acidly remarked that she did not expect us to spend much time in our rooms.

When I remembered them, I missed my family. Madame Carriera kept me too busy to brood, but sometimes I missed them very much. When, after just a few days, my father left me to return to Neven, my heart had felt bruised. Yet how could I regret staying in Aravis? It was my heart's desire to live there.

Aravis was at that time a thriving, beautiful place, one of the wonders of the world. Of course it is still beautiful in its gaunt way, but the culture, the society, the splendor, and the pride that every citizen knew in my day—all that is past and gone. Modern manners, that is what we have now instead of culture, drabness instead of splendor.

In those days, there was little formal activity at court. The king was old and ailing. The business of rule he surrendered to the prince-bishop, who thus represented church and state in one person. There were no obvious heirs, but no one doubted that the prince-bishop would choose the proper successor and control the next king as utterly as he had this one.

Stability, and confidence that stability would continue, was the great treasure of Aravis. The provinces that made up the Lidian Empire all looked to Aravis for direction. Aravis, in the person of the prince-bishop, provided it.

Aravis was rich in more than mere stability. There were some beggars, to be sure, but nothing to what we see these days. There was the usual amount of daily misery, there must have been, but we did not go looking for more by mourning each day that passed and making boast of our own sins.

The prosperity of Aravis was founded in trade, yet the merchants who made the city rich were no misers. Openhanded, they vied to demonstrate their worth through their devotion to the arts. No mere pious donors of votive objects, these merchants. They let their names be enhanced by all the arts. It was possible for a hard worker to earn a good living in those days. There were mummers and dancers and actors and singers, and the very liveliness of the city made the competition fierce. The degree of art and skill displayed, even by a band of mummers, made merely walking the length of a street fair a rare entertainment.

When someone wished for Madame Carriera to paint a portrait, the client did not simply saunter in and ring for service. Far from it. Most of Madame's patrons were folk of wealth, a few of them of high degree.

She was usually invited to wait upon them, which she sometimes would consent to do. More often, an exchange of messages would establish a mutually convenient time, and Madame would receive her prospective patron in her salon. She reasoned that most of the work was done in her own studio, so the subject would have to find his way there eventually. Why not start out with the upper hand if she could possibly arrange it?

It was such a negotiation Madame Carriera had embarked upon, a diplomatic campaign that would culminate in at least three sittings in a good north light, with Lord Stanimir, in February of my second year of training. She dispatched me with a message to Lord Stanimir's quarters in the palace. I had never been inside the palace before, though of course I knew precisely where it was. It loomed over Aravis.

I was leaving Giltspur Street for the palace when Gabriel caught up with me.

"Ho, Madame Rosamer." He fell into step beside me. "Off to the palace? What time is your audience with the prince-bishop?"

"I'm to deliver this message to Lord Stanimir." It was better not to correct Gabriel. Firm statements of fact worked best.

"I know. I heard Madame Carriera. But you haven't been to the palace yet, have you? How could you know the way?"

"I can't miss it."

"Do you know the way inside, I meant. The palace is a city within a city."

"I'm sure I can ask for directions if I go astray."

"Ah, but whom will you ask?" He pinched my cheek. "You don't realize how tempting a morsel like you can be. If you ask the wrong man, you may be led even further astray before you know it."

I caught his earlobe and held on firmly, letting him feel my nails. A good hard pinch there hurt more than it did on the cheek. "Keep your hands to yourself."

"Yes, Madame Rosamer. By all means, Madame Rosamer." Gabriel eased back a step, and I released him. Chastened, he asked, "Would you like me to show you the best way?"

"You don't have to. The palace doesn't intimidate me."

"Doesn't it? That's odd. Palaces are supposed to intimidate every-one."

"Then I'm surprised you are so eager to go there."

"It's for Madame Carriera, isn't it? Lord Stanimir awaits her message. Why delay?"

"That's true. The sooner he gets the message, the sooner they can agree on terms. Very well. Since you know the best way there, I'd be grateful for your help."

"Think nothing of it, Madame Rosamer. Pray, take my arm."

I didn't take Gabriel's arm, but I did let him show me the way into the palace.

Hardly had we been admitted (through the servants' entrance, naturally—so much for Gabriel's savoir faire) when his motives became all too clear. Foolishly, I followed Gabriel blindly through corridor after corridor, not marking my way. Then I allowed him to hold the door for me, as I preceded him into what he referred to as Lord Stanimir's antechamber. While I gaped around me at the splendid room, Gabriel plucked Madame Carriera's message from my hand and closed the door behind me, latching it so that I could do nothing but rap on the iron-bound oak and call out in vain.

Need I explain that I was not in Lord Stanimir's antechamber? Far from it. I found myself alone and locked in, for the time being, in one of the most beautiful rooms in Aravis, if not the world itself. Gabriel had lured me into the Archangel Chapel, the chapel royal, in which I found that wonder of the world, the two-century-old altarpiece painted by Miriamne Giuliana at the order of Queen Andred herself: the Archangel Nativity.

I daresay there were benches, choir stalls, and a pulpit too. I saw nothing but the altarpiece. It drew me from my tantrum at the locked door. I forgot the message Madame Carriera had entrusted to my care. I forgot the perfidious Gabriel. I forgot everything but the play of light on that treasure of an altarpiece.

There, at the heart of everything, was the Christ Child in the manger. Miriamne Giuliana must have known her stables. This was a real manger, and she had caught the glint of a divine light on real straw. Beyond that central radiance, the Holy Family was there, and beyond them, slightly—but only slightly—shadowed, the shepherds and the three kings. The ox and the ass, the sheaf of wheat on the stable floor, symbols that hold their meaning as the rosebud holds the rose, all were there in the perfect chiaroscuro that had made Miriamne Giuliana famous. And in colors that only Giuliana's palette could have captured and kept down the years, angels filled the panels, spilled outward and upward over the walls and ceiling. Seraphim, cherubim, thrones, dominions, virtues, powers, principalities, archangels, and angels—partaking in a heavenly flight, an orderly beat of wings toward the miracle in the manger, a dance of light.

It might have been only a moment that I stood there, transfixed. It might have been a year and a day or an eternity. Most likely, it was an hour.

The choristers roused me, throwing the chapel doors wide and filing in for their rehearsal. I seized the choirmaster's sleeve and tugged him close to the lower left corner panel of the altarpiece. "Tell me," I demanded, "who are they?"

I knew the repertory players in the company, the shepherds and the kings. I had picked out the attendant saints and deciphered their identities by the attributes they carried: St. Barbara and her tower, St. John all unkempt and cuddling his lamb, St. Rieul and his frog. But in the lower left corner, modestly trailing the saints, were three figures I could not identify, a man and a woman, richly dressed and crowned, and behind them, another man, bareheaded, a crusader's tabard over his armor. They were painted as well as the saints, yet there was something more in their faces, something that made me sure that Miriamne Giuliana had taken care to portray them exactly as she saw them.

"Those are the donors," the choirmaster told me. "That is King Julian the Fourth and his queen, Andred the Fair."

When I was a girl, we would often say, when some good though unlikely thing was anticipated, that it would happen "when the king comes home." I remember my mother telling me as much when I, at the age of eight, announced that my next pair of shoes would be red. "Perhaps," Mother said, which I was already old enough to know meant no, "when the king comes home."

Master Nicholas had once enlivened a school day by explaining to us some of the history behind the unconsidered phrases in common use. "Ashes, ashes all fall down," for example, was a relic of the Black Death. That contagion, as we have never yet forgotten, announced itself in its earliest stages with a fit of sneezing. Thus, "ashes, ashes" was a relic of *"achoo, achoo."*

The king of "when the king comes home" was Julian IV, Good King Julian himself. He was reckoned Good King Julian for winning us honorable peace with the Austrians after persuading the Viennese of his subjects' might and valor. He died unexpectedly, some said of a fever, some said of poison, on that visit to Vienna, and there was difficulty involved in returning his remains to be interred with appropriate ceremony at the Abbey of St. Istvan in Dalager. He died in high summer, and the means of preserving bodies were no more advanced then than they are now. His bones were preserved and, at the conclusion of a lengthy series of treaty negotiations between his royal successor and the Austrian government, returned for burial at Dalager. Hence, the belief that there had been a delay in the king's coming home and, inevitably, the rumor that the bones the Viennese sent to Lidia belonged to someone else, that the true King Julian IV did not rest with his royal kin in the dimly lit Abbey of St. Istvan.

In its own way, this story tells you everything you need to know about how we Lidians of Aravis think of the Austrian Empire. Yet perhaps in the expression *when the king comes home* there was captured another grain of truth, which Master Nicholas never dreamed of. Or perhaps Master Nicholas was merely wrong from first to last in that lesson. He sometimes was mistaken.

One day, all well-meant promises would be made good; that's what it meant, when I was a child, to say "When the king comes home." Wishes granted. Dreams made real.

I never hear the phrase used any more. No one refers to it. It is as if it has been lost to all memory save mine, vanished away, like the bits of some broken spell, some prophecy fulfilled. *When the king comes home.*

"They commissioned this chapel," the choirmaster told me, as if I were about six years old and a bit backward. "King Julian the Fourth is holding a votive crown. Queen Andred holds a model ship, for the dowry she brought to Aravis was a fleet of ships. This chapel is not open to all. How do you come to be here alone?"

I pointed to the armored man. "Who is he?" The chiaroscuro was much deeper in the lower corners, but I could see that he was watching the king and queen, guarding them, and that his nose was crooked, as if it had been broken in a fight, but crooked in a noble, aquiline fashion that would have pleased even Saskia. "Who is that?"

"That is King Julian's champion, Istvan. They called him the Seraph in the old stories."

"Because he was so beautiful?" I ventured.

The choirmaster looked at me as if I had taken leave of my senses. "Beautiful? Hardly! Because he was as deadly in battle as the Angel of Death."

THREE

(In which I discuss politics.)

The choirmaster must have had a quiet word with someone, for as many times as I came to the palace with messages—I never allowed Gabriel to trick me again in that particular fashion—I was able to visit the Archangel Chapel. I tried my hand at copying the donor panel into my notebook—several times. Never to my own satisfaction. I could render the pale queen's profile adequately, but the king and the knight never looked a bit like the painting.

Gabriel's visit to Lord Stanimir's quarters resulted in a commission, though not merely the one Madame Carriera arranged with Lord Stanimir.

As he approached the end of his seven years' apprenticeship, Gabriel was anxious to choose a good subject for his masterpiece, the sooner to win entry to the guild and establish his own fame. In Lord Stanimir's retinue were several dashing young bravos, one notable for his golden hair and the perfection of his features. Gabriel had taken advantage of Madame Carriera's message to Lord Stanimir to speak to this perfect young man, whose name was Tallant. Tallant had agreed, eventually, to sit for Gabriel, who planned to paint him as Apollo, or else the Angel Gabriel, a tour de force that would, with luck, become Gabriel's masterpiece.

At the appointed hour, Saskia, Piers, and I watched from the landing of the stairs as Gabriel answered the door. It was not every day that a young man with perfect features was expected. We wished to see the paragon.

We were surprised, all four of us, when the dark young man who entered swept off his hat and shook the rain from his cloak, for no one ever had less perfect features. Not that he wasn't passable. Taken individually, his features were well enough. His dark eyes were particularly fine. But it was a trick of personality and proportion that made him interesting to look at; there was nothing of the classical in that long nose or stubborn jaw.

The young man was a trifle under middle height, but he carried himself so that he seemed taller than he was, an illusion aided by the breadth of his shoulders. Of course, the cloak helped too. He was booted and spurred, as if for the hunting field, as young bravos at court usually were. Slung behind him, scabbard half-concealed in the damp gray green folds of the cloak, was the largest sword I have ever seen in my life. Beside me, Piers gave a squeak of pure envy.

Gabriel stared for a long moment, then caught himself and apologized. "I'm sorry. I was expecting someone. May I help you?"

"Are you Gabriel Wex?" The man with the sword had a northern accent, pleasant to my homesick ears.

"I am."

"Then I think you may help me. My name is Ludovic Nallaneen. I have come to sit for a portrait. Otto Tallant sent me."

Gabriel made a helpless little gesture. "I'm afraid there's been some confusion. I am expecting Otto Tallant. I agreed to paint his portrait."

"As Apollo." Ludovic Nallaneen had a most ingratiating smile. "No confusion. He sent me in his place."

"I'm sorry. It isn't possible. I agreed to paint Tallant."

The young man's air became confiding. "Yes, but Tallant owes me money. That's not something that happens very often, other people owing me money. But since he owes me, it stands to reason he owes everyone else more. So he can't pay me. Are you following this?"

Gabriel hesitated. "I'm afraid it isn't a question of money." I could tell he was thinking of Otto Tallant's fair hair and perfect features. Not much of the masterpiece about Ludovic Nallaneen.

The confiding air became, if anything, more conspiratorial. "Of course it is. It's almost always a question of money. Now, since he has no cash to speak of, we agreed between us that I'd take the portrait sittings he'd arranged with you in exchange." That smile again. "I quite understand your dismay. I'm no Apollo. Yet I'm sure you'll paint Mars just as well, won't you?"

Gabriel regarded Nallaneen with stiffness bordering on hauteur. I knew that expression well. He'd used it often enough on me. "It simply isn't possible."

"Are you sure?" Nallaneen shrugged slightly. It was hardly a lift of the shoulders, but somehow the hilt of the great sword seemed to strain eagerly forward. "How unfortunate. Because I want my portrait done. It would make my mother so happy."

All hauteur vanished. Gabriel swallowed with almost audible difficulty. "I . . . it isn't possible."

I felt sorry for him. Gabriel knew the risk he was running, offending a man trained to fight at the slightest nudge to his honor. Yet he couldn't agree to paint Nallaneen's portrait under threat. His pride wouldn't permit it.

Nallaneen knew all that as well as any of us. He seemed to enjoy Gabriel's wide-eyed discomfiture, but he didn't press his argument. He waited, smiling gently, as if he were at a play, interested to see what Gabriel would say next. It had to be acceptance. Gabriel was no fighter.

"I'm afraid I keep my apprentices much too busy to accept commissions of their own," said Madame Carriera from behind us on the landing. She stepped daintily past us and made her way down to join Gabriel and Nallaneen.

Nallaneen had already removed his hat, but he flourished it a little as he swept Madame Carriera a bow worthy of royalty. "I am your servant, Madame."

"And Gabriel is my servant. I'm afraid I cannot allow you to take up any more of his time just now. But perhaps you would agree to a sitting with me instead."

Another bow, deeper still. "Madame is graciousness itself, but I could never afford such an honor. Otto Tallant's entire substance is not worth a tithe of it, and he didn't lose a tithe of that to me."

"Tell me," Madame said thoughtfully, "if you were seriously displeased with someone, would you draw that sword?"

Wide-eyed, Nallaneen touched the hilt protectively. "Madame, that would be foolish of me." Reproachfully, he added, "I am never seriously displeased with anyone."

"Draw it now. In friendship. Such weapons were rare a hundred years ago. I never thought to see one at close quarters."

"It is not wise to see one *too* close, Madame. But to please you . . ." Ludovic Nallaneen drew his great sword and wielded it as easily as Madame Angelica Carriera wielded her brushes. It made a blue gray arc, and another, and another, as he ran through the sword drill from start to finish. The very air seemed to glint with steel, a dark glint like sun on deep water. Deep, *cold* water.

He held the final position a long moment, allowing Madame Carriera to look her fill at the light on the blade. Then he sheathed it, and the room seemed the least bit darker, as if the daylight faded a little when the sword went back into the scabbard.

Madame Carriera's eyes blazed with excitement. "Thank you. That was well worth a portrait. I will be glad to paint you."

For a moment, her generosity seemed to take him aback. He hesitated, as if on guard against hidden mockery. "As Mars? Or Apollo? Or in some other shape?"

"As yourself. Come up to the studio now, and we will begin. Hail, attend me. Gabriel, go about your business, if you have so much to do you can turn away a client. Saskia and Piers, busy yourselves elsewhere. I can't work while you gossip. Quickly, while the light lasts."

Delight seemed to overcome Nallaneen's hesitation, and he swept her another bow. "You do me and my family a very great honor, Madame. It will make my mother so happy."

Once in Madame Carriera's workshop, Ludovic Nallaneen took his time looking about before he accepted the chair he was offered. It was the only chair on the low dais, but the exposed position did not appear to make him uncomfortable. Even seated, he continued his study of the room. Though he made no remark, he seemed to miss nothing.

I busied myself assembling Madame Carriera's tools. She wouldn't need her palette, not so soon, but I set forth the materials for the preliminary sketches.

Madame Carriera took her place behind the easel and studied him. That keen scrutiny did not appear to discomfit him either. "Standing," she said at last. "I'm sorry to renege on the offer of a chair, but I'll have to paint you standing."

Nallaneen rose promptly.

"Hail, move the chair back. He can use it when I give him time to rest."

Under Madame Carriera's direction, I pulled the chair away and made slight adjustments to the fall of the cloak Nallaneen still wore. It was excellent material.

"That's fine. Out of the way now."

In the silence that followed, I took up my notebook and a stick of charcoal. The folds of his cloak were good practice for me.

Madame Carriera made several studies of the first pose, surprisingly detailed for the speed with which she worked, and said, "Rest now."

Ludovic Nallaneen looked surprised. "So soon? You haven't finished?"

"I've only started. You should move around a bit. Stretch while I give you leave. It's hard work, keeping still."

"A good deal of it goes on in the army, and for longer periods than this."

Madame Carriera looked amused. "Truly? I had no idea a soldier's life was so sedentary."

His innocent air was perfect. "Oh, yes. Complete inactivity punctuated by bursts of terror. That's the military life."

"You'll make an excellent model, then. If you're ready, we'll start again. Turn to your left. A bit more. You may keep talking."

"I can see complete inactivity goes on here routinely," Nallaneen said. "Where do the bursts of terror come in?"

I wanted to remind him of Gabriel but decided it would be unwise. I held my tongue.

"It's a dangerous business, portraiture. What if I offend my subject? You're armed." Madame Carriera started another sheet. "Hail, pull his cloak back and pin it—I must see the leg."

I put my notebook down and went to find a horse-blanket pin in the clutter of gear on the workbench.

"Surely your subject is more likely to offend you. Gabriel Wex seemed offended by me. If he weren't your servant, I might have been obliged to notice that."

"But he is my servant. Fortunately. And more fortunately still, you resist the urge to be displeased with anyone."

"Seriously displeased," he amended.

"Gabriel's a clever young man. He'll learn soon enough about the peril of making his opinions known to his clients. Such arrogance comes at a price. He's already lost the chance of painting you."

I stood close behind Ludovic Nallaneen and fiddled with his cloak. He smelled of soap and leather, and just faintly of horse. It was difficult to find a spot to anchor the folds of cloth without interfering with the angle of the sword.

"More, Hail. Pull it right back. You can make up for the severity with more folds on the other side. That's good."

"Are you her servant too?" he asked me.

I concentrated on not pricking him with the heavy pin. He was armed, after all. "I'm Hail Rosamer, her apprentice."

"Gabriel Wex is an apprentice too. So you are both her servants or neither."

I met his eyes. Sword or no sword, he had no right to make me feel like a serving maid. "We all serve art."

Ludovic Nallaneen laughed at me. "Ah, there's the burst of terror I've been waiting for. Don't be angry with me. Or at least, don't glare so. What if your face were to stick in that expression?"

I looked past his amusement to Madame Carriera. She was watching me with interest. "Pride comes at a price, Hail."

I turned back to Nallaneen. "Whom do you serve, sir?"

"Why, Mars." He looked at me more closely. "Surely you don't mean more specifically. These days it's most impolite to express an interest in anyone's politics."

"I mean, whom do you serve? We all serve someone."

"Oh. In that case, I serve my commanding officer, Colonel Anyz. Does it take all your energy, defending your fellow apprentice?"

"I'm not defending Gabriel. I'm defending myself. Gabriel is . . ." I bit off my words. To list Gabriel's tricks—from bumping my elbow when I was doing under-drawing in ink to sneezing on me while I sized gold leaf—in Madame Carriera's hearing would be treachery. "Gabriel looks after himself."

"He's not in your good graces, then?"

"He wouldn't wish to be." I went back to my notebook.

"Lucky youngster, to be so talented that he can weather such dislike from a fellow apprentice."

"He's skilled, but no one has so much talent that they can be allowed to run wild in the atelier." Madame Carriera did not let her conversation slow her work. "Rather, there are students one knows will enjoy success. With Gabriel, there is an unerring sense of how to achieve an effect. His gift is to know the pleasing thing—his fortune will be made by delighting his patrons. This Apollo he has in mind will be scholarly enough to earn the admiration of the guild. Not only will it win him admission to the guild, it will be beautiful enough to cause a stir. People will want to know who Apollo is. It will be popular."

"That's good, isn't it?"

Madame Carriera smiled but refused to answer.

"Not every apprentice is chosen for the guild," I said. "After seven years of training, a master can send a failed apprentice away."

"Gabriel will be chosen," said Madame Carriera. "Don't fool yourself. He works hard and he's eager to have a workshop of his own."

"That's all he wants, though. He doesn't serve art, not really. He serves himself."

Madame Carriera was severe. "He craves fame and independence. That's no crime, Hail. You do yourself."

"Not like that," I said, but it sounded weak even in my own ears.

"Pay less attention to Gabriel's work and more to your own," said Madame Carriera. "After all, you've only studied a year and a half with me."

"It was a year and a half in December, ma'am. This is my twentieth month in your service."

"Are you sure it isn't twenty minutes? Never mind. You still have much to learn."

When Ludovic Nallaneen returned for his second sitting, I made sure I was the apprentice asked to help in the workshop. I'd never known Madame Carriera so willing to discuss her apprentices, and I hoped that her conversation with Nallaneen would yield more confidences.

Instead, on the second occasion, Madame Carriera seemed intent on learning all she could about Ludovic Nallaneen.

"I am from Galazon," he said. Madame Carriera's interest won a genuine smile from him. There was pride in his voice as he added, "I am a captain in the prince-bishop's guard."

That explained his northern accent. Galazon was farther north than Neven, and even sleepier.

"Who taught you to handle a two-handed sword?" Madame Carriera asked. "Do they still use such things in Galazon?"

"My mother arranged lessons for me. She had me tutored in all the arts becoming to a gentleman and an officer."

"You astonish me." Madame Carriera looked up from her underpainting. "Keep still now." She worked intently for a space, then gave him leave to rest.

Nallaneen picked up the thread of their conversation unerringly. "What's astonishing in that my mother arranged my lessons? Don't I seem a gentleman and an officer?"

"You do, which is what astonishes me. My understanding is that the principal arts required by a gentleman in this age involve women, politics, and drinking."

"Say rather, my mother had me tutored in the arts required by a gentleman of a more demanding time. I learned a bit of Latin and Greek along with my fighting. Since my tutelage ended, I plan my own education. Women still tutor me, Madame, for I am old enough to realize my education in the gentlest of arts will never be complete. And as for wine, I study that on occasion, since it forms part of my duty as an officer."

"And what of politics?"

"I am a captain in the prince-bishop's guard, which is all the politics my duty demands. Ask me again when the prince-bishop chooses a successor to the king, and it may be my duty to be a trifle more political. Until then, let it rest."

"You, Captain Nallaneen, are made of milk and water. Do you let your commanding officers dictate your loyalties?"

"I let them dictate my duties, Madame Carriera."

"Could I dictate your loyalties, Hail? Would you stand for it?"

I was still intent on the notion of women tutoring Captain Nallaneen. Tutoring him in what? I knew about what men and women do in bed, but what sort of tutoring would that require? Or could they be talking about something else? "I'm your loyal apprentice, ma'am," I said absently.

"But would you change your politics if I desired it? Could you do that?"

"Leave the child alone," said Nallaneen. "You know she hasn't any politics, and no one can change what they don't have."

Goaded by his condescending tone, I stated, "I am loyal to the Crown."

"No matter who wears it?" asked Nallaneen.

"Who could wear it but the king?" I countered.

"What if it gives him a headache? What if the king can't wear it?" Nallaneen asked. "To whom are you loyal then?"

I frowned at him. "Are you more loyal to the prince-bishop than to the king?"

"I'm exactly as loyal to the king as the king needs me to be," said Nallaneen. "I'm as loyal as a captain ought to be."

"What if you're promoted?" I asked. "Will you be more loyal then?"

"That sort of thing usually works in reverse," said Madame Carriera.

"If ever I am so fortunate," Nallaneen replied, without taking his attention from me, "you ask me again and see."

Ludovic Nallaneen's third sitting for his portrait was postponed more than once, first through the press of his military duty and later through illness. When he was recovered, Nallaneen resumed his pose on Madame Carriera's dais and held it doggedly.

Madame Carriera worked for perhaps half an hour and then set her palette aside. "Sit down before you fall down," she commanded. "Hail, run down to the kitchen and mull some wine for Captain Nallaneen."

"I'm fine," said Nallaneen, sinking into his chair with relief. "It's only a head cold."

"You're green," Madame Carriera informed him. "I can't work on your skin tones when you're green."

"His nose isn't usually that red either," I added. I would have said Nallaneen looked gray, not green, but there was no denying that but for the tip of his nose, he was too pale.

"Mull wine for both of us," said Madame Carriera, "and remember to clean up after yourself."

I mulled wine for all three of us, and tidied up too. By the time I returned to the workshop, Madame Carriera had put things aside for me to clean. I drank my wine while it was warm and then set to work on the brushes. Just as well I hadn't made any more. I could feel my own nose turning red.

"Thank you for the wine," said Nallaneen to me. "It's very good."

Madame Carriera said, "Hail is a handy youngster, when she pays attention to what she's doing."

I was surprised into silence by the praise.

"Not so young as all that, surely," said Nallaneen.

"She's young for her age," said Madame Carriera.

"I'm seventeen," I stated. I was, but only just.

"A fine age for an apprentice," he said.

"How old are you?" I asked.

"Twenty-three."

I would have guessed more. To cover my surprise, I said the first thing that entered my head. "Do you ever play knucklebones?"

"Not since I was a small boy. But I think I can remember the basics. Make your toss, sweep up the bones, and catch your toss again. Right?"

"Right. Basically."

"Perhaps you'll show me the finer points sometime."

"I will. But not until you're over your head cold. You'll need a clear head and a steady hand."

"Let me know when you think I'm ready."

FOUR

(In which I study my craft.)

February yielded eventually. The days began to soften. Nights were not so long. My second spring in Aravis was perfection. I had friends. I had work to do. I had more to learn than I had time to learn it in. Best of all, I had the most beautiful city in the world to study, making my way through every winding street, every crowded market in Aravis, until I had it by heart.

When fair weather finally came, the city welcomed it with every window flung open, every clothesline hung out heavy with fresh laundry. The gray stone of the city looked blue in the young sunlight of spring, and every roof tile gleamed after the long rains of winter.

In May came the days of ivory and gold, when the sun rose before we did, and made even the fly-specked windows of our garret glow with splendor. On such days, the gifts that we were trying so hard to refine seemed undeniable. Our boldness matched our gaiety. We learned our craft and our art with the appetite of our years. That which did not come at once, we trusted would come in time.

Gabriel, Saskia, Piers, and I studied Aravis at Madame Carriera's bidding. I learned which apothecary sold the best quality gum arabic, just as I learned how to use it in compounding colors to meet Madame Carriera's standards.

Madame Carriera sent us out for more than mere errands. In the Chapel of St. Mary's by the south gate, there was a Madonna painted by Andrea Mantegna of Padua. Madame Carriera thought highly of this panel, though it seemed lumpish and gaudy to me. She sent me to visit it often, as she could see I was not impressed.

I went willingly to the mercers guild hall, where there was a pair of bronze doors wondrously made. They were of Tuscan workmanship. Six panels to one door, six panels to the other, the months of the year were represented. The figures symbolizing the cavalcade of the year were arranged simply, a large central figure in each panel sometimes flanked by smaller figures to each side. January was the old man keeping the gate, February the water carrier, March the fishmonger, and so on around the calendar. Every line of those doors was inevitable. The pair could have been crafted of wood or marble as easily as bronze, and every composition would have made as fine a fresco as it did a bronze.

Who could tell what mischance brought them to our end of the world? The merchants of the Lidian Empire were a canny lot and those of Aravis the canniest of all. Small wonder they knew a bargain when they saw one and brought such treasure home.

There was no quarter of Aravis that did not have some point of interest, whether a grand portal on an old building or a good view over the slate rooftops to the tangled streets of the wilder part of town. The city walls were my favorite spot. They were guarded, of course, but most days we could walk along the battlements and look out at the world beyond our walls. I liked the north ramparts, for there one could see the Lida flowing down from the misty blue of the hills.

Saskia showed me the north ramparts first. It was a favorite of hers, as she had the true city dweller's love for a beautiful landscape. Easy to admire the woods when one has never known a wood tick. The more distant a view was, the better she liked it. "Lovely, isn't it? Aren't you ever homesick for Neven?"

"I am when I remember to be, but I don't remember very often. I like it here. I belong here."

"No one who really belongs here ever admits they like the city. That's hopelessly provincial."

"I like it, and I belong here."

"Keep talking like that and you'll be marked for life as an out-lander."

"Oh? Will I? Well, I don't care. Aravis agrees with me." I didn't feel at all provincial. I felt the very curl of my hair improve every time I washed it in the water of Aravis. To me, the water of the city even tasted different from the water I'd known as a child. In Neven, the water had a faint iron tang to it and was always slow to lather. The water of Aravis felt more kindly to me. It had an indefinable sweetness, just a shading, like the faint color in old glass. It never seemed as cold to me as the water of Neven, nor did it take quite as long to boil.

Saskia studied me curiously. "Don't you even miss your family?"

"Of course I do. I write to them all the time."

Saskia shook her head. "They write to you all the time. You only write back when there's something good to tell them."

"Madame Carriera keeps us all busy. I'm sure they understand."

"I'm sure they do. They'd be mad to expect anything else of you. When will your father come to Aravis again?"

"This summer, with the woolpack."

"This time are you going to let us see him—if only from a distance?"

"I'd have introduced you last time, if I'd known you were interested." This was not quite true. The summer before, Father's visit to Aravis had been cut short by the press of business. I'd been so glad to see him, even for a few days, that it had never entered my head to bring him to Giltspur Street to introduce him to my fellow apprentices. Truth to tell, I hadn't trusted myself not to cling to his sleeve like a child. Not the way to behave in front of Saskia and Piers, let alone Gabriel.

"Well, promise to bring him next time."

"Promise."

That June we studied the pillars in the ambulatory at the little church of St. Lefko's. This was an exercise set by Madame Carriera. The pillars

were of the Corinthian order, done in the best classical style. One of
the pillars was a true work of antiquity. All the rest were copies. Madame Carriera instructed us to study the pillars, decide which one was
original, which were copies, and explain why we thought so, with
sketches to back our argument.

Gabriel taunted me in St. Lefko's. "What, don't you know the
classical when you see it, Madame Rosamer?" He seldom missed an
opportunity to call me Madame Rosamer. I could hardly conceal my
dislike of that nickname, and he knew it. "You're sketching them all."

"That was what Madame Carriera told us to do."

"No, she told us to identify the original." He held out his open
notebook to show off a beautifully detailed drawing of an acanthus
capital. "Why waste time on the copies? Oh, you need the practice,
perhaps."

"I'm following Madame Carriera's instructions. I want to be ready
to defend my argument." I could have added *Master Wex*, but I knew
it would please him more than annoy him, and anyway the words
would only stick in my throat.

"What argument? It's obvious which is the original and which the
copies. Can't you tell?"

I thought it was obvious too, but just in case I was wrong, I wasn't
about to reveal my choice to Gabriel. He mocked me at every small
opportunity. I didn't want to give him a chance to ridicule me over
something serious. "She told us to be able to explain how we know. I
want to make some measurements."

"What for?" Gabriel gave a dismissive flip of his hand. "How will
you measure them? Ask the verger if you may climb up on his shoulders?"

"I'll just estimate. You needn't stay." I returned to my notebook.

"I wouldn't dream of leaving you on your own."

He meant that, but only to annoy me. I ignored him and eventually
he left. With great care and all the attention to detail I could muster,
I drew the floor plan of the ambulatory, sketched the views from each
direction, and did details of each pillar's capital. The foliation of the
copies was as detailed as the original, but the overall effect was stiff. I

thought I detected at least two styles in the copies. It seemed pedantic, taking Madame Carriera's task even further, but I was interested in the variations of the copies, so I recorded all I could. Only the one I'd chosen as the classical original seemed to combine both grace and ease of line. I wondered how old it was. Even the copies were stained with age. In the calm silence of St. Lefko's, time seemed irrelevant. The rest of the world could bargain and bicker. Serenity filled St. Lefko's.

Each of us identified the correct pillar. Gabriel had done it with ruthless efficiency, drawing just one capital. Saskia had approached the problem the same way I did, though her sketches were far more detailed and she'd included diagrams of the vaulting overhead. Piers outdid us all, having gone so far as to redesign the entire church to bring it into proportion with the ambulatory. Yet even my dogged attempt to identify the similarities among the copies was greeted with approval.

Madame Carriera was pleased with our work. "You see it. You've absorbed it. Both the classical and the copies. You must be able to replicate either. But when you copy, know that's what you're doing. Don't confuse it with your own work."

"Yet we copy you," said Piers. "That *is* our work."

"For now," said Madame Carriera. "No artist worth the name copies forever, else there would be no seven-year limit to your apprenticeship. You imitate only as long as you can learn from the imitations. The day will come to leave copying behind. You will need something of your own to say, and a way of your own to say it. Or why would anyone ever want to copy you?"

"For his line," I said, without meaning to.

"For his way with color," said Gabriel, pleasantly enough, for him.

"For his beautiful brown eyes," sighed Saskia.

Piers blushed.

That summer was very dry, so dry that the Lida's usual deep flood steadied to a sullen flow. Instead of sending our woolpack to market in the old-fashioned way, on rafts made of our own timber, Father shipped it as freight on a flatboat. That way, if the flatboat encountered difficulties, the loss to Father would be the value of the freight alone, not the woolpack and the timber besides. The crew were professionals and the owner of the flatboat would be liable for any losses they endured.

As his fellow passenger aboard the flatboat, Father brought Amyas, my favorite brother and the one closest to me in age. There was no need for me to beg them to call on me at Giltspur Street. Instead, they came looking for me.

It was a quiet day, so hot in the streets that no one wanted to venture out of the shade. Madame Carriera was away on a social call. Gabriel and Piers had gone to the baths. When Father knocked, Saskia and I were down in the kitchen, as it was the coolest place in the house.

"Father!" I threw myself on his chest and he half staggered under the onslaught.

"Girl, you've grown." Father held me at arm's length to get a better look. "You're as tall as I am."

"It agrees with me, living here." I urged him indoors. "Come in off the doorstep. Would you like something to drink?"

"So I see." Father turned me toward Amyas. "Look who came with me."

I couldn't help laughing. "Amyas, you've grown a beard!" Amyas's hair grew in soft brown curls, which he kept severely short lest they become him too much. Predictably, his beard had come in as soft brown down. It made me want to pet him like a puppy.

"Yes, I know," said Amyas. I could always provoke him to huffiness.

I introduced Saskia to them. "Madame Carriera is out, I'm afraid. But I'm sure she would offer her hospitality. May I get you something to drink? Are you hungry? Please, sit down."

"I'll call on Madame Carriera when it's convenient for her," said Father. "For now, come with us, the pair of you. I'll buy you a slap-up dinner, the best the Sheepcrook has to offer. You can tell me all about your life as a famous artist."

"I'm only an apprentice, Father."

"For the moment, love. It's only a matter of time."

Father had ordered a fine reunion feast at the Sheepcrook. Saskia accompanied us and ate like a young wolf, while I was almost too busy talking to take a bite.

I had wondered what Amyas and Saskia would make of each other were they ever to meet. I thought they were alike, both very fluffy and soft looking on the outside, quick and cynical on the inside. Talking to each of them, to me, seemed like biting into pastry wrapped around what you expect to be marzipan and finding it's wrapped around an artichoke heart or a bit of crabmeat instead. It's not worse. It's just different.

At first Amyas seemed a little awed by Saskia. He sought to impress her with tales he'd heard from the flatboatmen. Saskia, always delighted to tease me about my provincial background, was eager to play the cosmopolitan artist for my brother.

When I had run out of anecdotes and was finally applying myself to the fish stew, Amyas said, "The Lida hasn't run so shallow in fifty years. The boatmen say it's proof that Red Ned has sold his soul to the devil."

Saskia did not ask who Red Ned was. Amyas waited for her to say something all the way through the poppyseed roll she was busy with. She had finished it and started on another before he gave up and continued.

"Red Ned is what the boatmen call the lord of Ardres; that's the castle on the heights where the Lida and the Arcel meet. It's a great defensive position, right atop a crag. An army of Turks couldn't take it. His name is Edward, but they call him Red Ned. He's a terrible man, the boatmen say."

Saskia smiled at my father and asked if there was by chance a morsel of cheese left. As Father called for more cheese and more rolls, Saskia turned to Amyas, her dimples still showing. "His name is Edward so they call him Ned. I think I grasp that much. But why do they call him Red Ned, I wonder?"

"Because he's so terrible." It was a struggle to get the words out intelligibly around a mouthful of stew, but I managed it. I knew that Saskia, like many redheads, was peculiarly sensitive about the traits red hair was supposed to signify. Sometimes there was no telling when she would take offense.

Too late. Amyas rushed in. "Because his hair is red, of course. And his hands are bathed in blood, the boatmen say."

Saskia's dimples faded. She gazed forlornly into her empty bowl. "Is it so terrible . . . to have red hair?"

Father called for more stew. More wine. More everything. Amyas said, very patiently, "It's superstition. There's nothing wrong with red hair. That's all rubbish about Judas Iscariot."

Saskia looked up sharply. "What about Judas Iscariot?"

"Judas-colored. People say Judas had red hair. So they sometimes call red hair Judas-colored. And they associate red hair with evildoing. It's nonsense. The same sort of people say Red Ned can bring people back from the dead. Pure rubbish."

More food arrived, but Saskia could not be distracted so easily. "In the first place, my hair is not red—"

"I never said it was—I never noticed it was—Oh, I *do* apologize. . . ."

Saskia ignored him. "My hair is red gold. Ask anyone with an eye for color."

"Hmm." I tilted my head a little and took a long, considering look. "No. It's red all right."

"Ask anyone with an eye for color," she repeated tranquilly. "In the second place, one *can* bring people back from the dead."

"Hmm." Amyas took his turn at a long, considering look. "Perhaps *you* can."

Saskia did not quite smile, but I could see her take a new measurement of my brother. All her archness left her, and she continued in her more usual downright way. "No, really. If you want someone to come back from the dead, you can fetch them back. If you have something that belonged to them, you can call them right to you. If you say the correct spells and if they died unshriven. That's why war is so terrible. So many die with their sins still on them."

Intrigued, Amyas rushed in again. "What about plagues? Lots of people die unshriven in a plague."

Father poured more wine. "Now, Amyas. It's one thing to listen politely to the boatmen, no matter what tales they choose to spin. But it is quite another to discuss this kind of rank superstition at the dinner table."

"Plagues too," said Saskia cheerfully. "Sometimes they want to come anyway, because there was something they forgot to tell you. Like where the family treasure was hidden. Or if they feel bad about something they did and want to apologize. You must have played green gravel when you were little. It's all about how to keep someone coming back from the dead."

I remembered the circle game we'd played as children. *"Wash her in milk, dry her with silk,"* I sang. *"Green gravel, green gravel."*

"That's the one," said Saskia. "Over time the words have changed. We learned *green gravel*, but once it was green grave, o."

We sang the round through twice. Father gave up and helped himself to more stew.

"You can see to it that your family are safe if you bury them properly. Or you can bring them back to life and make them stay, if they care enough about what it is of theirs that you have. That's why it's dangerous to put too much value on the things of this world."

Amyas put on his loftiest expression. "Oh, rubbish. Father's right. That's rank superstition."

"It is not. It's necromancy, and very wicked, but it isn't superstition. My grandfather is a healer. He only deals in the white arts, of course, but he has to know all about the others."

"Hmm." Amyas studied me. "So if Hail died unexpectedly, say, by talking herself to death . . ." He flicked a fingertip at my earlobe, but I pulled away in time. "I could bring her back just by saying a spell.

And I could make her stay, if only I could manage to get hold of one of those fine gold earrings she's so proud of. How did you come by those, I wonder?"

"They were a gift," I replied haughtily, "from a young man who admires my skill."

Father began to look appalled, but Saskia took pity on him. "She won them from Ludovic. Knucklebones."

Amyas smiled at me. "Very nice." He smiled at Saskia. "Do you play?"

"Not with you. Hail told us you taught her everything she knows."

"About knucklebones," I added. It's foolish to let even a favorite brother know just how helpful he has been. (Come to think of it, especially a favorite brother.)

I could tell well enough from his conversation what Amyas thought of Saskia. That night, in our room under the roof, I tried to guess what Saskia made of my brother. I hinted that he had seemed to like her. She would not catch my meaning and did not allow me to talk about it for long. In anyone else, that brusqueness would have convinced me there was something afoot. In Saskia, whose most amiable moments were lightly seasoned with vinegar, it was impossible to be sure.

FIVE

(In which I study Maspero's craft.)

Only autumn brought relief for the weather that baked us that summer. The turn of the season brought storms, the kind of high winds usual in spring, and constant soaking rains, but brought them too late. After such a dry summer, the harvest was meager. Chill rains waterlogged what crops were left. The produce for sale in the city's market stalls dwindled, and prices rose.

That October marked the end of Gabriel's seventh year in Madame Carriera's workshop. On the first day of the month he began his masterpiece, painting in a corner of her studio. It was an allegorical piece, a large canvas depicting the drunkenness of Noah. By the end of the month, the work was all but complete. Only the final glaze remained to be done. Gabriel was off celebrating with his friends when Saskia, Piers, and I had our viewing of the masterpiece.

"He's sure to be admitted into the artists guild for this." Piers pointed to Noah's hand, outstretched helplessly toward his sons. "Look at those halftones."

"The drapery's good," said Saskia.

"Oh, very good," I said. "So much of it too. Looks like the laundry day of Noah, in fact."

"Cat," said Saskia amiably. "You're only jealous."

"I can do drapery."

"I never said you couldn't. He's a brave one, I'll give him that. Not a very safe subject to choose these days."

"Noah?" I tried to look as if I knew what Saskia was referring to. "Or drunkenness?"

"A helpless old man," said Saskia. "People find political references everywhere these days."

"It's not a political reference," said Piers firmly. "It's the drunkenness of Noah, and it's good. Leave it at that. The guild will."

"It's going to cause a sensation," said Saskia. "The guild may not be as blind as you expect them to be."

"Noah is still Noah," Piers insisted. "His sons still owe him their filial piety. That's the text Gabriel chose. This will be talked about—it deserves the attention. But it isn't political. Or if it is, it isn't treasonous."

I remembered Madame Carriera's conversation with Ludovic. "Will this really cause a stir?"

"Oh, yes." Saskia put the canvas cover back very carefully. "It will be interesting to see when it sells, and to whom, and for how much."

"Will it please someone?"

Saskia said, "Probably. And that's how we'll know who, and how much."

"Then all I'll really be left wondering is why," I said.

On the last day of November, Gabriel's painting was presented to the artists guild as his masterpiece. He was accepted into the guild, and the *Drunkenness of Noah* earned a short-lived notoriety when it was purchased, at three times the going rate, for the private collection of Otto Tallant. Gabriel Wex opened a workshop of his own on the proceeds. Would-be apprentices flocked to him.

Saskia, now the eldest and the most accomplished of us, became our leader. The kindness she showed me, and the patience, which came not at all easily to her, was in sharp contrast to my experience with Gabriel. I learned all the faster.

Madame Carriera was commissioned to limn a Crucifixion, a devotional piece for the prince-bishop himself, a miniature to be fitted in its own cruciform jeweled case. The work was exacting. Madame

Carriera did the painting on vellum smaller than a playing card. She designed the filigreed case but left the casting to Saskia.

Saskia rose to the occasion. With me to help, she used the skill of a goldsmith to carry out Madame Carriera's wishes. The finished case was a jewel to match Madame Carriera's most delicate work.

"Well done," was Madame Carriera's verdict, and she halved the commission with Saskia.

"Glad to be done with it," was Saskia's private opinion. "I hope she won't want any more."

"Why not? It's beautiful."

"It's nice enough. Old-fashioned, though."

"You loved the casting."

"I do like metal. But I'd rather do something with some weight to it. A medallion, for example. Filigree is jewelers' work."

"Isn't a medallion just as much a piece of jewelry as filigree is?"

"That depends on the medallion."

The next errand that brought Saskia to the palace, I accompanied her. At Madame Carriera's written request, we were admitted to the palace archive. There, in a glass-topped case, were two portrait medallions, one bronze, one gold.

"There," said Saskia. "Call that jewelry?"

The bronze medallion looked unthinkably old, a Roman emperor with curly hair and a double chin. "Is it real?" I asked.

"They don't bother with copies here," Saskia reminded me.

I looked at the gold medallion.

There are faces that proclaim the character within. Let the proportions of a face be never so odd, if the heart within is strong and fair, the face reveals that quality. We look and say, this is not beauty, yet still we look. We are drawn to that mysterious quality of the visage, even when the likeness is of someone we have never met. Likewise, who has not known someone who is fair of face yet negligible of heart? We are struck with the proportion of the features at first, but the impression does not last. A single deed or, at times, even a single word spoken in sufficiently plangent tones can banish that first impression and leave us wondering where we found beauty at all. It is the task of art to give us all these impressions and qualities, both the inward and the outward, and to give us something more, something that keeps us looking and wondering.

"I've seen him before," I said. The portrait was similar to the Roman medallion in that it showed the profile of a man somewhere in his thirties. There the similarity ended, for where the classical portrait idealized everything but the double chin, this portrait seemed a realistic representation of a man who was at once strong, honest, wise, and sad.

"Of course you have, you idiot. That's Good King Julian." At my silence, Saskia nudged me in the ribs. "What did they teach you in Neven? Anything at all? That's Julian the Fourth. The siege medal, remember? It's by Gil Maspero."

"Gil Maspero? What else did he do?" The name was not as familiar as Julian's profile. He was my Good King Julian, from the Archangel Chapel. I ought to have recognized him at once, for the siege medal was the model for the Julian dinar, the backbone of Lidian currency, a silver coin so famous that even in these degenerate days it is used as a measure for goodness. You may put this to the test yourself.

Ask if a horse is sound and you will be told, without any hesitation, that he is as sound as a Julian dinar. That the horse is touched in the wind, or has a bowed tendon, or is spoiled in some other way, is simply the way of all horseflesh and must not be allowed to reflect on the soundness of that beautiful old coinage.

"Gil Maspero?" In her exasperation, Saskia nudged me in the ribs again, this time a bit harder. "It takes less time to think what he didn't do. Ever hear of a little thing called the Mathias Bridge?"

Everyone knew the Mathias Bridge. It crosses the Lida above Shene in a three-arch span, a feat believed to be impossible until the bridge had been finished. "I've heard of it."

"Maspero designed it. He also improved the city's defensive fortifications, cast portrait medallions of the royal family, painted miniature portraits of everyone who had the money to pay him, frescoed the palace throne room, and when she died, he carved Queen Andred the Fair in marble to ornament her tomb. Oh, and when Good King

Julian broke the Turkish siege and saved us all—Maspero cast the siege medal to commemorate the famous victory."

"He did all that?" Without meaning to, I dropped my voice to a whisper. "And he knew Good King Julian?"

"I suppose he must have. It's a good portrait, I think. More than the usual sort of official likeness. About the only thing Maspero didn't do was find a way to turn lead into gold. Not that he didn't try that too."

I stared reverently into the glass case. For me, the portrait of Julian IV held something even greater than the appeal of the donor panel in the Archangel Chapel. Miriamne Giuliana had known something of the king. But Maspero had known something greater than that, something that showed in every elegant, economical line. "He knew him. Maspero really knew him."

"Maspero knew everyone, I imagine." Saskia pulled me away from the glass case. "Since I've made my point, I suppose it's time we were getting back to work."

"Your point?" With great reluctance, I followed her out of the archive. "What point?"

"There's nothing like a good portrait medallion, is there?"

"You're right. I've never seen anything like it."

I saw Maspero's siege medal again as soon as I could persuade Madame Carriera to write me another letter of recommendation. I studied it. I sketched it. To the best of my ability, given the glass case, I measured it and recorded its dimensions exactly. After repeated pleas, the archivist opened the case and turned the medal over, standing guard while I sketched the obverse, which showed a view of the city of Aravis. That entire winter, I made a pest of myself over the siege medal. I longed to have made it myself, to have known the king as Maspero had. I yearned for the siege medal. And gradually, so gradually that even I cannot be sure when or how the idea originated, I became resolved to make a copy of the medal in bronze. This would be my siege medal, made for no reason but to please myself.

My notion was no simple undertaking. To craft and cast a bronze medallion is very different from the charcoal drawing and oil painting that had been my former inclination. All my training had to be begun anew, and privily.

Madame Carriera would not approve of my copying Maspero's work. To copy her style was my duty as her apprentice. To copy other work for purposes of instruction was part of my education. To copy slavishly, merely to satisfy my wish for ownership, was a self-indulgent waste of time. More than that, it was an embarrassment, as I could never copy Maspero's work adequately. There would always be something stiff and clumsy in it, something that was mine. Despite all that, I kept on with my study of Maspero's medal.

One spring day when I had been in Madame Carriera's workshop nearly three years, I looked up from my notebook to see Ludovic Nallaneen standing beside the glass-topped case, his head cocked to watch me as I sketched.

I was pleased to see him. "Hello, Ludo. Come to guard the palace treasures?"

"Hello, Hail. Nice earrings. I came to ask you to take a walk with me."

With care, I put my notebook away. "How did you know I was here? Did Saskia tell you?"

"Madame Carriera asked me to find out why you have become so studious that she needs to write a request to admit you to the palace archive twice a week."

I laughed. "She should ask me that."

"That's what I said."

Ludovic Nallaneen led the way out of the palace. I'd gone in on a gray morning. It was now late on a gloriously sunny afternoon. I felt vaguely cheated by this, though I couldn't decide if it bothered me more to have missed the fine weather or to be distracted from my medal. "Why didn't she ask me, then?"

"Perhaps she doesn't want to discourage serious study."

I considered the matter. Before I could think of a reply, Ludovic said, "No, I don't think that's too likely either. Why don't you just tell me and the whole question will be settled."

I frowned at him. "Why should you ask?"

"I'm a friend. I can be—unofficial. If Madame Carriera has to ask Saskia, Saskia will have to answer. It's her duty. Madame Carriera doesn't want to put anyone in that situation."

"What does she think I'm doing?" I demanded. "Plotting to steal something?"

Ludovic cleared his throat. "Well, no. *She* doesn't think that."

"And you do? How dare you?"

"I don't really think it either. But you were staring at it as if it were your one hope of heaven."

"It's good, that's all. It's Gil Maspero's masterpiece. I'm supposed to learn from the best, aren't I?"

"Madame Carriera is the best. You can learn far more from a living artist than you can from a gold coin, however old." He held up his hand. "Now, calm down. No shouting at me until we're back at the workshop. It's bad breeding to argue in the street."

"I have no intention of arguing with you." I swept along with all the speed dignity permitted me. I was particularly angry that there was nothing in what he'd said that I could disagree with, barring his reference to the siege medal as a mere gold coin, of course.

Ludovic kept pace without effort. "Oh, good. Here's the turning for the north ramparts. Are you sure you wouldn't like to take the air with me?"

"Quite sure, thank you."

"I see." In silence, Ludovic accompanied me all the way to the Giltspur Street door. Plainly reluctant to go in, he asked only, "You are going to tell her, aren't you?"

"Of course," I said. "Thank you for walking me home."

"My pleasure," he said, and took his leave.

Madame Carriera disapproved of my interest in Maspero's siege medal, as I'd known she would. "It's one thing to study an object and learn what you can," she admitted. "But you've spent far too much time on this already. The palace archive is a wonderful place. Why focus on just one thing there?"

"It interests me. I love it. And my time is my own. You can't say I've been neglecting my duties."

"No, I can't fault your work here." Madame Carriera looked troubled. "It's just that your enthusiasms are so—violent. And so ill chosen. Why Maspero? Why not Mantegna? Someone *good*."

"Maspero's good."

"All right. I'll yield that point. But emulating Maspero isn't going to win you a career. His kind of symbolism is old-fashioned."

"Is the Mathias Bridge old-fashioned?"

"You're studying to be a painter, not an engineer. Though if you're studying more of Maspero's work than one portrait medallion, I'm relieved to hear it."

"I saw the ceiling fresco in the throne room," I confessed. "The cleaners were in, and I pretended to be carrying buckets for them. It's beautiful. It's a trellis."

"I've seen it. Given the dimensions of the room, it's a good solution."

"Would you really let me study more of Maspero's work than just the medal?" I asked. "There's the gisant at St. Barbara's. I could study that."

"Oh, yes. Queen Andred's tomb. Maspero did that?"

"It was his last work. The only time he had ever tried a full-size sculpture in stone. It's thirty leagues." It was a bit farther than that, closer to one hundred miles than ninety. Most of the members of the Lidian royal house were buried in the Abbey of St. Istvan in Dalager, but Queen Andred had spent her widowhood among the Sisters of St. Barbara, and in death she refused to leave them. So fair was the queen's tomb, it had become a shrine to rival that of St. Barbara herself. Of course, there was only a finger bone of St. Barbara to revere at her shrine, and unseen beneath Maspero's masterwork lay an entire queen, so perhaps the devotion the queen inspired was understandable.

"I'd forgotten that was his." Madame Carriera looked sad. "The queen's shrine attracted one pilgrim too many. Some Philistine has robbed the tomb. It was all they were talking about at the guild hall last time I was there."

"No! That's sacrilege!"

"More than that, it was folly. There couldn't have been much buried with her. A few jewels, perhaps. I suppose they'd have done it for no more than the coins from her eyes. Barbarians. Clumsy barbarians at that. They levered the lid off the tomb, and it shattered. I'm sorry it was Maspero's work that was ruined."

"Shattered?" I gaped at Madame Carriera. Saskia and I had talked of traveling to St. Barbara's as pilgrims ourselves someday. Thirty leagues was not too far for two healthy young women. We'd known Madame Carriera would refuse to give us time to make the journey, but we would both be members of the artists guild one day, free to make what pilgrimages we pleased.

"Not shattered into dust. But certainly badly damaged," said Madame Carriera. "I'll ask for more details if you're so interested."

"Yes. If you please." I shook my head wearily. "I can't believe it."

"I'm sorry you hadn't heard. I suppose the miracle is that it lasted this long."

If the weather the year before had been too dry, the weather that year was too wet. The rains were heavier than anyone could remember. By the time the fields were dry enough to sow, we were weeks past the planting season. I was grateful that my family's business was not as subject to the tyranny of the weather as most.

For my own part, I hardly noticed the chilly dampness. Saskia knew someone who knew someone who had a casting furnace I could afford to hire. I modeled and remodeled my waxen copy of the siege medal, cast and recast it, smelted and resmelted the same few ounces of bronze, until my eyebrows were half singed from the heat.

When I finally made a copy of Maspero's medal that satisfied me,

I rejoiced. It was a thing made to be held in the hand, to be cherished. To me, my medal never quite lost the heat of the furnace. Even as it nestled in my palm, it seemed to give back some of the fire of its creation, some of the warmth I'd felt as I labored to craft it. Before I even began the burnishing that would complete the medal, I showed it proudly to Saskia, to Piers, even to the man who owned the furnace.

A few days after midsummer, when I was almost halfway between my eighteenth birthday and my nineteenth, Gabriel came back to Giltspur Street.

He was there to help Piers with repairs to the ceiling of the garret room they had shared. In an attempt to fresco the ceiling, Piers had brought down much of the cracked old plaster. When the worst of the patching was done, the conversation turned from the design of Piers's fresco—he insisted it should be Venus and Adonis, over all our protests and suggestions—to the works we had been concentrating upon that spring.

"Saskia, you must be nearly finished," said Gabriel. "Let me see."

With grave serenity, Saskia led the way to the studio, where her portrait of Madame Carriera held pride of place.

"A shameless piece of self-promotion," said Gabriel, "but rather good. Yes, rather good, my dear."

Saskia gave him her sweetest smile and said nothing.

Piers showed us the Madonna and Child he was working on. Gabriel complimented it lavishly, as was only right, then turned to me. "And you, Madame Rosamer? What masterpiece from your hand?"

My hand itched to slap his face, but I tried to be as benevolent in aspect as Saskia. "That would be premature. I'm not half finished with my apprenticeship yet. Time enough to decide on a subject for my masterpiece."

"Waiting for your craft to match your ambition?" Gabriel inquired solicitously. "Is that wise? I fear in your case, the latter will always outstrip the former. But I heard from the fellow at the bellows that you've been at the casting furnace lately, melting anything not fastened down. Won't you show me what you've been working on?"

"I don't know what you mean. Do you get much gossip from fellows with bellows?" It was a feeble rejoinder, but it served my turn. Gabriel dropped the subject. Piers demanded we help tidy up after the plastering, and the rest of the rainy afternoon was spent in cleaning tools.

Gabriel hadn't forgotten the subject, however. He met me the next day, as I was out on an errand of Madame Carriera's. I returned his greeting and allowed him to fall into step beside me. I was glad to walk slowly. My basket was heavy, for in addition to the pigments I had purchased for Madame Carriera at the apothecary shop, I had been to the market and spent a crown of my own on a bent bronze candlestick, which I planned to recast into several small pieces. Not medallions, anything but that. A cloak pin, a pair of shoe buckles, any simple small thing I could show Madame Carriera to account for my time if she too heard some gossip from the man who owned the furnace.

The first thing Gabriel said after he'd bid me a good morning was, "You've copied the siege medal."

I stared at him. He looked as he always did, well groomed and cheerful. But for the only time since we'd known one another, he wasn't patronizing me. There was nothing of mock jollity in his tone. He was speaking equal to equal.

"I hear it's good. I suppose you worked in lost wax because you didn't have the wit to cast it as a die. That's necessary to stamp out the coins, but I can help you with that." The patronizing tone came back then, as he explained how much help he would be to me, making more copies of the siege medal. "You haven't thought about the cost of the silver either, I can tell. It's one thing to cast bronze, and quite another to cast the real thing."

"What are you talking about?" I asked him finally.

"Don't try the ignorant act with me," Gabriel snapped. "I know you too well to be fooled. Play it my way, or I'll turn you in to the authorities."

"Play what?"

"All right. Let's go. You could've turned the medal over to me, and I'd have kept quiet. Since you insist, we'll go tell the magistrate all about your hard work spent counterfeiting Julian dinars."

"What?" That brought me up short. "You're mad."

"Am I really? I'm an established member of the guild you can only aspire to join. I have a workshop and more commissions than I and a studio full of apprentices can fill. The magistrate knows me well. He'll listen to me."

"Listen to what?"

"The truth about you, *Madame* Rosamer."

"Don't call me that." I stalked away.

Gabriel matched my speed. "Why not? You love it. It's the only time you'll ever hear it, and you know it."

"You call me that to plague me, that's all. I hate it."

"Liar. You know you're never going to be in the guild. Madame Carriera took you on as a favor. You came here with your nose in the air and you looked down at all of us. Do you know how hard I had to work before she would even consent to let me try for an apprenticeship with her? I was better trained before I ever set foot in Giltspur Street than you'll be on the last day you see it. You, with your little copies—you make me laugh. You've always made me laugh."

"I never looked down on anyone. You spent all your time thinking of ways to make things harder for me—you sneezed on my gold leaf!" My voice shook with indignation, and I bit back my words lest I shame myself with tears of rage.

We had reached the mouth of Giltspur Street. Gabriel took my arm to stop my flight home. "Give me the medal. I won't say another word about it. Give me the medal or I'll report you. Do you know what the penalty for coining is? First they'll slit your long nose, Madame Rosamer, and then they'll hang you."

Here was no prank, no sand in my sinopia. Here was something I had never encountered in my life: hatred.

"Think of the shame you'll bring to Madame Carriera. Think of the pain you'll cause her, the discredit to her workshop. Give me the medal."

His words burned in my ears as his grip on my wrist ground my bones together. I tried to free myself. "Why? What would you do with it?"

"Why, I'd turn it in to the proper authorities. I'll say I found it somewhere. There'll be nothing to connect it with you." I was looking him in the eyes and I saw the lie there, clear behind the pious words. Gabriel truly thought I intended to use my medal to fake Julian dinars. Once he had the medal, he would have a secret to hold over me always. He could threaten to reveal my supposed crime any time it suited him.

As I could see his lie, he could see my fear. The sight fed his hatred, and he went on telling me what my misdeeds would do to Madame Carriera's reputation, to my family's reputation. He let himself make every threat he could think of.

Such words. It would not repay my effort to recollect them and set them down on the page. But the result served me better than it served him. Young, I was. Foolish, I was. Female, I am and have always proudly been. But even a brass farthing can buy trouble. Even a market basket can dent a head.

He fell at my feet. I stared at him for what seemed like quite a long time, but it must have been a minute, no more. My blow had broken the skin at his temple and the blood came fast.

My thoughts were clear. If I had hurt him very badly, he might die. Then I would be arrested for murder and put to death. If I had not hurt him badly enough, he might live. I would be arrested for counterfeiting and put to death. As desperately as I wanted to be a great artist and create all the things that I had in mind to make the moment my skill allowed, I wanted even more to live.

Given time, and a good hot furnace, I might have destroyed the medal. The casting furnace was half the city away and I knew that by the time I'd fired it to the proper temperature, too much time would have passed. Gabriel would have been discovered. Charges lodged. An arrest made.

My thoughts were clear. Yet my thoughts were not all that ruled me. I ran away. I put the pigments where Madame Carriera would find them, lest she come to chide me sooner than she must. I gathered up the siege medal, a few poor items besides, tied them in a scarf, and fled.

Six

(In which I take a long walk.)

It is one thing to plan to walk thirty leagues and quite another to do it. Saskia and I never planned to make our pilgrimage to St. Barbara's unprepared. I had far more than thirty leagues ahead of me the day I ran away from Madame Carriera's workshop.

It was ninety leagues north to Neven from the city of Aravis. More than that, for I could not take the main road. Even if I had dared to brave the easiest route, where any pursuit would be sure to look for me first, my conscience kept me to the longer, ill-traveled river roads. The season's woolpack would be in by now, and soon the raft would bring it downstream to market. If I missed them en route, my family would float serenely past me and try to sell our goods in a city where I was deemed either a murderer or a counterfeiter. I was determined to stay within sight of the river, to shout, to wave, to set something afire, anything to prevent that.

I walked ten miles the first day, no more. My legs were strong enough for more, but I was frightened and dread is tiring. That night I hardly slept, and the next day I set off as soon as there was a smear of light in the east. Fear spurred me thirty miles before the light failed at last. The third day I did not do so well. Weariness, remorse, hunger, and blisters plagued me. That day I had hardly gone eight limping miles before the long summer evening began to close in. When it did, I sat down under a barberry bush, put my face in my hands, and wailed like a two-year-old. Before I was finished weeping, exhaustion caught up with me. I curled up under my bush and slept.

Sunlight woke me the fourth morning. I watched the river while I soaked the last of my bread in water until it was soft enough to eat. The sun was well up before I set out stiffly, with no food left, and with the nagging worry that the raft had passed by while I slept the dawn away. I cursed myself for a laggard, a sluggard, ten sorts of a fool. Oh, but I was in a sour mood. So of course it was that day, about noon, by which time I had gone scarcely twelve miles, that it began to rain.

It is wonderful what fear can overcome. It is wonderful what hope can bring to pass. But there is nothing in the least wonderful about what walking in even a summer rain can do to a hungry person with blisters. By late afternoon I had come as far as the bridge at Folliard. There, under the bridge, at the water's edge, where I could be out of the rain and still see the river, I halted. Fear of pursuit, fear of arrest, fear of execution—all these paled before my hunger, my blisters, and the constant, unyielding, relentless fall of rain.

The seven-arched bridge at Folliard is a very old one, Roman stonework upheld only by the perfection of its design. Such arts are long lost to our modern stone craft. The river must have run wider or deeper in the Romans' day; even after all our rain, there was still a gravel bank between the first pier of the bridge and the river. There was no food for miles, of course, or any cure for blisters. But the stonework kept the rain off, and when I reached it, that was enough for me. I stopped.

I thought at first glance that a large bundle of old clothes had washed up at the river's edge. When I realized there was a person in them, I was startled and afraid. It is all very well to plan to venture forth as a pilgrim. To be alone, without even the symbols of staff and cockleshell to keep the world at bay, is quite different. It would be folly not to be wary when one finds oneself alone with a stranger, far from any help.

He was on his stomach, one arm in the water all the way to the shoulder. His face was turned away. He might have been sleeping. He lay so still, he might have been a drowned man, washed up there on the riverbank. He was wet enough for it.

I remembered how still Gabriel had lain where he fell. Fear twisted my stomach. If this man were dead too, perhaps he hadn't drowned. Perhaps he'd been killed by someone hiding nearby. My fright made everything around me into a threat.

While I was still fumbling for some kind of defense, a stone— Lord, even a bent candlestick—he stirred. On one smooth movement, he rose and pulled free of the river—and threw a fish at me.

It was a mudskip, all whiskers and fins. I am ashamed to admit I screamed as it fell on the gravel at my feet. I don't think the man had even noticed me until then. He lunged at me, a knife in his hand. I sprang away. He fell upon the fish and gutted it before I had drawn breath for a second scream. With a few precise cuts, he sliced the fish and began to eat.

Instead of screaming again, I said, "You shouldn't do that. Mudskip tastes bad enough cooked."

He paid no attention.

After a while, I said, "You must be hungry."

He looked up at last. "Do you have anything to eat?" He laughed at my expression and added, "Spare a crust for a poor beggar, mistress?"

He was dirty but he was no beggar. His eyes were terrible, red rimmed with exhaustion. Weariness marked him as plain as the mud did. The concentration he brought to the simple act of putting food in his mouth said his remaining strength was small. But he was strongly made, well able to work for his keep. Nor were his clothes those of a beggar. They were fouled with mud, but the fabric was rich and from what I could see, the garments well made, though wildly out of fashion. He even wore a chain of office, heavy S-links, like a king on a playing card. Had he been clean, he would have seemed as out-of-date as a figure in a stained-glass window.

For all that he'd scared me, I studied him closely. I couldn't rid myself of the notion that I knew him. From Aravis? From home? Or had he been one of Madame Carriera's subjects, met only on canvas or vellum? Was he a player, costumed for a masque?

I was frowning with the effort of memory. My scowl seemed to amuse him.

"What do you have in that pack of yours? A parcel of bread and cheese? Some apples? A sturdy lass like you never set off without packing nuncheon."

"I ate it all."

"Of course you did. You look like a good eater. Want some fish? Sorry—there's not much left but bones and whiskers."

"No. Thank you. My name is Hail Rosamer. Who are you?"

"What I am, mistress, is a stranger. You are forbidden to speak with strangers, I'll warrant."

I looked upstream—no sign of any river craft. He followed my gaze. In the instant when I'd turned back and he still looked upstream, I recognized him. It was the profile, of course. Madame Carriera taught us that the profile makes the best portrait, the finest likeness caught in the fewest lines. This stranger's profile was the same as that on Maspero's siege medal. My voice was half strangled by my surprise. "Who *are* you?"

He frowned at me. There was a silence between us, but I was sure my thoughts could be read on my face. Finally he said, "Who do you think I am?"

When the king comes home. I managed not to say the words aloud. Instead I fumbled in my pack and found the medal I had made. Gingerly, I put my hand out, as if I were offering a biscuit to a strange dog, possibly a dangerous dog.

With wariness to match his weariness, he craned forward to see what I held. I saw the recognition strike him. He drew back, as if I'd offered him a blow. "Put it away."

I obeyed him, as much because of the pain in his voice as because of the note of command.

We looked at each other then, really looked. Our eyes were level, for he was still hunched over the ruins of the mudskip, and I'd dropped down to crouch on my heels before him.

"Tell me your name again."

"Hail Rosamer. From Neven. Upriver."

"I know Neven. Good sheep country."

I nodded. "What shall I call you? Your majesty?"

He rejected the words with a shake of his head. "Nothing. I'm no one."

"Julian?"

"No. I'm not him."

"Well, are you related to him?"

If something that sounded that tired could be called a laugh, he laughed. "No."

Here was more reticence than I could overcome. I chose another tack. "You were fishing just now. I'll call you Fisher. If I may?"

"If it pleases you. You're far from Neven, surely?"

"I've lived in Aravis for years. I'm apprenticed to Madame Angelica Carriera."

"You're not too near Aravis either. Funny place to choose for a walk in the rain."

"It wasn't raining when I started. I'm going home."

"On foot? From Aravis to Neven?"

"Unless our raft comes. Then I'll signal them and they will pick me up."

"And take you back—to where? Neven? This river flows the wrong direction for you, doesn't it?"

"I have to signal them. It's very important."

"Better start, then."

I looked where he was looking, far upstream. It was easy to miss in the rain, but a raft was coming, just a smear of gray against the paler gray of the river. I leaped up, I and my heart together.

My father saw me wave from the bridge. I watched them pull the sweeps to steer toward shore. It was like a dream, the slow kind, while

I turned over so many things in my mind, so many greetings, so much to say, that it seemed time scarcely moved at all. It seemed the raft would never touch the shore.

I came back to wait with Fisher under the bridge. "I'll make them give us something to eat," I told him.

He'd been meaning to leave—I could tell by the line of his shoulders and back—but the thought of food tempted him. He relaxed a little, just enough to let me see the moment of temptation clearly. Then he braced himself again and said, "No need." His tone was flat, as if he had a lot of experience in resisting temptation and had become so good at it, he no longer needed to give it much thought.

"You recognized the medal. That deserves some sort of reward. Where did you see it before?"

"I don't remember." I had a feeling he remembered all too well and didn't wish to tell me. After a pause, he added, "He was from Ardres, wasn't he? Perhaps I saw it there."

"Who?"

"The craftsman who made it, your precious medal."

"Gil Maspero was from Ardres?" It was the first I'd heard of it. It was a revelation for me to imagine Maspero being from anywhere. Easier to think of the Archangel Michael coming from Ardres.

"Perhaps. Perhaps not. My memory's faulty."

"But you know about Maspero. You know he was a great artist."

"He was?"

"You'd be surprised how many people have never even heard of him. What else do you know about Maspero? How did you learn of him?"

For some reason, my enthusiasm seemed to discourage Fisher. He fell silent. We watched as the raft came slowly in to shore some hundred yards downstream from the bridge. I thought Fisher would stay under the arch, but he walked with me down to join my father and brother. I was glad. I wanted to know a lot more about him and if he knew anything more I didn't about Maspero.

"Hail, what's amiss?" Father called. "What's wrong?"

I didn't even try to answer until I was safe in his arms. Then the whole story came out, punctuated by my sobs.

My father did not behave at all the way I'd thought he would at the news that I was either a murderer or a counterfeiter. He lectured me—no other word for it—for deserting my obligations in Aravis, and he ordered me out of the way among the baggage. "We'll settle matters as soon as we have you back safe in Giltspur Street."

"But the magistrate . . ."

"I'll speak to the magistrate. An articled apprentice has every right to pursue her craft without being molested in the street by rivals jealous of her ability."

"Gabriel wasn't jealous of my ability. He didn't think I had any."

"That's more proof he was unbalanced. Let me handle this. Don't make a nuisance of yourself there. Just sit down and be still." Father then thanked Fisher courteously for his care of me, just as if there had been any reason whatsoever to do so. From the angle of Father's gaze as he inspected him, I could tell he was trying to decide if it would insult the stranger to offer him money. The circumstances allowed it, but the quality of his bedraggled costume argued that it might be rude to patronize him.

Nothing in Father's manner suggested that he saw the likeness to Good King Julian. I wondered if I were the only one who noticed it. Would it take study of the siege medal to teach one the resemblance?

"There's a smoked chicken here," I announced. The chief reason I'd retreated obediently to the baggage was to investigate the supplies. "Won't you join me?"

"I thought you'd prove a good eater."

"Where are you headed?" Father asked.

"I need a priest."

Father looked intrigued but said only, "We are traveling to Aravis. Would it serve your purpose to accompany us?"

Temptation again, in every line of him, and I could see he was going to resist it. I swear that's the only reason I started on the smoked chicken.

"Is there any mustard?" I asked Amyas. He passed me the little stoneware crock. As I opened it, Fisher accepted my father's invitation with a nod and stepped lightly aboard the raft. I made room for him beside me. Amyas passed him the oatcakes.

Father called to the men at the sweeps. They and my brother set to work poling us out into deeper water. The current took us and we moved steadily downstream. As we drew away, I looked back and saw the Folliard Bridge from midriver. From there it seemed to me the arches met their reflections, and despite the steady rain on the surface of the water, the mass of the bridge and the darkness of the reflections made half circles whole against the pale river. I admired the sight as I ate, until the view was lost around the next bend of the river.

I finished my drumstick and one oatcake in the time it took Fisher to consume six oatcakes and the rest of the smoked chicken. Before I'd cleaned up the bones and put the mustard away, he was asleep.

I stretched my legs before me, winced once more at my blisters, and settled myself to watch Fisher sleep and plan what questions I would ask him about Maspero when he woke. We had not gone a mile downstream before I was asleep myself.

I grudged every mile I'd walked, even as I watched them pass from the simple comfort of the raft. Every blister on me, I blamed on Gabriel. If I'd killed him, and at times I hoped I had, he'd had his revenge of me. Only once I was safe with Amyas and my father did I realize how frightened I'd been, how far from clear my thoughts had been.

"What possessed you to disobey Madame Carriera?" Amyas demanded. "If you hadn't spent so much time mooning over the siege medal, you'd never have found yourself in such trouble."

"I was studying it. I mean to study all I can of Maspero's work."

"That won't take long," said Fisher quietly. "He only worked when he had to. The rest of the time he spent scribbling in his notebooks."

"How do you know that?" asked Amyas. "Have you studied this Maspero too?"

Fisher gave a snort of scorn. "I'm no student." He made no reply to Amyas's questions, nor to mine.

Eventually I gave up asking questions about Maspero. Instead, I devoted myself to my notebook. In addition to recording any reference Fisher had made to Maspero, I sketched Fisher. If I had Good King Julian there in front of me, I didn't mean to waste a moment of my time.

On his usual visits, my father spent much of his time in Aravis at the guild hall conducting business. His acquaintance, as I had always assumed, was largely drawn from the wool merchants of the city. But I now learned that my father did more in Aravis than just conduct business and that his acquaintance was not exclusively among those who practiced his own trade.

True, he knew no magistrates of the Court of the King's Bench, but he knew several members of the Chancery Court, and they were glad to provide introductions to clerks, attorneys, chancellors, and all. He was not as familiar with the proceedings of the King's Bench as he was with the civil suits of Chancery, where matters of the wool trade usually ended up, but he knew who to ask and how.

By the time we were tied up at Shene Wharf, my father had planned his campaign to clear me and the Rosamer family name. My presence in Aravis formed only a small part of his strategy, fortunately, and so I was bidden to stay with the woolpack, safely out of the way until summoned, with my brother Amyas to guard me. My father thanked Fisher again, then left to start work on clearing my name.

Fisher clambered from our raft to the quay and made a vague gesture of farewell to Amyas and me. "I thank you for your help."

I joined him on the quay side. "Wait, where are you going?"

"Hail, get back here," Amyas called.

"I need a priest," Fisher said, turned on his heel, and left.

"Hail!" I heard Amyas scolding behind me but paid no attention. He was welcome to follow me if he wanted to.

Fisher paused and looked around as he left the wharf, as if getting his bearings. But he didn't ask directions from anyone, just walked from there to the old church of St. Peter the Fisherman. Amyas caught up with me as I followed him in.

Once inside (and a nice little interior it was too, simple but well proportioned), he wasted no time. He interrupted the priest's conversation with the verger.

"Your pardon, Father. I beg of you, help drive me out of this man. I am a damned spirit, brought back to possess the hapless body before you. The rite of exorcism, I beseech you."

The priest and the verger goggled at him. After an astonished moment, the priest said, "My son, this is no matter for joking." Something in Fisher's expression made him think better of that answer, for almost at once he added, "Nor a matter that can be hastened, even if I wished to. I cannot simply sit you down in a chair and perform the rite of exorcism here and now."

"Why not?"

"I am not qualified, not prepared, and frankly, not inclined. Is there some other way in which I might help you?"

Fisher was absolutely still for a moment, a stillness that hinted at despair. Finally, he sighed and asked, "Will you hear my confession?"

"Will you be able to make one, damned spirit that you are?" The mockery was very gentle, and Fisher didn't even seem to notice it. He let the priest lead him away.

Amyas looked at me. The verger stared at us both. I turned my attention to the church interior.

Amyas whispered in my ear. "Don't you have ears? Father told you to stay with the woolpack."

"I'll go straight back there as soon as I can."

"You'll go back there now. I can't protect you from the whole city, you know."

"You don't have to. What's going to happen to me in a church?"

"I'm not leaving you."

"Then hush."

Amyas's whisper in my ear was hot with anger. "What's the matter with you, anyway? Anyone would think you were mad too, the way you follow him around."

I whispered back. "Don't you see it either? Amyas, he's either Good King Julian or he looks just like him."

Amyas closed his mouth and stared at me in disbelieving silence.

"That's right. When the king comes home, brother. I'm staying right here."

It seemed a long time before they came back. When they did, Fisher looked gray. He knelt before the altar, praying. The priest looked very white about the mouth. He whispered a lengthy message into the verger's ear. The verger's eyebrows climbed, and he left us in haste. The priest turned to Amyas and me.

"Your friend will be helped. You need not fear for him any longer."

"That must have been a remarkable confession." Amyas's murmur was faint, but I caught it.

So did the priest. "It was. I erred before. This is a matter of the most profound urgency. I was a blockhead not to realize it at once. The river could run with milk and I not notice sometimes."

Amyas looked surprised. "So you're going to do it after all? You'll perform an exorcism?"

"Not I. Someone more qualified. We will care for him. Thank you for bringing him safely here."

That sounded very like a dismissal to me. I crossed my arms. "Will it be done here?"

"No, no. It will be done somewhere more suitable."

"Where, precisely? By whom, precisely?"

Gentle mockery stirred beneath his words. "You are very protective of this unfortunate soul. You have brought him to safety and you deserve thanks. I can only offer advice, but it is good advice. Don't linger here."

"Do you think he's dangerous?" Amyas murmured. "Whoever he is, he's mad as mad can be, but he's been very quiet with us."

I frowned at him. "He isn't mad."

Amyas ignored me and turned back to the priest. "Where have you sent the verger?"

"He went to fetch help."

"Then you do think he's dangerous?"

"Without a doubt. But he isn't mad."

I glanced back at the altar, trying to see Fisher as they did. He knelt before the altar as if he were sheltering from a storm, head down, shoulders hunched. The priest's words made more sense to me than my brother's. He did look dangerous, yet I was convinced that Fisher was every bit as sane as I. But he was in trouble. "I'm staying with him."

Amyas frowned. "I should never have let you leave the raft."

I just looked at my brother. Where Amyas gets these ideas about being responsible for me—no, that's unjust. Father and Mother gave him the ideas. But how he managed to think they were practicable ideas escapes me.

"If I'm safe there, I'm safe here. And if I'm not safe here, I'm not safe anywhere."

"Didn't you ever listen to Master Nicholas? That's not remotely logical."

The priest had been listening for something all this while, and when he straightened and smiled a little as the sound of marching feet approached, I realized what he'd been waiting for. The verger had returned. As Amyas and I turned, ten soldiers joined us, all clad in the gray cloak and green tabard of the prince-bishop's guard. The tenth, their officer, was not much above middle height and had dark eyes and a stubborn jaw. He brought his soldiers to order and saluted the priest. "Father, we are at your service. Is this the unfortunate we are here to escort?" Ludovic Nallaneen studied me with interest. "Possessed, is she? I've often suspected as much."

"Good morning, Ludo." I thought of several pert remarks to add but made none of them. There was the distinct possibility he had come to execute a warrant for my arrest. I could think of worse people to do it. Ludo seemed more tolerant of me than most people ever dreamed of being.

The priest was impatient. "Here is the unfortunate in need of the prince-bishop's help."

Ludovic paused to study Fisher. When he addressed him, it was with soft-spoken courtesy. "Your pardon, sir, but I must interrupt your devotions. The prince-bishop wishes to see you urgently." He took off his cloak and offered it to Fisher. "Please wear the hood. It is His Grace's express wish."

I wasn't the only one to see the resemblance, after all. The hood could only be intended to conceal Fisher's face from anyone who knew what Good King Julian looked like. Judging from Ludovic's expression, he remembered Maspero's medal as well as I did.

Fisher rose, accepted the cloak, and put up the hood without question. He thanked the priest, thanked Amyas, and took my hand as if to thank me too.

"No need for that," I said. "I'm not letting you go off on your own."

"Not just yet, at any rate," said Ludovic. "The prince-bishop wants a few words with you too."

My stomach twisted. "About Gabriel Wex? Did I—hit him as hard as that?"

Ludovic looked intrigued. "You hit Gabriel? Whatever for?"

"Didn't he accuse me of murder? Attempted murder, at least? He threatened to accuse me of coining too."

"Gabriel reported your truancy to the guild. In leaving the city, you violated the terms of your apprenticeship."

"I ran away because he threatened me. He wouldn't let me go. I only hit him in self-defense."

"Strange. No such attack was mentioned."

Perhaps Gabriel had been embarrassed that I had knocked him senseless, too embarrassed to tell anyone I had bested him. I was filled with relief at not being guilty of murder, after all.

"The prince-bishop wishes only to ask you about the circumstances in which you and this gentleman met." Ludovic turned back to Fisher. "The prince-bishop awaits us."

I turned to Amyas. "Tell Father I've gone to straighten things out myself."

"You can't be serious. I'm not letting you our of my sight." Amyas turned to the verger. "If you please, sir, I need to get a message to our father."

Fisher and Ludovic set off with the soldiers. They marched away, a small, efficient mob in perfect step, Fisher hooded in their midst. I followed. Amyas followed me, scolding softly all the while.

SEVEN

(In which I learn more about Fisher.)

From the Church of St. Peter near the waterfront at Shene to the palace that crowns Aravis as snow crowns the highest mountains is not a long journey, yet in a way it spans the whole world. From the lowest to the highest we walked, from the beggars outside the church, past the boatmen at the waterfront, through Shene gate, upward through the crowded streets to the palace on the heights.

It took us an hour to cover the distance, for Fisher stopped in his tracks again and again. At first I assumed he was unused to the steepness of the way and stopped to catch his breath. Soon, though, it became clear that he was watching as he went, slowing to take a good look now and then, even stopping to stare. It was the new buildings that seemed to interest him, not the fine old ones. He stood for a long time beside the monument built to honor the relief of the siege of Aravis. I was glad, for that monument, carved with the little ships that had brought the relief, had been designed by Maspero. It seemed fitting that it should be admired properly.

Once we reached the palace, our progress grew more swift. Ludovic and his men led us by countersign and password through the security measures that guarded the heart of the palace. From there we were taken through the corridors to the prince-bishop's chambers and into the august presence of the prince-bishop himself.

I had never seen the man before. The prince-bishop wore black velvet despite the season, and his point lace collar was flat and stiff, yet as graceful as a bird's wing. His smooth gray hair was dressed severely back beneath his clerical cap. His face was soft: velvety jowls, round cheeks with a flush of health and good humor—or heat. His eyes were brown and moved all the time, measuring and memorizing. There was an indefinable softness about that face which had nothing to do with the bones. It was as if he had been ever so lightly powdered. He looked as if he might smell of cloves or lavender, something pleasant.

The chamber was simple, sparsely furnished, whitewashed walls and ceiling with a floor of chessboard black and white. Afternoon sun came full through the great windows that looked south over a jumble of rooftops from the esplanade to the lower city. It was a peaceful room. I was glad of Amyas at my back. Without him, I would have felt an utter rustic, intruding in something that was no business of mine. With him, I knew there was at least one person in the room who felt more out of place there than I.

Fisher knelt and kissed the prince-bishop's ring before Ludovic's men were at parade rest. Fisher kept his head bowed, and when he spoke I could hardly catch his words, muffled in the prince-bishop's velvet. "I beg you. An exorcism. Free the unfortunate I've been summoned to possess."

With the flick of his hand, the prince-bishop summoned his only attendant, a cherubic-looking gentleman, white-haired and simply dressed, from his quiet corner. "Rigo, your counsel, please."

The cherubic old man joined the prince-bishop. Gently he pushed back the hood of the cloak and rested his hand on Fisher's bent head. "You've traveled far."

Fisher's shoulders rose and fell with the force of his sigh. "Send me back, I beg you."

The old man's hand soothed him as if he were patting a hound. "That is not in my power. Nor is it in His Grace's power." He met the prince-bishop's piercing gaze and said to him, "This is not a case of possession. Your people know their business, as do you."

The prince-bishop's voice was cold. "What is it, then?"

"It is not what you fear. I can help a little. Not here though. I'll use the Archangel Chapel. It's protected." Without paying the slightest attention to the rest of us, not even the guards, the old man took Fisher's hand and helped him rise. Together, they led the way to the Archangel Chapel. We followed in silence, the prince-bishop first, the rest of us trailing after like ducklings.

At the chapel door, the prince-bishop paused to speak to Ludovic. Half his men were detailed to guard the door from outside. The rest of us were admitted to the chapel. "Rigo likes plenty of witnesses," the prince-bishop murmured to us.

Once we were in the chapel, Rigo made Fisher kneel before the altar, then turned back to the prince-bishop. With a touch on his shoulder, he bade him remain with us. "Stay at a distance, Your Grace. Kneel and say the Paternoster. All of you. Keep saying it. We must not be disturbed."

"You needn't tell me when to pray," said the prince-bishop, but he led us in the prayer without further protest.

Rigo circled the room, muttering and making small gestures with his gentle hands. He looked like an elderly terrier trying to remember where he'd left a bone. His route brought him steadily closer to Fisher until he was shuffling around him at arm's length. The muttering had dropped to a barely audible singsong tone, an aimless humming, like a preoccupied bee.

Rigo paused before Fisher, stared into his face for a moment, then brushed his fingertips from Fisher's hairline to his chin. I thought I saw something come away in his hands, a soft gray something, like a cobweb. He rubbed it in his fingers, humming all the while, and turned swiftly to the altar. He held it to one of the candles there, and for an instant it was as if a cloud had come over; there was an infinitesimal dimming of the light, not just of the candle, but all the light in the room. Then the whole chapel seemed to brighten, to recover light and color.

Fisher still knelt, still prayed, even as Rigo turned from the altar candles and came to stand before him again. This time, he put his hands on Fisher's shoulders as if to steady him. His voice was gentle. "That's all."

Fisher looked up. I could only see his back, the line of his shoulders, the curve of his spine, but I could tell he wanted something more from the old man. I don't know what it was he needed, but he needed it badly.

Rigo looked very sad, but he tightened his hands on Fisher's shoulders and gave him a little shake as if to encourage him, to urge him to brace up. "You're here. You're a whole man. That's more than some of us are given."

"I don't . . . I don't *want* it."

"Now, what has that to do with anything?" The words were harsh, but the old man's voice was kind. He helped Fisher to his feet and steadied him when he seemed about to stagger. "You're a fine strong fellow. You'll do well." He beckoned to us.

I rose and followed the others toward the altar. When I was nearly there, I stopped and stared. Fisher was standing on his own now, though he seemed reluctant to let the old man go. From where I stood, I could see his profile. I looked from Fisher to the donor panel of the Archangel Nativity. I looked back, blinked hard, and looked again.

Fisher's face had changed. I no longer saw any resemblance to the portrait of King Julian IV. The profile that I had seen was gone. But I recognized this one too. Fisher was still there in the donor panel. For the man standing beside Rigo now had a different face, a different profile. His nose was crooked, as if it had been broken in a fight, but crooked in a noble, aquiline fashion. His shoulders sagged and his eyes closed. He looked desperately tired.

While I stood there gaping, Amyas made a clucking sound of astonishment and grasped my sleeve. "What is this? How did he do that? A mask? I saw him burn something in the candle." He was far from pleased.

I pulled free, caught Amyas's wrist, and brought him with me to the altarpiece, as close to the donor panel as I dared get. "Look."

Amyas looked. First at the donor panel, then at me. He said nothing, but his eyes widened and he looked accusingly at me, as if his confusion was somehow my fault. He looked back at the painting.

Fisher joined us. Before I realized it, he was at my shoulder, staring where Amyas was staring. He reached out to touch the panel and Amyas caught his hand. "Don't touch it. You'll mar the glaze. It's very old."

"He can touch it if he wants to," I snapped, cross although Amyas only parroted the scolding I'd once given him.

Fisher's voice was ragged. "How old?"

"About two hundred years," I said. Two hundred and fourteen, but I didn't think it was the moment to be a stickler for accuracy.

Fisher's breath caught. He brushed a fingertip across the smooth surface of the panel, just touching King Julian's crown. His face was full of grief. "So long?"

The pain in his voice made my throat close up. I knew better than to try to answer. I knew that much, anyway.

"Are you finished, Rigo?" The prince-bishop asked as he joined us. "No more transformation scenes in this masque?" As we had grown more troubled and confused, he seemed more cheerful. He stood so close to me that I could tell, far from smelling of cloves or lavender, he smelled faintly of incense and gunpowder.

"That is his true appearance," Rigo answered. "There is no more I can do for him. We live in an age of miracles, but this is not the miracle you surmised."

"This is no miracle. I am cursed." Fisher pointed to the donor panel. "I am Istvan Forest. That man in the painting. I was dead and now I am alive."

"You have not risen from the dead. Only our blessed Savior has such power over our poor clay." The prince-bishop folded his hands. "Yet here you are. You are safe. You have witnesses. Speak. Tell us how you came to be here."

Istvan Forest let his breath go in a shallow sigh. "It was cold. It was dark. Someone was calling me. I had to answer. I remember pushing pine branches out of my way. I thought I knocked some snow off the boughs—but that was my mistake, because it wasn't winter. It was a summer night. My head cleared. I was climbing over a windowsill. Explain that to me, sir. I'll give you as much time as you'd like to think of an explanation.

"I was at the top of a flight of stairs. I had to walk down. At first I couldn't see where I was going. My head was swimming. Winter, summer, awake, dreaming, I wasn't sure of anything. I came down a step at a time, and as I did my vision began to clear. I could see there was someone at the foot of the stair.

"It was a woman, and I knew she was the one who was calling me. She had red hair and she wore dark clothes. She was standing in front of something shiny—a shield or a mirror or a window—I couldn't tell what. It reflected the light from the fireplace. There were no lamps, no candles, no other source of light. She was very quiet. She was looking at the floor, at her feet, as if she was thinking hard about something.

"I thought it might be warm down there in the firelight. I was cold.

"I walked down the stairs and stood in front of that woman. When I was in front of her, she looked up at me. Her eyes were green. She stared at me as if she'd never seen anything so wonderful in all her life. She smiled at me. Her smile made me afraid.

"She didn't say anything, but I knew she wanted me to come closer. I had come close enough. I didn't move. I *felt* her call me closer. I didn't do anything. She seemed displeased.

"She said, 'You heard me.' She sounded preoccupied, as if she was only picking words with a small part of her attention, while all the rest of her thought was aimed hard at something else. Her voice was a little rough. It made me want to clear my throat. It seemed strange that I'd heard her say so few words aloud. It felt as though we'd been having a longer conversation, none of it spoken until those few words. 'You heard me.'

"I wanted to say, 'I hear you.' I wanted her to speak again. But instead it came out, 'I'm here.' And she said, 'Come closer.'

"I looked past her, and I saw we were both reflected in that mirror. Only now my vision—or my mind—had cleared and I saw it wasn't a mirror at all. It was a window. The firelight inside and the night outside made it a dark mirror. In it I could see my reflection almost hidden by hers. In the mirror, I was looking at myself over her shoulder.

"Only it wasn't me. It wasn't me. It was the king." Istvan broke off.

Every one of us in the room knew exactly what he meant. I was the only one to say it. "Good King Julian."

Istvan looked at me. "Do you still call him that? Two hundred years in the future? He's still Good King Julian?"

"It's not the future," I reminded him. "It's now."

Istvan shook his head. "I didn't know that. I didn't know where I was. Or when. But I knew I wasn't Julian. I understood that she was calling Julian. I don't know why. I could have answered her call and perhaps she might never have realized the difference. But I knew that if I did, if I came any closer, I would never turn away from her again. But she wasn't calling me. So I could turn away. If I gave it all my strength, I could even walk away.

"I tried to turn to go back up the stairs. I couldn't reach them. It was like walking into a high wind or wading against a strong current. I couldn't go back. But there was a door, and I could open it.

"I walked out."

Istvan paused, and the silence lasted a long time. It was a solid silence, a silence that drew out until even he noticed it. He had been looking into nothing, into the past, perhaps. But gradually he remembered us, and finally he spoke again.

"I walked out. Two men tried to stop me. I'm sure I killed one. The other, I don't know. The woman wanted me to return. I wanted to leave. The farther I drew away from her, the easier it became. After a while, I could go quite fast. After a while, I could run away from the call. That was the only sense of direction I had. My bearings were gone. I only knew I had to get away from her. I did."

After another long pause he continued. "It took me some time to realize where I was, even after the sun was well up. I'd been to Ardres before. The last time, things looked quite different. I realized that a bit of time must have passed, for the damage to have been repaired so well. I had no idea how long it had been. Two hundred years . . ."

The prince-bishop's voice was extremely dry. "You traveled to Ardres? You are sure?"

"I traveled from Ardres. I am very sure. As soon as I had my bearings, I headed downriver. Away. By midday, I had reached the bridge at Folliard. There used to be good fishing there. I was hungry. That was where I encountered Hail."

The prince-bishop and Istvan looked at me. So did Amyas and Ludovic Nallaneen, but with a good deal less gravity.

"Hail helped you come here," said Rigo. "You needn't look so stern. She won't do it again."

I turned on Rigo. "What do you mean? I haven't finished helping him yet." Even if he no longer looked like the king come again, Istvan still knew Maspero. He remembered what Aravis was like more than two hundred years before. He was the Seraph, the king's own champion. Any help I could offer was his without asking. "I've scarcely begun."

Amyas stifled a groan.

The prince-bishop turned his attention back to Istvan. "Do you know precisely where the calling occurred? Was it in Ardres itself?"

"Not within the stronghold proper. I passed no fortifications."

"Nearby?"

"Not between me and the river."

"You said two men tried to stop you. Are you sure there were only two?"

"No. I don't remember clearly."

"Did either of them refer to the woman by name? Could you describe her?"

"I just have."

"Red hair, green eyes. Could you provide any more details?"

"No." Either in an effort at recollection or for mere weariness, Istvan closed his eyes. "She was small. Slim. I don't know. She had a gleeful look when she smiled. Like a fox."

"Or a ferret." The prince-bishop's voice was dryer than ever. "That is Dalet. I conjectured that she was working for Edward of Ardres. This may not prove it, but it gives me confidence to proceed in accordance with my beliefs."

"Dalet? Who's that?" I asked.

"Red Ned?" Amyas looked intrigued. "He really does call dead people back to life?"

"How?" I asked.

"Why?" asked Amyas in the same moment.

The prince-bishop looked disdainful. "Only our blessed Savior does that. I admit it seems as though something very like it has occurred here. Apparently Dalet has called back someone. Perhaps she miscalculated. For it seems clear she expected Good King Julian and someone else answered instead." He studied Istvan dispassionately. "Why did you answer when you were not called?"

Despair was plain in Istvan's face, but his voice was steady. "I don't know."

"A few months ago," the prince-bishop began, "there was a robbery at the convent of St. Barbara. The tomb of Queen Andred the Fair was violated. The jewels interred with the queen were stolen. After some difficulty in finding the records, the archivists here at the palace library succeeded in locating an inventory of the queen's possessions at the time of her death. Andred was buried with a copy of the Aravis siege medal, an enamel brooch, a gold band on her left ring finger, and, on the index finger of her right hand, a man's ring set with a piece of jasper."

All the prince-bishop's attention was concentrated on Istvan, so he could not have missed his startled expression. He continued. "The assumption, at the time of the queen's death, was that the ring had belonged to the king. It was the queen's express wish that she be buried with it."

The silence in the chapel was vibrant with unspoken speculation. Finally Istvan broke it. "That explains why I was the one who answered that woman. That was my ring, not His Highness's."

The prince-bishop spoke, his attention focused on Istvan. "Prompted by the robbery of Queen Andred's tomb, we made good use of the palace archives to learn what had been buried with her king. We know what was interred with King Julian's remains at the Abbey

of St. Istvan: a golden ring, a small prayer book, and a copy of the
Aravis siege medal. In light of your account, I think it would be wise
to keep close watch on the king's tomb. We will send someone north."

"Send me," said Istvan.

"One man cannot guard that place. I must send many. But not
you. Your account of Dalet's behavior is too valuable to us."

"Dispatch what men you will. Let me bear them company."

"You will remain here in the palace. Suitable arrangements will be
made."

"You think it will happen again. It mustn't." Istvan's eyes were
wide.

"That is no concern of yours. You wished our help. We must be
permitted to help as we see fit." The prince-bishop turned his full
attention to me. It was as if the temperature in the chapel increased
suddenly. I felt the heat climb my neck and arms, prickle up into my
scalp. I returned him look for look. It was difficult, but I did it.

"I understand you have crafted a replica of the Aravis siege medal,
and that you carry the fake upon your person. Please surrender it to
me."

Replica. Fake. Curious, what power words possess. I kept my temper, but the sting his scorn provoked dismayed me.

Rigo gave me a kind smile. "Do as he asks, child. At least here you
have witnesses to the confiscation."

Unwillingly, I brought forth my bundle, surprisingly small for the
amount of work and trouble it had cost. I fumbled the knot loose and
rolled the medal out of the scarf into the prince-bishop's outstretched
palm.

His appreciation of the medal was plain. I savored the long moment of silent appraisal. I would have enjoyed it more had it not been
mixed so obviously with astonishment.

"You are an accomplished craftsman. It is unfortunate that you
have forsaken your studies."

"I haven't." My indignation made it hard to pick out the right
words and speak them intelligibly. "I am an apprentice in Madame
Carriera's workshop."

"At the moment, however, you are here. While you are here, I trust you will accept the hospitality of the palace. You and your family. Captain Nallaneen and his men will be here too. The clergymen you spoke with at St. Peter's understand the need for discretion. There is no need for them to join us here."

Amyas looked fierce. "Are we all under arrest? For what crime?"

"You may call it house arrest, if you wish. It is for your protection and the protection of the realm. Those who saw this man in his earlier state may not understand the need for discretion."

"He doesn't look a bit like the king now," I protested.

"Even if he still did," said Amyas, "what of it? No one could think he really was Good King Julian."

"When the king comes home," said the prince-bishop. "Who knows what marvels might ensue if the king comes home?"

King Corin was old and ill. Any ceremonies held at court waited upon the wax and wane of his health. Thus the prince-bishop held us at the palace with no more explanation than that we had done some small service for the crown. We would be rewarded for it, some day when the king's health was robust enough to permit.

My father and Amyas and I were lodged in comfort. There was some prestige attached to the arrangement, and my father was able to conduct his business by messenger almost as well as he could have if he were free.

Amyas was bored, but he spent his time with those of Nallaneen's men who would permit him to listen to their tales. Some card games were played, but Amyas acquitted himself well enough that the sport of fleecing the newcomer soon palled.

Istvan spent much of his time in prayer, usually in the Archangel Chapel. I liked it there too. My notebook was soon crowded with studies of my favorite details from the altarpiece.

"Why do you pray so hard?" I asked Istvan. "Most people look calm. You look fierce."

"You ought to be praying yourself instead of watching other people."

"I do pray. Sometimes. But I must watch people. It's part of my training. Why do you pray so much?"

"It helps. I don't know what to do. If I pray, sometimes I can think more clearly. At least I can see what not to do."

"I thought you might say you were repenting. You were the Seraph, King Julian's angel of death. I thought you might have killed so many men that you were still repenting them."

Istvan studied the altarpiece. "The Seraph. Yes, sometimes they called me that. Ridiculous."

"Wasn't it true, then?"

"What?"

"Wasn't it true that you killed a lot of men?"

"Oh, yes. That's true. I don't repent that. I wish I hadn't let them give me such a nickname. It was the fashion, though. I thought it was better to answer to that one lest they find another, something worse."

"How could they give you silly nicknames when you were so dangerous? Why weren't they afraid of you?"

"I was the king's champion. How could I pursue a private quarrel? That would bring dishonor to His Highness." Istvan looked at me. "To be honest, most of them were afraid of me."

"Was Maspero afraid of you?"

"If I cut off your head, would it say *Maspero* inside?"

"In golden letters. Did he like you?"

"Why aren't you afraid of me? What have I done wrong?"

"I don't know. Perhaps I'm so afraid of the prince-bishop, I don't have room to be afraid of you too. Were you friends with Maspero?"

"No. No one was. Maspero was a lout."

"He was a great artist."

"He was an undisciplined churl who managed to fulfill a few commissions between bouts of drinking and fornication. If he'd been half as good at painting as he was at talking, he'd have been a passable artist. Only passable."

"So you didn't like him?"

"No. He talked a lot of rubbish about individuality and emblems and souls and symbols. He borrowed money and didn't repay it. He could hold his liquor, I'll grant him that." Istvan looked curious. "How came you to fall ill with this Masperous fever? Are there no artists here and now?"

"I have studied his work. Mistress Carriera says that there is no truer portrait than the profile, and no one did a purer profile than Maspero."

"He drew them purely enough down in the alehouses, for pints of stout or bitter. He'd wager he could capture a likeness in four lines or fewer, and then he'd scratch the portrait into the wooden tabletop. Nose first. That's what I know about Maspero. Take your bit of knowledge and be content. He always started with the nose."

EIGHT

(In which I leave.)

I was watching Istvan at his devotions two days later when Ludovic
Nallaneen found us in the Archangel Chapel.

"You're both here." He settled down to wait for Istvan to finish.
"Good."

"Is this an official visit?" I asked. "Are we wanted?"

Ludovic gave me a long look, as if he were trying to decide which
of my questions to answer, and with what degree of gravity. "Purely
unofficial. I may not be here at all. In fact, probably not." To emphasize
his supposed insubstantiality, Ludovic bowed his head and began to
pray.

As a courtesy, I prayed a little myself, but it was difficult to concentrate. Eventually, Istvan joined us.

Ludovic concluded his worship promptly. "I've come to ask you
for my cloak. Do you still have it?"

Istvan looked perplexed. "What cloak?"

"The cloak with the hood you wore so that no one saw your face
on the way from Shene to the palace. That cloak belongs to me. The
weather has been warm so I've had no need of it. Without it I am out
of uniform. There are some sticklers at the officers mess. I need it back
before someone notices."

"Oh. Yes, I have it. Shall I get it now?"

"I'll collect it tomorrow. To remind you of it is my true reason for
being here today, in case anyone asks. Mark this. My presence has

nothing whatever to do with the rumor that the prince-bishop has changed his mind and is going to charge Hail with her coining and imprison her."

"I never—" My words were cut off as Ludovic put his hand over my mouth. His eyes held mine.

"Don't tell me again, Hail. I know. You didn't. But if you are wise, you won't deny the rumor until it turns real. Put together what you can to take with you to the cells. It's cold down there, even at this season. Ask your father for what money he can spare. No matter how vile the cell, the necessities can usually be had, at a price." Ludovic released me.

"I never counterfeited anything."

"The prince-bishop's charges against you have nothing to do with his true motives. He ordered that Istvan conceal his face on the way to the palace. Anyone who saw him when he looked like Good King Julian has been ordered to stay here, under the prince-bishop's eye. But house arrest isn't sufficient in your case, it seems. You found Istvan. You and your family brought him to Aravis. He doesn't trust your discretion."

"Istvan isn't Julian. What is there to be discreet about?"

"See how right the prince-bishop is? You must ask him that question some time. No, to be honest, I don't recommend it. Don't you see? The prince-bishop doesn't expect the rumors of Good King Julian's return to subside. It doesn't matter that he knows them to be false."

"What difference does a rumor make? Good King Julian hasn't come again. We have a perfectly good king on the throne. Why does the prince-bishop care about me?"

"The harvest failed last year. It's going to fail again. There's going to be trouble. I don't know how long the prince-bishop can prop King Corin on the throne, and neither does he. You're the least of his worries."

"Then why does he want to lock me up?"

"You recognized Julian's face. You talk too much. He doesn't know what to expect from you."

"Do you really think I talk too much?"

"Yes. Never mind that. Tell your father what I've said. Warn him to be ready. Your imprisonment will be surety of his good behavior as well."

"Father hasn't done anything wrong!"

"Of course he hasn't. Nor will he, with you at risk." Ludovic rose. "Nor was I ever here. Remember." He left us.

The silence in the chapel after his departure was precious to me. Once it broke, I would have to act. As long as it lasted, Ludovic's words were mere possibility. I did not have to decide whether to accept them or ignore them. Either way, I would have to take action. But not just yet. Not while my beleaguered wits were trying to make sense of the threats, to me, to my father, to the rest of my family.

Istvan stared at me without speaking, almost stared through me. I thought he might return to his prayers, so intent was he on some inner vision. When he broke the silence at last, his voice was low and slow. "You'll come with me. I can't take you home to Neven. But you may come with me part of the way. Could you travel alone from Ardres to Neven?"

Too astonished to speak, I nodded. For the first time since Rigo had given him back his true appearance, Istvan revealed the intensity he'd shown when he'd endured our raft journey downriver in order to find a priest. What serenity he'd possessed was gone. What patience he'd employed to endure my questions about Maspero was out-worn.

"We can't spare the time to tell your father. Too many questions. I have a few things I've gathered, in case. Wait here while I fetch them. If anyone else comes in while I'm gone, pray. It will do you good."

Alone in the chapel, too distracted to pray, I folded my hands over my notebook and waited. I looked at the donor panel. Istvan was there, guarding the king and queen. It seemed odd to think that he was prepared to guard me too.

When he returned, Istvan had Ludovic's cloak bundled under his arm. At his murmured order, I followed him out of the chapel, along an unfamiliar corridor, and down two flights of stairs. At the landing of a third, he stopped and pulled me through brocade hangings into a window embrasure. It was a clear morning, and the sunlight caught between the glass and the brocade made the small enclosure breathlessly warm.

"Don't speak unless you must and then keep your voice down. Even a whisper may carry."

I nodded. "Where are we going?"

"Immediately? Out of the palace. Ultimately, Ardres."

"Not Dalager? The prince-bishop thought there would be trouble at the royal tombs."

"I must find that . . . woman. Dalet. I must find her, and I'd best start in Ardres."

"Why? What will confronting her accomplish? You've already broken free of her."

"She wanted Julian. Not me. I've prayed for guidance. This is a sign that it's time to go. Unless I stop her, she'll try to call Julian back. I can't permit that."

"How will you stop her?"

"I'll kill her. The sooner, the better. This way." Istvan fumbled with the paneling in the thickness of the window arch. A scrabble of fingernails against wooden molding, and a narrow panel slid inward. We sidled through, he shut the panel, and we were cramped in utter darkness.

One breath and the dust made me want to clear my throat. Instead I muttered indistinctly, "How did you know this was here?"

"Julian showed me. There were other passages then. Things have changed. This was the only one I could still locate. We go this way."

I caught his belt, squeezed my eyes tight shut to keep from straining myself blind in the perfect darkness, and followed him.

I was impressed at how few times Istvan had to backtrack in the cramped, dark passages. Guessing by sound and smell alone, our route took us near or through the palace laundry, the palace scullery, and possibly the royal mews, on our way to the dank little close where we emerged into the city streets.

"Now we leave the city," said Istvan. "They won't realize we've escaped yet, so the gates will still be open."

"You think they'd close the city gates just to stop us?"

"The prince-bishop would do more than that to keep us under his hand. Now, listen. No matter what, don't say anything. Just keep your eyes down and follow me."

I caught his sleeve. "We're going to walk out the first gate we come to?"

"Unless you plan to hide in the city. I don't recommend it. Anyone who helps you will risk the prince-bishop's displeasure."

"There are better ways to leave than walking. My poor blisters still hurt."

"We don't have time to nurse your feet."

"I don't propose to. We must take the time to get some food and transportation. That chain of yours must be worth quite a bit."

"This?" Istvan touched the heavy links and then pulled the chain off and handed it to me. "Sell it, by all means."

"Not the whole thing. That would attract attention, a transaction that large. It will bring more a few links at a time anyway."

I tutored Istvan in the essentials of bartering with a goldsmith. The guild of goldsmiths was closely affiliated with the artists guild, and I couldn't run the risk of being recognized. I stayed safely in a side street while he negotiated the sale.

"That's fetched five times as much as we'll need," Istvan said, when he rejoined me.

"Show me." I counted out the coins. "You have even less idea what things ought to cost than my brother does."

"A horse and a bag of oats, what more do we need?"

"You eat oats? I like a more varied diet. And we'll need two horses."

"You can ride pillion behind me. It will attract less attention."

"If you're going to Ardres and I'm going on to Neven, we need two horses."

Istvan conceded that point. While I had the upper hand in the argument, I insisted that we eat something at once, before we tried to bargain for the horses. "It takes time to buy a horse. If we're hungry, we'll be impatient. The horse trader plays on weaknesses like that. We need to behave as if we've all the time in the world."

"We don't. Speed is essential."

"Hurry, and we'll only draw attention to ourselves."

I found a bakeshop and persuaded them to sell me the next batch of rolls out of their oven. Istvan sat beside me under the chestnut trees. We watched the sun on the river while we ate.

"We won't have much time for dickering," Istvan reminded me.

"If you don't dicker, you'll be remembered for another two hundred years. I'll do the talking. Hold your peace unless you see something wrong with the horses. The more faults you find there, the better."

Make no mistake. If you are ever given a choice between setting forth on a long journey afoot with little preparation and less baggage or setting forth on a long journey on horseback with a minimal amount of preparation and a small though sufficient amount of baggage, choose the latter. There was no similarity between my first attempt to leave the city and my second. By the time Istvan agreed to stop and rest the horses, my knees ached a little, but nothing worth complaining about, once we were settled for the night.

Istvan was silent, even by his standards. I waited until the work of seeing to the horses and cleaning up after our plain little meal was finished before I tried to get him to talk about our journey. He wouldn't. Nor would he talk about anything else. He had built a small fire. Keeping it poked properly seemed to require his entire attention.

"Are you ill?" I asked finally.

He shook his head.

"Are you sure? You looked quite pale for a while there. I thought you might faint while we were waiting to get through the north gate. Did the rolls disagree with you?" Mother always told us hot rolls were bad for the digestion. I have never found this to be so, but she was very seldom wrong.

"No, I'm not ill."

"What's wrong, then?"

He shook his head again.

After a long pause, I asked, "How many men do you think the prince-bishop will send after us?"

He looked surprised. "Are you worried about that? We'll outrun them. Go to sleep."

"If they don't worry you, what does?"

I thought he wasn't going to answer. Eventually he said, "I thought someone might recognize him today. There were so many people in the streets, at the gate. I might have walked right past his wife. Or a child of his. If he had a wife or children."

I blinked. "Recognize who?"

"Him. The man who lived in this body before that woman put me into it."

"Your body?"

He shrugged. "Mine now. But this one isn't two hundred years old, is it?"

"Oh. *Oh*. That's why you thought you were possessed?"

"Not me. Him."

The thought made me sit up straight and sputter. "You mean, she put you inside someone else? Someone *alive*?"

"She found some poor fellow, put his soul out as if it were no more difficult than putting out the cat, and invited me in. She changed the looks of him too. Dressed him like a doll. Kneaded him like clay until he looked like Julian. I can't tell what he was like. But perhaps someone will recognize him just the same. Someone who loved him. You can't just pluck a man out of a crowd and expect no one to miss him. He must have had friends. Enemies. Someone who owed him money. God's bones, even I had that much."

"Who owed you money?"

"Gil Maspero. And if you ask me one more silly question about that mountebank, you can ride the rest of the way by yourself."

"I had no idea you felt that way about him."

"You don't listen, then."

"Maspero said—"

"Quiet. I don't want to talk about Maspero any more. You'll grumble tomorrow if you don't rest tonight. I'll keep watch. Go to sleep while you have the chance."

"But he said—"

"Not—another—word."

"Gold has no memory."

Istvan stared at me.

"When it's melted down—to be reshaped. 'Gold has no memory. What ancient coins have been new minted, what antique crowns lost to make earrings for a lady who cares for nothing but the vain fashions of today.' That's what Maspero said in his treatise on metalwork."

Istvan said nothing.

After a while, I added lamely, "Yet Maspero made treasures. No one remembers the coins and crowns they might have been once. No one regrets them." I didn't share Saskia's comments on Maspero's theory. She held it was nonsense. Gold couldn't be worked and reworked indefinitely. It could be melted again and again, certainly, but every time the metal was reworked, it changed subtly. As it grew less pure, it grew brittle, until finally it was unfit for anything but money. Even though I kept Saskia's opinion to myself, an awkward silence fell.

There was a long pause, in which the only sounds were the soft hiss and crackle the fire made, before Istvan spoke. "Maspero was wrong."

It didn't even rain, that's how different my second trip north was from my first. Neither horse went lame, though mine made odd coughing noises first thing in the morning and Istvan's bit him on the wrist once. We were even able to find a decent meal in Joretta, where a tavern offered us a chance to bait the horses while we made free with an excellent mutton stew, my first hot meal in days.

The route Istvan chose took us away from the river, and several times we crossed back and forth over the spine of hills west of the Lida, a more direct route than the river road, which made loops and arcs that paralleled the course of the river, much less traveled than the old royal road. Despite the poor farming weather, the hills were rich and green at high summer. All along our passage we met flocks of sheep and herds of goats.

I even had time to think while I rode, something I never take for granted unless the horse I've been allotted is exceedingly meek and mild.

One of the things I decided, as I kept my horse close to Istvan's along the high tracks (though not too close, for his horse was fond of kicking as well as biting), was that it would be hard to part company with Istvan when we reached Ardres. He had no way of knowing, after all, that the necromancer Dalet would be where he had last seen her. He had no way of knowing where that previous meeting had occurred, not for certain. He had no way of knowing where she could be found, though Ardres seemed a likely starting point for the search.

I had no way of knowing if the prince-bishop's guard pursued us. It seemed fair to assume they were. If they were, would they hesitate to look for me in Neven? It seemed a likely spot to hunt for me. I had no wish to bring down disaster on my home.

If any friend who helped me in Aravis was at risk of the prince-bishop's displeasure, how much more did my family risk if I hid with them in Neven?

I had no way of knowing if the road north of Ardres would truly be safe for me, riding alone as I would be. I had no way of knowing, even, if I would be able to force my mount to part ways with Istvan's. Notoriously reluctant to travel alone, horses are. I have never been so poor in virtues that I needed to brag of any I did not have. I never said I was the finest horsewoman in the world, though of course I've always been perfectly competent, given a horse of tolerably good character.

It began to seem to me that it would be a pity to part company with Istvan for no more reason than that we had reached some arbitrary crossroad.

For one thing, he did not seem interested in the necessities of the journey. I had to force him to stop so that I could arrange to provide us with even the barest of provisions. For someone with a hearty appetite, he was wonderfully indifferent to food, something I envied after our eleventh consecutive meal of oatcakes and goat cheese.

NINE

(In which I hear things.)

What is it that one sees in a line or a shadow or a shape? What is it that an object signifies to an artist when it expresses something that cannot be communicated in any other way?

The siege medal tells us something about royalty, something about Good King Julian, and something about pride. It is a very simple design, yet it conveys the heroism and the joy that victory required and resulted in. Such simplicity used in such a cause argues pride verging on astonishment that the Lidians actually won. That degree of pride tells us something about Maspero, no stranger to vanity himself.

It all comes back to spoons and cloak pins. It takes a great deal of skill, experience, and, yes, art, to make a spoon signify something. More art and skill in a well-wrought spoon than in a dozen frippery cloak pins. Yet one is not born with one's full complement of skill, experience, and art. One must come to it through striving and practice. If one wishes to signify that a dragonfly might look rather well as a cloak pin, well, one must begin somewhere.

I can't say what it was about Istvan that made me sure I would paint him. It was no resemblance to the donor panel. I was done making copies. Now I would make only what I saw only in my own way. Who I saw was Istvan. What I saw in him, I could not articulate, even to myself. It was this mute certainty of mine that made me realize that here was my subject. If I could not signify something of what

Istvan was in paint, there was no hope of expressing it in any other way.

When I looked at Istvan, what did I see that interested me so? It wasn't his face, though it was while he was wearing a semblance of King Julian that he first attracted my attention. It was not the way he moved, for it was nearly a week after our first meeting that he regained an easy gait. Until then, he had walked like an old man, or like someone who'd been held immobile for days. He'd lurched. Once he recovered his ease of movement, it was possible to see in him the grace that had made him a great fighter. At times it was possible to glimpse the swiftness and strength that had evoked his old name, the Seraph.

There was a balance to Istvan that pleased my eye. A good tool tells you in its shape what it is for. In Istvan lay something unseen yet evident. I longed to find a way to portray him so that what was unseen should be seen, not stated, but there for the eye with the skill to see it.

Whatever it was I saw in Istvan, my desire to set it down compounded with my sympathy for him. It led me to persuade myself that he needed looking after—not a role the youngest in a family is usually allotted.

Novelty, the desire to indulge in untrammeled bossiness, and a kind of girlish sentimentality that I blush to recall all combined to convince me that I ought to stay with him.

I tried to plan how to convince Istvan to let me accompany him. There was so much I did not want to say, it was hard to think of anything else. In the end, my persuasion was not necessary. We reached the milepost where the Ardres road crossed the royal road.

"There's the way north," Istvan said. He pointed and repeated the route to me painstakingly. One would have thought I had no sense of direction at all, the care he used.

"I'm not going north. I'm staying with you."

"Fine," said Istvan, and took the Ardres road, without wasting an instant to discuss my decision.

I gathered my wits and reins to follow. One might almost have thought it was a matter of no moment to him.

*   *   *

The terrain around Ardres is sharp and steep, rocky fields bounded by stone walls like untidy heaps of roof slates. Although it was high summer, the fields seemed barren. Wild mustard bloomed here and there, garish yellow against the sparse fields. There were no flocks of sheep there, and what goats I saw might have been wild, they clambered so swiftly and so warily along the ridges.

The Arcel and the Lida make a **Y** where the Arcel's flow joins the Lida; Ardres makes a bony spur that fills the bowl of the **Y**. Ardres Castle rode high and severe above the river valley, a prow of stone mastering the countryside for miles.

Istvan chose his route into the high country above Ardres from the Folliard Bridge. Unlike me, he'd approached it from the north and west. So to the north and west we rode, as fast as our weary horses could go.

I confess, I was growing somewhat weary myself. My blisters were unimportant, but a deep ache had taken up residence in the small of my back, and each of my knees had developed its own particular affliction: a shooting pain in the left, a steady twinge in the right.

Istvan seemed tired too, which was not surprising, since the only watch we kept at night was his. He grew more silent with every mile until we were a day and a half northwest of the Folliard Bridge. By then he was so weary he merely blinked at me when I spoke. At times he seemed to be looking at something just behind me, something I couldn't see when I turned to look. Sometimes he seemed to be listening to something I couldn't hear. It was a hard journey.

By great good fortune it was still hours before dusk when he reached a place he recognized. The shadows of afternoon were lengthening, but the sun was still well up when he led the way up a crooked valley to a place where a ford offered passage across a river the color of dark beer.

"I came this way."

I followed him through the ford. He led us upstream until the river dwindled to a brook. The terrain grew steeper and steeper, until the brown trickle of water dwindled to a spring and disappeared. We had to dismount and lead the horses. It was a slow climb. The long afternoon drew to a close. We gained height gradually, so that the daylight seemed unchanged, as if no time were passing.

I decided that we were never going to reach the top of the hill. We were going to climb eternally. We had missed dying somewhere along our journey, we had slipped past Cerberus, and trudged directly into purgatory.

We clambered upward until I could feel the little muscles around my kneecaps quivering like plucked lute strings. I stopped for a moment, puffing, but Istvan kept on. I knew without thinking about it that he would trouble himself no more about leaving me than he had about my decision to accompany him instead of carrying on to Neven. Whether I stopped or whether I kept on, it was all one to Istvan. He was in a hurry to find that red-haired woman, the necromancer who had called him back from whatever dreams death had allowed him.

I straightened my spine and trudged on, hauling my horse along, up and up, until the whole world dwindled to my labored breathing, the sting of sweat in my eyes, and the aches in my back and knees.

I hardly noticed it at first, I was so caught up in my assorted miseries, when the pitch of the hill eased. The world opened up all around me. I stood beside my horse—I would have leaned against him, but I thought that might tip us both over—and looked about. North, south, east, the barren hills fell away. We had reached the heights—and Istvan trudged on, oblivious to the stark beauty of the hills laid out before us. He was headed toward a square-built stone tower that commanded the summit to the west. Dark against the glory of the western sky, it was difficult to make out more than the silhouette. It looked battered, as if the weather on these heights were harsher than any ever encountered in the valleys below.

The slope upward to the tower was gentle. My knees were still twangling. I mounted and urged the poor beast after Istvan.

I suppose it is logical to put a tower somewhere high. From near its foot, I could see for miles. From the top, I imagined, one might see all the way to Chersonesa. A lookout post, this had been, for Ardres.

If there was a flaw in the defenses at Ardres, which commanded the valley so completely, it was that it viewed the hills to the north not at all. A watchtower provided a vantage point.

A watcher could see far to the north from here. But how could he tell Ardres what he saw? Perhaps a bonfire? It would take a series of bonfires to spread an alarm as far as Ardres. There was nothing larger than gorse growing anywhere near.

Or were there less tangible means? Maybe I was light-headed with exertion. Maybe I was full of girlish fancies. I thought I heard voices in the wind. Names called out by voices I recognized, voices I didn't, words, perhaps, in a language I couldn't understand. I tried to concentrate on catching my breath and staying as close to Istvan as I could.

At his command, we hobbled the horses. He circled the tower at a distance. There was no sign anyone was within. I walked with him to the door. It opened. He paused on the threshold, and I realized he was breathing hard. It wasn't the climb that had made him breathless. His eyes were nearly bulging. He was frightened.

I ignored what I thought I heard, put my voice into the steadiest register I could manage, and said, "No trees. Are you sure this is the place?"

He nearly fell off the step. "What?"

"No trees. You said there were pine trees near the tower."

"Perhaps there were once. Or perhaps I was traveling faster than I realized. Or perhaps the pines were farther than I thought. I don't know. But this is the place." He crossed the threshold. I followed him.

There were bird droppings. Problems with the roof, no doubt. Pigeons get in everywhere. There were sheep droppings too. There was plenty of dirt, but beneath it the floor was rough-dressed stone, well made. A flight of steps curved up toward the stout beams of a wooden ceiling. What light there was came through the door with us and from above in a few narrow bars of sunlight. Dust motes hung in the angled light. Either the roof was worse than it looked from outside, or there was something like a window up above.

I started up the steps while Istvan was still looking around, braced in one spot as if some unseen tide was rising past his knees.

"No one's here," I called down. The upper level was full of light and dust. There were three narrow windows, unglazed, and a flue and fireplace in the wall. It looked nothing like the place Istvan had described to the prince-bishop. It showed no more sign of occupation than the ground floor had.

The steps continued up and so did I. The upper chamber was cramped, windowless and small. In the interests of thoroughness, I found the trapdoor to the roof. It opened with difficulty, but curiosity made me strong. I skinned through to find myself at the zenith, the absolute summit of the world.

It was beautiful country, even if it was barren. The hills rose and fell all around me. Shadows had moved while we were inside the tower. The sun was almost gone. Only the top half of the tower still caught the light. It gilded the dark stone below me and all the hills south and eastward. Even a meandering loop of the river Lida was visible off in the blue distance, giving back the sky like an arc of light against the dusk.

To the north, I could see the dark line of the hills of Galazon. Beyond that, so clear was the day, a suggestion of deeper blue against the sky hinted at the round-shouldered mountains of Haydock.

I closed the trap and clambered down. It took me much longer to descend than to climb, for I was all but blinded by the gloom of the tower after the glory of the world.

It took me a few minutes to find Istvan. He'd left the tower and gone to stand with the horses, head down and shoulders braced. He looked ill.

"Now where should we go?"

He blinked at me.

"No one is here. What shall we do next? Track them? It looks as if it's been a month since anyone has been here. That's judging by the sheep manure. I know my sheep manure, you can trust me on that."

He made an effort. Still, I barely caught his words. "Can't you hear it?"

"Hear what?"

"I don't know."

"That's the wind."

"No." He shivered comprehensively, and the horses shifted away from him, ears flat back and eyes rolling. "It will be here she does it. She's going to come here because this is where she *can* do it. Perhaps that sound is souls she hasn't bothered to finish calling. Maybe that's what it is."

"What if she's already done it?"

"Listen to it. It—expects her."

"We wait for her then?"

He nodded.

"Where?" I looked around at the empty ridge. The closest cover was back the way we'd come, down in the folds of the hillside. "Inside the tower? There's a sort of loft just under the roof."

The thought of going back inside the tower seemed to dismay Istvan. "If there's light enough, we can see her coming."

"*If* she comes tonight."

"It will be tonight." Istvan opened the blanket folded and rolled behind his saddle. A heavy bundle of oiled linen fell into his hand. Gingerly, he unfolded the fabric and showed me the pistol he held. "Amyas told me what I would need. I stole it from the palace. Did you ever use one?"

I regarded the expensive weapon with respect. "Even Amyas doesn't use one. Put it away."

Reluctantly, he folded the linen around it, but he did not replace it in the blanket roll. Instead he tucked the bundle tenderly under his arm, as if it were a borrowed book. "I will use it when she arrives. If the light allows."

"How much did Amyas explain about such devices? Did he show you how to reload? You do realize you only get one try with it?"

"He told me the theory. Never point it at anything I don't wish to kill."

"Well, practice would be wise. It isn't loaded, is it?"

Istvan brought it out again, examining it with incomprehension that made me wince. It was loaded.

"Let me take it."

"You don't like it. I can tell."

"I know more about it than you do." I was exaggerating just a trifle. My experience with firearms consisted of accompanying Amyas once when he "borrowed" Father's pistol and went out potting rabbits. We didn't hurt anything. So little damage had we done that going to bed supperless was considered punishment enough.

"You wouldn't use it."

"I'll hand it to you when it's time."

"When I fire, will you reload it for me? I have everything Amyas told me I needed." He brought another bundle, lighter but a little more bulky, out of the blanket roll and handed it to me. Istvan was thorough, I must admit. He had brought it all: powder, wadding, balls, even an extra flint.

"I'll try. But it won't be much use in the dark."

"Practice if you need to. I'll hide the horses."

"I would rather practice braiding snakes."

He left me there, crouched in the wiry grass. I ignored the two linen-wrapped bundles in my lap. My hands were cold, so I folded my arms and pretended that it was a pleasant change from the heat of the summer day. I watched the first stars come out. I listened to the things the wind said. The night came up the hill like a river rising, like the tide coming in, like the world ending.

When Istvan rejoined me, it was so dark I couldn't see him; but I could tell easily enough that he was shivering, and I could smell that he was sweating. I even guessed the reason. It was because he knew we were going to have to go back up into the tower. It was far too dark to hope to keep watch anywhere else.

I led the way. He didn't want to climb the steps. He didn't want to crouch in the cramped, dusty little chamber under the roof. He didn't want to stay quiet. I made him do all that, even though I had to lean against him to be sure he'd stay still. No wonder I dozed off, propped against his back for hours.

When he moved, I thought he was going for the door. Instead, he put his hand over half my face. He meant to silence me. I nearly suffocated before I freed myself. "It sounds like lots of people," I gasped finally.

His voice was hardly a breath in my ear. "Six, at least."

One of the six was in the chamber below us, making a steady whimpering sound that was more painful to listen to than the wind itself. Someone else was giving orders. I couldn't quite catch the words, but the inflection was impossible to mistake. The voice was pitched soft and low, very pleasant. I thought it was a woman's voice. From Istvan's shuddering, I judged it had to be Dalet.

The whimpers broke off for a while. The voice ordered, quite distinctly, "Guard this place. I won't lose more time through your carelessness." Four sets of footsteps departed, clattering back down to the ground floor. One set of footsteps continued, swift and light, around and around the plank-floored chamber below us. The rhythm of the steps turned and varied, as if in a dance without music. Or a dance with no more music than muted whimpering and a relentless cry of voices on the wind. It was impossible to listen to anything but the pattern of those steps.

I don't know what Istvan was thinking. I forgot everything but that relentless dance. The pistol, the urgency that had brought us here, the certainty that had held us here, the vigil we kept, all faded.

I put my fingers in my ears and squeezed my eyes shut, despite the dark, until stars bloomed under my eyelids.

The stuffy warmth beneath the rafters of the tower grew cold. I bit my tongue to keep silent. The footsteps quickened their pace. Beside me, Istvan was shivering. The whimpers crumbled into muffled sobs. The sobbing seemed to make the voices worse. It stirred them.

I crossed myself and began to whisper the Paternoster beneath my breath.

"Stop it." Istvan caught my hand and nearly crushed it in his. His words were little more than warm breath in my ear. "She'll *know*. She can smell out the good. Be still. Don't even think."

I nodded. He released me. In the darkness, the voices fluttered everywhere, above us, below us, piping, squealing, dragging out their strange syllables in painful need.

The footsteps halted. The silence dragged at me. I could no longer hear the voices in the wind. The sobs were still there, a weary counterpoint to my own hushed breathing. I shrank against Istvan, but the stone of the tower would have offered as much comfort.

The voice was very pleasant, soft and musical. Pitched to command, I found her words unmistakable. "Come down, lambkin. I hear your prayers. Come down to me."

TEN

(In which I pray.)

I could not keep myself from moving. As I got clumsily to my feet, Istvan rose too. He brushed past me, not gently, and he took the pistol away from me as he did. With sword and pistol he went down to her. With a squeak of relief, I huddled alone in the darkness. But I'd been the one she called. After a deep breath, I followed. I was half down the steps to the room below when my knees betrayed me. I huddled on the steps and stared.

Dalet was surprised to see Istvan. Her voice betrayed that much, though all she said was, "Lambkin—"

Istvan fired the pistol. The screaming began. It was all around us, not just from the room below. Every voice in the air around us protested. I winced, and winced again when the pistol hit me. Istvan had thrown it back up the steps to me and I'd missed it, my eyes squeezed shut against the noise.

Reload it. I scrambled to retrieve the pistol, to find the bundle that contained the ammunition.

Heavy footsteps coming up from the ground floor—her sentries— and the stamp and clash of swordplay.

I pawed at the bundle of cloth, set the materials out on the step beside me by touch. *Primer. Charge. Wadding. Ball.* Was that the right order? I squeezed my eyes shut again, hard, only because I couldn't squeeze shut my ears. All I could do was make my own racket.

Aloud, and very loudly, I said the Paternoster as I fumbled my way through reloading the pistol. Was it done properly? I had so little faith in myself that I took it up in my left hand when I was done. In a tower full of necromancy, with death and madness waiting for me, I took the trouble to hold that pistol in my left hand, lest anything untoward happen to my right.

I do not say this was a sensible precaution, nor even a realistic or useful one. It is what I did, that's all, and I think it may serve to show how, even when farthest from the tranquil concerns of art, the true artist is mindful of her destiny.

No. Not true. Even I am not quite *that* full of porridge. I held it in my left hand because I was sure I'd done it all wrong and somehow it would blow to bits even as I held it.

It says something about Istvan's skill that the fight was still going on, even after all the time I'd taken attempting to reload the pistol.

I peered downward. Two guards had fallen already and lay motionless. A third was falling, and the fourth hesitated, terrified equally of Istvan and Dalet. There was a man lying supine between them, bound hand and foot, his sobs and whimpers silenced. By the fireplace, Dalet leaned against the wall and only a dark stain on her sleeve showed that Istvan's very first attempt at a pistol shot had done anything at all. I saw the gleam of gold on her finger and at her breast. The ring that had summoned Istvan? I wondered. And the other? I looked, but I couldn't see well enough to be sure.

Dalet had the straight, silky kind of red hair, not wild like Saskia's. Her eyes were too widely spaced, her chin too sharp, her mouth too narrow for good proportion, and her long neck too long. Yet the first thought anyone would have of her was *beauty*. The second thought was likely to be more prudent, for the burning eyes and pallid complexion spoke of zealotry, scholarship, and a rich diet. She was like a child's drawing of a princess.

Dalet was watching the fight with avidity. She was waiting, I thought, for a little more bloodshed, a little more excitement before she intervened. Even though she'd been injured, her confidence was unshaken.

Istvan engaged the fourth guard and the vigor of his attack backed the puffing man a step or two closer to the stair. I could see Dalet's appreciation of the maneuver. Any more, and the man's retreat would send him backward down the flight of steps. Instead of warning him, she licked her lips. Waiting.

Our Father who art in heaven . . . I steadied my left hand with my right, brought the barrel down as steadily as my loathing would let me, and squeezed the trigger.

The gunshot made me scream.

Dalet screamed louder.

It hurt her no more, I think, than the first had, but I managed by luck to injure her other arm. The surprise was a greater factor than either injury. She sprang up, calling out in a voice that made all the voices in the air fall silent. Then there was an owl where she had been, a white owl, small but fierce, its wings barred with scarlet.

She flew to the window and was gone. The fourth guard recoiled—and was gone—a step too many and the stairs took him in a series of ever-diminishing thumps.

Istvan panted and looked around and cleaned his sword. I lowered the pistol as soon as I realized I was still aiming it, my arms gone stiff, elbows locked, at the spot where Dalet had stood.

Istvan knelt beside the captive. In better times, the bound man would have had a steady strength about him. He seemed stocky, yet well made, like an oak in a grove of beech trees. Not a young oak either. From his thinning hair, the lines on his face, his calloused fingertips, I would have guessed this man had spent at least sixty years working hard, with his brain as well as his back. He had fainted, apparently, and the strain of his captivity shadowed his slack features.

When Istvan released his bonds, the sound of the knife on the ropes seemed loud, that's how quiet the tower was once the voices had fallen silent. It was so quiet that Istvan's indrawn breath sounded like cloth tearing.

"God's bones. I'm too late. That damned dance of hers. . . . When the crying stopped, that's when the change took place. It must have been."

It took me several moments to understand Istvan's loss of composure. Then I saw the resemblance in brow and chin, breadth of chest, jut of nose. Julian again. This time, the king as he had been, perhaps in Vienna, when the fever (or the poison, if the tales are to be believed) brought his reign to a close. Good King Julian, worn and weary, come home at last to Lidia.

Istvan put out his hand, as if to touch Julian's face, but he stopped himself. The delicacy with which he'd touched the donor panel in the Archangel Chapel was brusque in comparison to the gentleness with which he finally touched the king's face.

I couldn't watch. It was private, never meant for my eyes. Istvan had forgotten I was there. I knew that much. I busied myself retrieving the flintlock and the parcels I'd left in the upper chamber. By the time I was finished reloading the pistol, Istvan was kneeling beside the king, who was blinking up at him sleepily.

"Istvan. I've just had the strangest dream. . . ." His voice was like the very best India blue, well ground and perfectly compounded, smooth and rich, deep and heart lifting. He broke off at the sight of me. His face betrayed his curiosity, but his courtesy, even in these extremes, was too perfect to allow him to ask the obvious question.

"Allow me to present Hail Rosamer, my Lord."

I found my knees knew how to curtsy, even if the rest of me had never been sure.

"Your lady fair, Istvan?"

"My bailiff, more like."

"You've long needed one, heaven knows. I give you good evening, Mistress Rosamer. Keep a careful watch on this fellow. He needs steady sharp eyes like yours to look after him."

"Your Majesty." I curtsied again and stepped back. "You've . . . traveled far, I think. May I offer you something to eat? We've some oatcakes."

The king got to his feet, with much help from Istvan. "Traveled far? I feel it." He looked it too. His rich garments were crumpled and dusty from his captivity.

Istvan was grim. "Farther still to go. We can't stay here."

"But can we leave?" I handed Istvan the pistol and took a good look down the stairs. "Will we be able to?"

"You keep it," Istvan said, eying the flintlock with distaste. "It likes me not."

The king was looking from my face to Istvan's as horrified suspicion blossomed into certainty. "What device is that? Istvan, have I been dreaming? Am I dreaming still?"

Istvan took the king by his shoulders, a brotherly embrace, even to the slight impatient shake. "We all dream, Your Majesty. All of us. And this is the longest, fearsomest dream yet. We are exiled here, out of our long rest, and no way home that I can think of, without a sore change of hard heart by that witch who summoned us."

"Which?"

"Dalet. The woman with red hair."

"Oh? Oh. I remember now."

I thought for a moment that he might faint again, he grew so pale, but Istvan steadied him.

"I remember. She told me her name in my dream. I wanted to come home, and she was asking me to do so. But this is not home, is it, Istvan?"

"No. Not this place. Nor any other in all the wide world."

The weariness in the king's face caught at me, and the more familiar weariness in Istvan's voice drove me to speak. "We must go."

"If we can." Istvan retrieved his sword and led the way, warily, down the stairs.

We found the horses where Istvan had left them, far down the hill. We rested there a while, beside the beck. Julian was hungry, as hungry as Istvan was the day I found him fishing. He ate oatcakes and drank water scooped from the stream in his cupped hands. Not very regal. I don't know what I expected. Perhaps it was his age. I never had the slightest difficulty believing that Julian was a king. His habit of command had nothing to do with it, for he never commanded anything that I can recall. But he seemed well able to command himself.

He had a quiet face, with nothing of the unease and fear that Istvan had displayed when wearing the same features. He looked and sounded tired to me, but I was the one who curled up in a blanket beside the beck. Istvan and Julian merely sat there, an arm's length apart. If they regarded one another, I don't see how, for it was hours until daybreak. If they spoke, the fall of water on stone drowned out their words. I let the sound of the beck lull me. I slept.

The sky was ultramarine when I woke, the deepest blue broken as it gave way to a tinge, just a tinge, of the coming daylight. Painters used to reserve that blue for Mary's robe.

It always lifts my heart to see a whole sky of that color—deepening to the west, bleached ever so slightly at the eastern hem by the promised day. Very seldom do I need to be awake that early, so the sight retains its rarity for me. It would be a shame to earn a living as a baker and to rise early so often that such a blue grew commonplace.

I had plenty of time to admire the sky, for we were off on our journey before there was enough light to see each other by, let alone the path before us. Istvan insisted that Julian take his horse. Mine was not merely gentle but large as well, and strong enough to bear both Istvan and me, if the pace were not too fast.

During the night Istvan and Julian had reached an accord. We were going to Dalager, to ask for help from the prince-bishop's men, if any were there.

"Why Dalager?" I asked Istvan. "Why not Aravis?"

"Dalager is closer, only two days from here. We'll need more provisions and another horse. You're right about riding pillion. No one should have to endure you asking questions in his ear for long."

"If the prince-bishop did send men to St. Istvan's to guard King Julian's tomb, how will you persuade them to help us?"

"They don't have to help us. Julian will be safer in St. Istvan's than anywhere else. They can guard him as well as his tomb."

After that, Istvan paid me no attention except when I dug him in the ribs to make him draw rein for the day. Julian seemed to bear the strain of travel better than I did. Never a word of complaint out of him. Still, we weren't precisely moving at a breakneck pace.

We traveled with maddening deliberation eastward to the royal road. Once we picked that up, the way was easy though the country-side was hard. Steep and stony, even after an overly wet spring, the land around Dalager was forbiddingly bleak. Only the inns on the pilgrim's way offered simple comfort, as they had provided it for the centuries of travelers who had come seeking, as we were seeking, Dalager and the shrine of St. Istvan.

Dalager was like a city built on a staircase. Here and there a landing provided space for a little square, just room to turn around and look up or down the steep little valley. Every shop and stall and house in town was built in a jostling row along the steep ravine that led up to the abbey. There, carved from the living rock, St. Istvan's held the shrine and the royal tombs.

We left the horses at an inn in the valley. In Dalager itself there was seldom space for two to walk abreast, so crowded and narrow were the streets. For horses, no hope. Julian had all his attention on the abbey church far above us. Istvan had all his doggedly set on Julian. And I? I drank in the sights and sounds; I reveled in the fripperies of Dalager.

Dalager's stony valley was a bleak place for such excess. Perhaps that is why the frippery seemed all the brighter. Everywhere we saw the emblem of St. Istvan's, the sign of a heart held in two hands.

There were hearts in hands everywhere: brooches, badges, even ginger biscuits came in the shape of such a heart. Elsewhere, I'm told, this is a symbol of true love. In Dalager, it refers to another kind of fidelity, through which the remains of St. Istvan were brought mirac-ulously to safety among the monks of the abbey. Only his heart—Lidian kings had since brought whole carcasses—but that heart began the tradition of St. Istvan's that had lived on for centuries, a sacred trust, and the only source of prosperity in the whole bleak countryside for miles around.

Before he was a saint, that ancient namesake Istvan had been a fighter too. He was a chieftain, and he led his people against the Turks. In his last battle, though sorely wounded, Istvan promised his captains that he would lead them once more. The last charge was glorious, but Istvan fell. His captains mourned him even in their victory. So hot the battle had been, they could not find Istvan's body among the men who had fallen with him.

Istvan's captains went to the abbey at Dalager and prayed for Istvan's soul. They distributed alms to the poor in his name. Masses were said for him. The infirm were healed when they prayed to Istvan for a cure. The word got round, and the devotions increased. A miracle: two angels brought Istvan's heart to the monks of the abbey. The cures increased. A shrine was built at Dalager, and by the time it was finished, the transformation had taken place. Istvan had become St. Istvan, and he was revered.

Dalager welcomed the pilgrims who came to the abbey church. Every new angle of our climb up to the shrine brought us fresh distraction. Vanity of vanities. The whole city was vanity. I stopped and bought some ginger biscuits.

Julian and Istvan climbed on without noticing until I caught them up and offered to share. Istvan looked and shook his head, wordless. Julian beamed at me. "I love these. May we get a garland too?"

"All right. Why?" I started to take a bite of my biscuit. Julian's expression stopped me. "What is it?"

"You don't just *eat* them, do you?"

I gazed blankly at the inoffensive biscuit in my hand. "I don't?"

"Very bad luck." Julian broke his carefully in half. "You have to break them first. Then you eat them." He demonstrated. "Delicious."

I broke my biscuit as symmetrically as I could. "Which half first?"

"It doesn't matter."

I ate the right half first. It could have been a thought fresher, but it made a welcome change from oatcakes. I finished my biscuit and offered the others again. This time Istvan took one too. He and Julian broke theirs with great ceremony. I finished the last biscuit and brushed the crumbs away.

"And now a garland, if you please, Mistress Rosamer. Rosemary, lavender, or bay?"

"Are those our only choices?" I asked.

"The garland is an offering to St. Istvan. We dedicate it in hope and gratitude. Rosemary for recollection, lavender for protection, bay laurel for victory. Which shall we choose?"

"Bay." Istvan's tone brooked no argument.

Julian's reproachful glance was a masterpiece. "Not rosemary? Does remembrance mean so little?"

"It's for St. Istvan, isn't it? I think the bay laurel is more appropriate."

"Ever my champion." Julian sighed. "Nothing changes, does it? The next thing you'll say is that rosemary would serve very well—with lamb."

Istvan looked at me. "I tried to prevent this. You're my witness. I tried to keep him from coming back."

"We could have both," I said. We had done pretty well out of the dickering for the links of Istvan's chain in Aravis. "We could have all three."

"No. The rosemary," said Istvan.

Julian looked horrified. "No. On no account. A garland of bay laurel."

I bought both. It did no good. Instead of being annoyed with each other, they were annoyed with me. I don't know why.

We made our way upward toward St. Istvan's shrine. The abbey church was smaller than I'd expected, and much darker. It was almost windowless, set deep into the hillside. Candlelight was reflected in pools of water on the floor. If the stone around us wept in the middle of summer, I could only wonder what the damp chill of winter must be like there. My knees twinged with sympathy for the monks kneeling at their devotions then.

The shadows made the interior of St. Istvan's seem as crowded as a box room. There were side chapels in which gisants reposed, some

cold white marble, some painted wood, cheerful in the blaze of candlelight. Dozens of stone memorials were set into the walls and floor,
a jumble of names and dates and pious inscriptions. The air of clutter
owed most to the trophies that hung everywhere from the vaulted
ceiling: crutches, which looked well used; garlands in every state of
decrepitude, all the way to the freshest circlets of rosemary, lavender,
and bay, such as we'd brought for the altar; model ships, hung as a
plea for safe voyage, some elaborate with sails and rigging, some no
more than chips of wood; here a pair of spurs, there a sword; all was
disorder—yet every votive offering spoke the same wish, a cry of devotion, a plea made manifest.

The altar was an island of order amid the artifacts of faith. There
was a fine sculpture of the Madonna there, the Child on her knees, his
stiff little hand held out in benediction. I lit a candle, and my traveling
companions made their offerings, the garlands joining the day's drift
of fragrant greenery that festooned the place. I prayed too.

I was grateful for a quiet moment to make my devotions. I prayed
hard for the welfare of my family, of my friends, of Neven, and of
Madame Carriera's house in Giltspur Street. I then returned to my
oldest prayer, even in trouble my most constant and heartfelt, that the
Lord should find it in his gentle heart to make me a true artist.

St. Istvan's was a good place to pray. The prayers of so many
monks might have eased the way, worn the path to heaven smooth
with centuries of devotion. I forgot my aching knees, my tired back,
and my selfish fears. Even Dalet could not prevail against such holiness
as St. Istvan's. I was doing the right thing, I was sure of it, to stay with
Istvan and Julian, to help them all I could.

When I looked up, Ludovic Nallaneen was standing by the altar,
his guardsmen behind him. It seemed right to see him there, as if God
had dispatched him to guard Istvan and Julian with both the temporal
and the holy might of the prince-bishop himself.

I might have expected surprise and disfavor when he recognized
me, miles from the prince-bishop's house arrest. Instead I saw fear and
disbelief in his eyes as he recognized Good King Julian, come home at
last.

ELEVEN

(In which I listen and learn.)

When Ludovic had seen beyond the impossible presence of Julian to Istvan and me, he said, "You might as well keep the cloak. I had to order another."

With calm to match Ludovic's, Istvan thanked him. "I hope our departure did not cause you any hardship."

Ludovic frowned. "Your arrival poses the difficulty, I'm afraid. The prince-bishop was not happy to have you at large even without your resemblance to the king. It will cause His Grace concern to learn King Julian the Fourth is here with you."

"You agree he is King Julian?" It puzzled me that Ludovic would accept Julian's presence with such aplomb. From the look of Ludovic's men, they shared their commander's serene acceptance of the situation. I didn't see how anyone could question that Good King Julian had returned, but it seemed wrong for Ludovic to let the miracle go meekly by. He was so good at asking questions.

"Oh, yes." Ludovic looked at me. "You're all right? They're taking care of you?"

"I'm taking care of them."

"Yes, of course."

"I am Julian, yet I am not your king." Julian's reminder was gentle. "That much is spared us."

"King Corin still rules in Aravis," Ludovic agreed. "Long may he do so. The prince-bishop will be most interested in the circumstances of your return."

Julian was rueful. "As am I. Two voyages across the river Styx and I remember neither."

"It was the river Lethe you crossed. Small wonder you don't recall." Ludovic looked thoughtful. "Yet here you are. The prince-bishop is sure to ask us why."

Istvan had listened long enough. "Dalet called him. She must have had some talisman to conjure with."

Ludovic nodded. "It follows. Yet the abbot assured me that the royal tombs are undisturbed."

Istvan looked grim. "She called him. Somehow. We must learn what she's done. Julian's tomb must be opened."

"It's not a tomb. It's an urn," I said. "Alabaster, of Viennese workmanship." They ignored me.

"Let me speak to the abbot," said Ludovic. "It is an awkward situation. Still, I have the prince-bishop's authority to do what must be done."

The abbot was notified. The proper members of the monastic order were informed and the proper cleric called upon make appropriate prayers. The king's remains would be surveyed with respect. All would be done with the most perfect reverence.

We would learn what was missing from the effects interred with the king's remains, and we would have to guess from that how Dalet had managed her necromancy without alerting the guards or the monks of the abbey.

I followed the discussion as we drifted along the clutter of St. Istvan's, Julian and Ludovic exchanging views with the abbot, Istvan putting in a word or two as required. I trailed in their wake as we passed chapel after little chapel, among which was the well-guarded chamber that contained the alabaster urn the Viennese had sent to Lidia all those years ago.

Istvan followed Ludovic and the others into the chamber. The guards would have let me pass too. Belatedly I realized what I was doing. I backed up a step and bumped hard into the wall behind me. Julian turned to look at me, and I recognized the stiffness in his expression. It matched my own.

"It's just occurred to me," I said, trying not to sound as apologetic as I felt, "what's in there."

"My person, or what remains. A disagreeable thought." Julian looked up and down the curving passage of the ambulatory. "Mistress Rosamer, would you care to bear me company?"

"Please, don't call me that. Call me Hail."

"Hail, then. Help distract me, I beg you. I find I would rather talk than think. On my last visit here, I made an offering of my own. It held pride of place then. Is it still here somewhere, I wonder?"

"What sort of offering?" I followed him back to the nave. We craned our necks to study the trophies overhead.

"A votive crown. A replica of St. Istvan's crown. We'll be hard-pressed to find it, if it hangs too high among the cobwebs."

"A replica of St. Istvan's crown . . . Who made it for you?" I was sure I knew the answer.

"Gil did. He grumbled when I bade him use gold foil over base metal. If he'd had his way, this place would have been a shrine to attract thieves, not pilgrims. The less gold, the less occasion for larceny."

I managed to squeak the name. "Gil Maspero?"

"Heard of him, have you? He had a good opinion of himself, and he always claimed he'd finish famous. Was he right?"

"Yes."

Julian crowed with laughter. "I hope he never knew it. Insufferable, that would make him. He was hard enough to bear while he was merely the finest craftsman at my court."

"Or any other."

"Just what he would have said. How do you know of him?"

While we walked slowly along the nave, necks aching, eyes strained to pick out the shape of a crown, however dusty, among the vast clutter overhead, I told him of my interest in Maspero's work. Julian listened attentively and I think we were both careful not to let our thoughts stray back to the memorial chapel, back to the urn and its contents.

I spied the crown at last, hanging between a battered dulcimer and a mason's trowel. Only the gleam of gold, all but lost beneath the dust, betrayed its presence. I had to narrow my eyes to study it, hanging in its wire cradle five feet above my head.

As grimy as it was, the circlet was still beautiful, a ring of linked panels. It did not look merely gilded. Maspero had given it solidity as well as grace.

Julian regarded it with satisfaction. "The original is far older, far heavier, yet no better crafted. I assume it is still safe in the royal regalia."

"Yes. What was this crown an offering for?"

"Why, for nothing save pure piety, just as with all these other offerings," Julian said with weary resignation.

"No, truly. I want to know." His friendly ease with me made me feel that I could say anything to him. Any distraction I could offer him was my duty.

"Andred was ill. I had to travel to Vienna, and I didn't wish to. I made a pilgrimage here and offered this up with my prayers for her recovery."

Had that been his last journey, the one to Vienna? I found there were some things I did not dare to ask after all. Instead, I said diffidently, "She is so beautiful in the donor panel. But remote. Like a mountain with snow all year around. Was she like that?"

"That's Giuliana's Andred you mean. The one in the Archangel Chapel?"

I nodded.

"I thought so. She didn't like to sit for Giuliana. She said Giuliana painted her with the wrong sort of ship, but there was no remedy. It ought to have been a cog-built coaster or a coaster-built cog—something of that nature. Whatever sort it ought to have been, Giuliana thought it was ugly. So she insisted on a more regal sort of ship. Andred was displeased. She preferred substance to appearance." Julian looked up at the crown again. "Andred was made to rule Lidia. She should have been born to the throne. Instead she married it."

"She married you. The king."

"Oh, yes. Thank God. The substance of our marriage far out-
weighed its appearance. When Andred swore her marriage vow, the
ring I set on her finger was fragile in comparison. What she promised,
she fulfilled. I did my best to match her. Though I was but crown
prince when we married."

I held my tongue while Julian looked back at memories that made
the corners of his eyes crinkle. His voice was warm and gentle as he
continued. "She was such a pretty child, you see, no one thought she
would amount to anything. Flaxen blonde, she was, and when they
called her Andred the Fair, at first that was all they meant by it. She
was like a doll when we were wed, a blue-eyed, stiff little painted doll.
Not a word out of her. I was impatient. I had work to do. I was twenty-
two, a grown man, with serious matters on my mind. She was scarcely
seventeen, frightened mute by the ladies-in-waiting and by my
mother."

Julian smiled to himself and strolled slowly on. I kept pace with
him, straining to catch his words.

"Andred was shy, so the courtiers let her alone. Waiting for me to
get her with child, I suppose, though we never had that particular
piece of good fortune. They seemed to think that because she never
said anything, she never thought anything. Even I knew better than
that, though I never knew *what* she was thinking. I could tell by her
eyes that she never stopped thinking, never stopped trying to make
sense of it. It took Istvan to draw her out. They were always a pair.
She was as speechless as he. At first . . ."

Julian's voice trailed off. We paused before the altar containing St.
Istvan's heart, a golden reliquary shaped like a heart held in two angelic
hands.

"Istvan doesn't say much now," I prompted at last. By comparison
with Julian, he was nearly mute.

"Istvan's never needed to. Deeds, not words, that's my Seraph.
Hands and heart. He left the fine speeches to the courtiers. Yet almost
from the first he spoke to Andred as freely as he does to me." Julian
shifted his weight, moved his shoulders a little stiffly. "Thank all the

saints that he could find something to say to Andred when she needed a friend. She gave him her favor, and he wore it in the lists. How he could fight. It made me want to cry to watch him sometimes. I had lessons all my life. I recall a dozen scoldings for every technique I mastered. I was competent, but there's only so much that muscle can do when the will alone is giving orders. With Istvan it was muscle and will and heart and soul together, a lyric all his own. He made her name more famous than I did. He was my champion first, but he was her champion best."

"Who did he fight? Did he fight duels?"

"No one would let a quarrel turn into a challenge with Istvan. They'd seen enough of his fighting to know that to duel with him would be folly. He fought only in the lists, only according to the laws of chivalry. Andred the Fair, they called her, and Istvan made them see how fair she was. Quite beautiful and so *young* it wrenched your heart to see her. What she gave Istvan in return was the power of speech. She knew what quotations he could cap. She let him finish her couplets. It drove the courtiers wild to see them at it. Like Paris and Helen of Troy."

How much like Paris and Helen of Troy? I was so afraid I'd say the words aloud I forced my tongue against the roof of my mouth and hoped it would dry there.

Julian looked at me and saw my thoughts. His eyes narrowed with amusement. "Launcelot and Guinevere, is that what you're thinking? Oh, don't deny it. The courtiers thought so. My mother thought so. Fair enough, I thought so too, for about a fortnight. But Istvan never thought so, and if it ever did cross Andred's mind, she was wise enough to know that Istvan would never touch anything that he thought belonged to me."

But the ring, I thought, *her ring.* I managed to keep silent.

"It was a very difficult fortnight," Julian continued. "The Austrian ambassadors were in Aravis, *and* the Venetian ambassador, and the Carinthians as well, and the Russians were worse than all three put together. There was a tournament, and a masque of courtly love, and a spell of unseasonably hot weather. Andred flirted as if she'd invented the art. The ambassadors thought she was Aphrodite come again. I thought I would go mad or die of jealousy before it was all over. If it had been left to me, I would have slain the Carinthian champion in the lists. Mother pointed out to me the little glances Andred shared with Istvan, the confidence they had in each other. I was too blind to see they shared the same looks with me, to realize their confidence included me." Julian paused for a moment and frowned at his recollections. "There's a calmness that comes only when the ones you love the most are near. I never realized how badly I needed it until my jealousy drove it away. Envy is a deadly sin." He fell silent, eyes on the reliquary.

When I could bear the silence no longer, I prompted him. "You were lonely?"

"I was miserable. Yet even that success of Mother's betrayed her, for that misery was the thing that made me realize how much I had come to love them both, depend upon them both, trust them both. My mother resented the power they had over me. She thought Istvan was an ignorant commoner—not too far from the truth—for if he ever read anything beyond a prayer book, I never heard of it. She thought Andred was a puppet—which must have begun as wishful thinking and which ought to have ended when Andred betrayed her by having a keen wit and a great heart, instead of the empty head and fertile womb she'd counted upon."

"She sounds powerful herself, your mother."

"Oh, yes. What she had, she used. Wisely, for the most part. She kept what she considered my best interests in mind. It was no fault of hers that I disagreed."

"What did you do?"

"I was too proud to do anything. I would have held my peace until doomsday. What a dunce I was. Fortunately, Istvan came to me when he realized I believed the rumors. He was hurt, though he tried not to show it. He knelt before me, as if I were a relic of St. Istvan, as if I were somehow holy, just because I was the king. Yes, I know that is what the crown and chrism do, they make me somehow holy. So I have always been told." Julian trailed off, looking back into his memory with an air of gentle abstraction.

Listening to the story was like riding my horse. I had to prod at regular intervals. "What happened?"

"Istvan lay his sword on the floor between us. He offered to go on a pilgrimage for me. I asked him what pilgrimage, why? One to the Holy Land for choice, he told me, but any pilgrimage. He would go gladly to the farthest corner of the world. He would climb a mountain in Cathay and bring me back a handful of snow. He would travel with a trade delegation, with courtiers, even with *ambassadors*—he offered any amends I wished. He didn't know his misdeed, but he would make amends." Julian shook his head. "I was stung out of all reason and I had no idea why. It made me cruel, my confusion. So I asked if Andred had told him to speak so."

"Had she?"

"No. I thought it would hurt him to hear me ask, that's all. It did. He stared at me so sadly. He said, 'I serve only you. Unless you no longer wish me to.' I realized that he had set that sword of his down before me and meant not to take it up again. I was not the only one, it seemed, who had been hurt by the past fortnight of misdirection. Istvan had hated it. He had been patient long enough. Any more, from anyone, most particularly me, and he would take his life away from me and spend it somewhere else.

"Such men do not last long, be they never so good at fighting. For a moment I saw how it would be. He would find someone else to fight for, and he would fight too long, and all that I would ever know of him would be rumors and gossip until the news came that he was dead."

I protested. "But he's a good fighter, the best. Who could beat him?"

"Rarely do men like Istvan die in battle. They kill themselves privily, either by the bottle or in some quarrel provoked by reputation."

"So you didn't let him go."

"I could live without a great many things, but I found that I could not spare Istvan. He trusted me, even I could see that, though I was but a dunce. I trusted him. Belatedly, I saw the nature of my malady. At court honesty is very like dishonesty. I tried to be careful not to dress matters up too formally and hurt him by putting more distance between us. 'You honor me,' I told him. 'I cannot be without you. You must let the fools' tongues wag how they will. I know it's hard.'

"He didn't understand me, but he understood that our misdirections were at an end. No pilgrimage. No penance. He took up his sword and we both understood that he was mine again."

"Did Queen Andred understand that too?"

"She always understood that. She understood more than I ever did. I have no idea how she accomplished it, but Andred persuaded the lot of them, even the Venetians, to sign the accord on the alum trade."

Even if I hadn't known how important it was in making dyes, I would've known what alum was. It's nearly as important to the wool trade as sheep are.

Julian continued. "Fine stuff, alum. It's the only useful thing ever to come out of the Haydocks. We bartered our borders with it. Andred succeeded in getting the Austrians to open the negotiations. Their ambassador assumed she was a light woman, the way she had behaved that fortnight, and that she could be persuaded to ask me anything. He assumed that I was so besotted I would grant her anything she asked. Once my wits were about me again, I found it diverting to watch her handle them. Better than a play."

"She tricked them?"

"Not with words. Her speechlessness played to her advantage at times. One can't record a lingering touch, a smile, or a tilt of the head. Once the trade agreement was signed, she let herself be put back on the pedestal, where no one was able to tempt her with verses or songs of courtly love. But I realized that she was an accomplished mummer in our royal acting troupe and that she knew it too, and that she would perform for the benefit of our crown and not just for her own amusement. It was then I realized I was her friend in addition to everything else and that she was my friend, much the way Istvan is—a friend who trusted me, whom I could trust. That frightened me at first."

"What's frightening about a friend? It would be more frightening not to have one."

"Ah, but who was I to befriend anyone? I was the king—my duty had made me do terrible things. I knew that if I had to, I would sacrifice anyone for the crown. How could I accept their trust when my duty might make me betray it? Yet I did. They trusted me, and I let them. For my sins, I behaved as if I deserved them both."

"But you did deserve them. Istvan understands about duty. I'm sure Queen Andred did too."

Julian shook his head. "I did my best. I claim no more than that."

Ludovic Nallaneen came into the nave to find us. Istvan was beside him, and they both looked grim.

"The abbot has resealed the urn," Istvan said. "Only the siege medal is missing."

"The inventory is specific," said Ludovic. "The—other things are there, but the seal has been broken. It was intact when the abbot checked last, six days ago. The abbot is questioning the brothers and the servants. We must find out who saw the urn's seal intact last and learn who came and went since. It will take time."

His calm appalled me. "How could Dalet have stolen anything from a place like this?"

"Dalet might have employed someone else." Ludovic's eyes narrowed. "Let's hope the culprit left some trace to help us."

"You think it was the siege medal that Dalet used to call me back?" Julian looked intrigued. "My medal?"

"The prince-bishop's inventory seems depressingly thorough," said Istvan. "Do you think it might be incorrect?"

"No, no. I don't question its accuracy. It would make great good sense that my medal would work. After all, it had my blood in the casting."

Ludovic was horrified. *"Blood?"*

"Maspero studied alchemy as well as art. He believed that blood would clarify the gold, enhance the casting."

I blinked. "He did?"

"He had a theory about representing the soul of the sitter in material terms. It's in his notebooks. He recorded the theory with care."

"He did not." It was my turn to be horrified. "I've studied Maspero—everything I could find—and he says nothing about it in his published work."

"It was all in the notes he took while casting the siege medallion. He wrote a treatise later. There's a copy in the royal archive." Julian caught himself. "There was a copy there in my day."

Istvan said, "Dalet called me back by your name and the jasper ring that was buried with Andred. Anything of yours would have done as well as the medal. She needn't have known about the blood. When we were in the tower, she seemed surprised to find me there—as if she cannot sense me without seeing me. But you she called back by your own name, Julian, and her grip on you is unhindered. She may know all your comings and goings. She may be able to control you. You felt her, just as I did. I am sure she could control me, save for the accident of the ring."

"It doesn't matter, does it?" I asked. "We shot her, didn't we?"

Ludovic caught my wrist. "You shot someone?"

I shook myself free. "Dalet. She turned into an owl and flew away." I examined my wrist but it didn't seem likely to leave a bruise, so I refrained from scolding him.

Ludovic's relief was obvious. "You shot an owl."

"No, no. Istvan shot her first. Then I shot her. Then she turned into an owl and *then* she flew away," I said.

"So we know she wasn't injured seriously," said Istvan. "If she could fly away—"

A new thought drove Ludovic to interrupt. "What did you shoot her with, Hail? You can't pull a long bow. I've seen you try. You don't have a pistol, do you? What criminal fool of a gunsmith would sell you a pistol?"

"It's really Istvan's." I had it with me, but I was certain that if I showed it to him, Ludovic would confiscate it.

"Amyas told me what I'd need," Istvan explained.

Ludovic closed his eyes for a moment. When he opened them again, he was resigned. "I might have known that brother of yours would be in this somehow. It frightens me to think what he's been doing back in Aravis with no one to stop him."

"Father would stop him if he needed stopping," I reminded Ludovic. He seemed unconvinced.

Julian was very thoughtful. "If Dalet has such power over me, why hasn't she exerted it? If she used the medal to fetch me, she had it when she worked her spell. That's sure, and it may aid the questioners as they try to find who stole the medal and why. Yet it doesn't explain why she hasn't moved against me since."

Istvan frowned. "She might have tried. Perhaps we outstripped her on the journey here. Perhaps she cannot harm you while you are in a consecrated place. Perhaps her wings hurt her."

"Perhaps the moon is made of cheese," Ludovic put in.

"What do we do next?" I asked. It seemed time for a new subject.

"For the moment, I must insist you remain here," Ludovic said. "The brothers of the abbey will extend their hospitality to you. We will stay here until we learn what happened to the urn and until I receive new orders from the prince-bishop."

Somehow Istvan was between Julian and Ludovic, his eyes hooded. His voice held lazy interest and an edge of something that matched his eyes. "Must you? Must you insist?"

Before Ludovic could answer, Julian did. "Where else would we go? There's nowhere safe for us in all the world. Rest here for a few days. See what advice our friends can give us. Rest, Istvan, and then think again."

TWELVE

(In which I am given advice.)

The abbot questioned the brothers under his authority. His report to Ludovic was private, but crumbs of it emerged. The initial delay had occurred when the abbot waited to question Brother Tobias, who was responsible for the chapel in which King Julian's remains were kept. Brother Tobias could not be found. At length the abbot learned that Brother Tobias had left the abbey five days before and hadn't been seen since. There was no absolute proof that Brother Tobias had opened the urn and closed it again before his departure, but no better explanation presented itself.

Ludovic stated his theory in the report he sent to the prince-bishop. Brother Tobias had stolen the siege medal from the urn, left the abbey, and conveyed the medal to Dalet, who had used it to conjure up the king.

Though injured, Dalet remained at liberty. Ludovic was convinced of her alliance with Edward of Ardres. If she had pursued Julian and Istvan to Dalager, there was no sign of it. Ludovic's men reported no untoward activity around Dalager, and there were no discernible rumors from Ardres.

Ludovic and his men kept close watch on Julian and Istvan. Until further orders, we would remain at the abbey of St. Istvan.

*   *   *

After all our oatcakes, the hospitality of the abbey was a relief. In addition to providing safe beds for us all, the abbot played host to us at wonderful meals. Loaves of bread warm from the abbey ovens were brought forth to the plain scrubbed wooden tables, accompanied by deep crocks of butter and a huge comb of honey on a silver tray. Sometimes it was lentil soup instead, fragrant with herbs, or a capon roasted with such care it challenged the golden perfection of the honeycomb.

At the end of thirteen days, the prince-bishop's reply arrived, carried by a fresh detachment of men, but no higher officer. Ludovic broke the seal and unfolded the paper with a troubled look.

"I am to bring Julian and Istvan back to Aravis with all speed. There I am to commit them to the care of the prince-bishop himself. He will undertake their safety in these uncertain days. King Corin's health does not permit him to afford his guests the welcome His Majesty would wish. The prince-bishop will serve as His Majesty's proxy with a glad heart. All the comforts the palace can provide will be made ready in anticipation of our arrival." Ludovic put the letter away. "I am not to fail in my duty as escort."

Istvan puzzled over the message. "Why Aravis? Wouldn't it serve the prince-bishop's turn as well to let us stay here, safely obscured?"

"King Corin's health is poor?" asked Julian.

"His Highness has been confined to his bed for years," said Ludovic. "For his age, his health is exemplary. Unfortunately, he's nearly ninety. No heir in sight."

Julian looked grave. "I see."

"The prince-bishop wants you under his hand," said Ludovic.

"What about me?"

"Yes," said the abbot. "What about young mistress Rosamer? I'm afraid our brotherhood will not be able to shelter her once you've departed."

Ludovic frowned. "I'm afraid I can't spare you an escort back home to Neven. My orders are explicit. We must return to Aravis as soon as we can."

"Then it's settled. I'll go with you."

*   *   *

Thirteen days were long enough for word to spread in a place as small as Dalager. When we departed, we had a quiet but interested audience. Ludovic and his men seemed to notice nothing out of the ordinary. Neither Istvan nor Julian paid the watching townsfolk much attention. I gave back stare for stare without a qualm. The crowd did not seem hostile, though they certainly were not friendly. They were watchful, and mostly silent. I heard a boy ask his mother, "Is that the king?" If she answered, I did not catch her words, but she put her hand on his shoulder and moved him back behind her skirts. That was answer enough, in its way.

The prince-bishop's guardsmen had very fine horses, yet I was happy to have my own solid beast back. The race is not always to the swift, and comfort counts for much in travel.

After the interest the townsfolk of Dalager had taken in our departure, I was intrigued to find a similar, though smaller, group of villagers at Vanca, where we crossed the ford. There were ten men, no women, no children, and for all the notice Ludovic's men took, they might have been invisible.

But we were of great interest to the men of Vanca. As Julian's horse splashed into the ford, a low cry went up from the watchers. I was in the rear; I saw the reason.

As Julian's horse moved forth into the current, the water of the Silverrod, which had been churned brown by our passage, flowed milky white where the king passed. Had I poured a bucket of white-wash at each step, just so would the water of the river have seemed. The whiteness faded in a few strides, the Silverrod wholly brown again the moment the king's horse had crossed, but the low murmur of the witnesses followed us on our way.

Istvan and Julian exchanged a look. Ludovic and his men paid no attention. It occurred to me to wonder if there was a local tradition, some legend peculiar to Vanca, which had to do with the river turning to milk when the king came home. I asked the guardsman riding closest to my beast.

He made the sign of the fig at me, which is what the ignorant do when they wish to avert the evil eye.

"Rudesby," I said.

"Witch," he countered. He looked the same age as Amyas, but his rough manners made him seem older.

"I'm no such thing. I am Hail Rosamer. I am an artist's apprentice. What is your name?"

"You are a nuisance. You may call me 'Sir.' "

"Not likely. Come, tell me. What happens when the king comes home?" I persisted.

Rudesby looked thoughtful for a moment. "That draught horse you are riding waddles a little faster?"

"Go on without me, then, if you don't like it."

"I like my ears. Both my ears. The captain would cut at least one of them off for me if I let you stray. And then how would I keep my hat on straight?"

"It's not on straight now. What happens to the Silverrod when the king comes home? Does it run milk instead of water?"

"I don't know. I'm not from these parts."

"Where are you from?"

"Look, you are going to get me into trouble with the captain."

"Any novelty in that?"

He didn't answer. Eventually I gave up.

Traveling with the prince-bishop's guard was different from any traveling I had done before. We moved fast—at least, it seemed fast to my beast and me—and we put up for the night when we wished to, where we wished to. There was belligerence in the way Ludovic and his men ordered the innkeepers about, and all the authority of the prince-bishop's warrant could not win us a welcome. No, we were tolerated, that was all the prince-bishop's bidding claimed for us. Fodder for our horses, food for us, and that was all.

The third morning, as we were leaving the town of Tariel, where another throng of grim onlookers had gathered, a dozen dark, swooping birds flew past us, circled, and returned. It took me a long look to identify them. Martins, I was sure, though they never paused for an instant. They flew as martins do, so swiftly that their elegance defeated the eye. As they returned, more joined them. Swooping, calling, dipping, diving, the martins flew in greater and greater numbers, until it seemed a ragged scarf of birds traveled along with us as escort. They made the horses twitch. Istvan and Julian carefully did not look at one another. Ludovic and his men paid no attention to anything but the road ahead. Rudesby seemed to notice nothing whatever out of the ordinary.

The townsfolk of Tariel called out in wonder, and we had not gone so far down the road that I could not hear those calls. "The king comes home," that's what they were saying.

I tried to draw rein. I wanted to go back and ask those onlookers what sort of things were supposed to happen in Tariel when the king came home. Did their water turn to milk? Or wine? What other wonders were in store?

But Rudesby had his own ideas. He must have been quite frightened of Ludovic, the way he hauled at my beast's headstall. He shepherded me along after the others, and he refused to respond to my objections with anything more than a look of dogged endurance.

Before we had left Tariel a mile behind us, the martins lost interest. We rode on without their escort for many leagues. By dusk, the horses were tired. I was exhausted. Julian looked weary. Even Istvan was looking a little worn, as if he'd been out for more than a mere saunter. As we approached the bridge at Folliard, the martins returned. This time there were three times as many, swooping and crying, and in the failing light the flight circled us until we could see no beginning to them, nor any end. We moved forward in a ring of swift wings, until we reached the span of the bridge.

The horses had been nervous in the morning. At dusk they were weary, too weary to spook and startle. But they balked, eyes rolling, and refused to move forward to the bridge. My beast put its four feet together and dropped its head. I hauled at the reins as lustily as if I were pulling a full bucket of water out of a deep well, but I could not get the creature to stir. Rudesby, I was pleased to see, when I could spare a glance at him, was reduced to much the same case with his mount. So much for the proud steeds of the prince-bishop's guard.

All the while, more martins joined us, and more and more. Never any slackening in that sweeping flight, the ring around us grew more solid as we watched. The little cries the swift birds made, some pitched so high they lay just within the edge of my hearing, grew more plaintive, as sharp and knifelike as the pattern the flight cut in the air. I began to think I could make out words in those little cries, and the voices I thought I could just catch made the back of my neck cold.

"The king," the voices said, and they said it over and over again, mindlessly, relentlessly. "The king, the king."

"O God," said Istvan.

I looked where he was looking.

Ahead of us, waiting patiently in the center of the Folliard Bridge, stood Dalet, hands folded, eyes bright. Her white robes had scarlet bars across the sleeves. There was no other color about her, save for the gold medallion—the siege medal—blazing at her breast.

Rudesby uttered a low exclamation, a wordless compound of fear and wonder. Ludovic snapped out orders his men could not possibly follow—for even as he spoke, Dalet lifted her hands and the horses went mad.

I fell off my beast at once. The others clung to their mounts for slow moments longer. Thus I had the best idea of what happened, for once I'd pushed myself up to stare, I was free to watch as Julian rode toward Dalet. The martins flew with him as his horse ambled forward, untroubled by noise, by birds, by pitching, squealing horses, straight toward Dalet.

Julian took his left foot from the stirrup and put down his left hand to her. She took his hand, slid her foot into his stirrup, and swung up to ride pillion behind him, as elegant in her own way as the flight of the martins all around them. Together they rode across the bridge, the martins wheeling and sweeping along with them. Her sleeves were white against the worn richness of his tunic, and she held him lightly.

Istvan roared, and his horse regained its senses for a moment or two, just long enough to bound forward on the bridge. If I never hear that sound again, my ears will still ache at the memory of it. My heart aches at the memory, even now, of the cry that Istvan made.

Dalet lifted one hand, a careless over-shoulder gesture, and Istvan's horse was possessed of a fury. Blind with madness, shrieking in terror, the poor beast sprang aside, desperate to flee the bridge. Istvan hauled back on the reins. Obedient to his great strength, the strong neck curved—and the horse went over the side of the bridge. And down— Istvan with him—down screaming to the Lida below.

Say what you will of Rudesby, he was an impolite young man, impatient, and sullen by any measure. But when I scrambled down the riverbank and threw myself into the water, he was right beside me. Right beside me he remained, until we clawed our way to Istvan's dying horse. I was crying, so was he, as he pulled out his pistol. He shoved me in place at the horse's head.

"Keep its head still. Sit on its head if you have to. Don't move. Cry all you want to—scream if you have to—only *God* don't move."

Praise God. The powder was dry. He found the place, pulled the trigger, and ended the broken animal's agony. After that great noise, I could hear myself again, and I wished I couldn't. I was making terrible sounds myself, gasping and sobbing, squeaking and squawking.

Once the horse was still, he could work with his knife, and work he did, quickly and neatly. The harness came free. Istvan's legs were twisted in the stirrups, tangled in the leather straps. I lurched forward and tried to keep his face out of the water. I managed so ill it is a wonder we weren't both drowned.

Ludovic Nallaneen was beside us then, and for the first time I understood why he would've been a leader in any group of men. Out of the madness, he brought order in a few barked sentences. By the time Istvan was carried back to shore and put down as carefully as could be wished, there was already a camp being made, a fire being lit.

I could not quite trust myself to lift my feet for that last step up on the riverbank, so I waited a moment, gasping and trying to collect myself. A hand came under my elbow, and Rudesby's voice was in my ear. "Nearly there, Mistress Rosamer. One more step. You can manage."

I turned and looked into his face. All the sullenness was gone, all the doggedness. He looked even younger than Amyas. Possibly only my age. I stared at him until he urged me up the bank again.

"That's right, that's fine. Sit here by the fire. I'll take care of your horse for you."

I gulped and tried to muster words. "You never told me your—" I had to break off for a fit of coughing.

When he smiled, he looked even younger. "They call me Tig."

"Tig." I coughed some more and decided to stay where he'd put me.

Istvan lay where Ludovic's men had carried him. He was still breathing. I watched him and wondered how he'd escaped drowning. To survive the fall had been marvel enough. To survive our clumsy attempts at rescue was nearly a miracle.

My stomach twisted at a new thought. Perhaps he would have recovered without us. Perhaps he would have recovered without even being pulled from the river. Perhaps there would have been another bundle of wet clothes at the river's edge the next morning, ready to eat mudskip raw. Perhaps Dalet's magic was stronger even than the river. It hardly seemed likely that Dalet would create a puppet that could be broken before she was ready to break it herself.

The men built a fine fire so that as the afternoon turned to dusk and then to night, there was light and warmth. Istvan was wrapped in blankets, still but for the steady rise and fall of his chest. If any of Ludovic's men spoke, it was in tones so hushed that I heard nothing.

We had one piece of good fortune. It was high summer, and that night we were spared a thunderstorm. Instead we were given a fine moonshiny night—warm and soft as fresh milk. If we had jumped in the river and huddled on the bank while our clothes dried on our backs at any other season of the year, surely one of us would have come away ailing. As it was, we were only clammy and uncomfortable.

Ludovic must have spent the night planning. I don't know what or how. I wasn't paying attention. I was sitting beside Istvan, just watching him breathe. I was waiting, no more. Not a thought in my head beyond that. I was careful to keep my mind blank. Because if I let myself think, I would have to remember the dreadful grace with which Dalet moved. I would have to remember the sound that Istvan made when he saw her take Julian as deftly as ever queen checked king at chess. I would have to remember the cold, sharp, ever-rising edge of wet as I ran into the water, the struggle with the dying horse, the smell of blood and mud and gunpowder.

I stared vacantly at Istvan while my clothes grew clammy on me. Eventually, they grew almost dry. Ludovic's men saw to the horses, pulled the carcass out of the river, tended the fire, prepared a simple meal. I think Tig offered me something, but I wasn't hungry. I tried to keep all my attention on Istvan, wholly and only, and on the moment I was in. I wanted nothing of the past and still less of the future.

It was dark when Istvan stirred. I leaned close at the first small movement he made. The firelight was bright enough to betray him as his memory returned. Hardly a moment of grace was allowed him before he recollected what had become of Julian, what had brought us to this place.

Istvan flinched away from my hand. That slight motion brought Ludovic close. His grip pulled Ludovic still nearer, in range of the whispered words. "I must go after them."

Ludovic's voice was soothing. "I set two of my best on her trail. Not to catch them, just to mark the way."

"A horse."

"You shall have mine." Ludovic gestured, and men came nearer to support and counsel. I was elbowed away into the shadows. The soft voices were edged with purpose as Istvan and Ludovic laid their plans.

I waited. Freed of my vigil, eased of some of my worries, my mind was at liberty to wander. I could no longer keep it steady and still.

How could Maspero have written an entire treatise that I had never even heard of? And upon alchemy, of all subjects? I felt a vast irritation with the man. How could you write something as sensible as "gold has no memory" and then temper a casting with blood? Well, say it was so. There must be many treatises I'd never heard of. Might someone who truly knew the intricacies of magic be able to free Julian? Rigo seemed to know all about such things. He had removed the miscast spell from Istvan as easily as I could tear paper. Perhaps Rigo could remove Dalet's spell from Julian?

What else was there for me to do? Keep a weather eye on Istvan? Pretend to myself I was his sister and responsible for him, as my brothers had always fancied themselves responsible for me? Small chance of that. Istvan was a hunter, and once his business with Ludovic was settled, he would be off after Julian at once, relentless as a hound unleashed.

"She *can't* control him if she's dead." Istvan's voice was soft but savage, unmistakable over the murmur of voices.

I listened to as much of the fireside council as I could catch. Relentless, almost thoughtless, Istvan had a single, rapidly fraying tether to the world—his bond with Julian. Ludovic was willing to aid and abet. Where that took him, even Ludo could not follow. I was nothing but baggage.

The fury now in Istvan made mockery of what I'd seen in him before. Who was I, to think of this creature as a brother? As well try to claim St. George, once he had been set on to slay a dragon. Not that Istvan had anything of the saint in him. He was an absolute sinner and he knew it, judging by the length of his confessions. Perhaps that was why this fate had been measured out for him. He had been summoned back to walk the world. Punishment enough in that.

For the first time, I appreciated what a torment the world could be. I shivered in my damp clothes. Istvan had died. To suffer that and still to have no hope of rest, no hope of morning to end the night that seemed to go on so long—it would be hell, to have a life after life. Purgatory had a limit, even though a long one. But endless life in a world where everyone else would die? I thought of the inevitability of death and wept a little more for pure self-pity. My mother and my father would die. My brothers would die, and their wives and children. My friends would die. My enemies, even, would someday die. And I would die. That was the only certain relief that I could muster.

I wondered what relief, if any, Istvan had been able to muster since his return. Whatever it might have been, it was long gone from his thoughts, judging by his expression. Lost souls must look so.

He was not quite lost to all but his own pain. When the horse Ludovic had given him had been saddled, and when his pack was filled with the supplies Ludovic's men had shared out for him, when his arms were in order, when his cloak was nearly dry, he remembered me.

Istvan looked around resignedly, almost absently, as one looks around when it is time to put the cat out for the night. I realized that he was looking for me, and I suspected that he could not remember my name. Before he could confirm the impression, I stepped close.

"Do you want to take the pistol with you?" I asked.

A little of his preoccupation drifted away while he, with obvious effort, recollected the pistol. "No. You keep it."

"How will you kill her then?"

"Ludovic has loaned me his sword."

"His two-handed sword?" I glanced, amazed, over at Ludovic. "But that's his own true love."

"I'm out of uniform when I carry it," Ludovic said. "Istvan will make good use of it.

Istvan's eyes cleared a little. Amusement gleamed and was replaced with something like fondness. "Remember this much advice when I am gone," he said to me. "If you want someone to support and help you, ask them for a favor."

"What will you ask of me, then?"

"Go back to Aravis. Be safe. Be careful."

"Oh, is that all?"

Istvan flicked a finger lightly at one of my earrings, enough to set it swinging. "Be civil to these poor fellows as they try to guard you on the way. They're only doing their duty."

He left us then in the rising day. We watched him go in silence. His way would be well marked by the men Ludovic had set on Dalet's path. None of us, I think, held any hope that we would see Istvan, or Julian, again.

THIRTEEN

(In which I am confined.)

It took three days to travel from the Folliard Bridge, where I had first seen Istvan, where I had last seen Istvan, to Aravis. The prince-bishop's guardsmen, under Ludovic Nallaneen's command, could have done the distance more quickly. For some reason, they, particularly Tig, seemed determined to show me some consideration.

Unfortunately, I was too weary to appreciate it. Although my clothes had dried on me as I watched through the night at Istvan's side, the chill of the river had not left me. I was well able to ride, to walk, to do whatever was expected of me. Yet there was a kind of fuzziness in my head, my appetite had vanished, and by the end of each day's ride my bones ached with fatigue. Two steps away from the horses, with Tig steering me, and I'd fall into my place, wrap the blanket around me, and sleep until the morning racket as the others made ready for off.

After the journey, I was taken to the prince-bishop. I ought to have dreaded this considerably. I was too tired to care. The fuzz in my head seemed to interfere with my eyes, my ears, even my balance. The footing of perfectly ordinary streets seemed as unreliable as deep sand beneath me, and my sense of direction had deserted me completely. I had Tig to guide me, thank goodness. Ludovic had ordered him to guard me. "Stay with her. Understand? If she leaves, you leave—and send me word where. But don't let her leave. Don't let her do anything."

So I had Tig at my elbow, looking disgusted at the world in general, when I knelt before the prince-bishop. I waited for him to speak. I remembered that it wouldn't be right to address him before he had acknowledged me. I couldn't remember why. I only knew Tig wouldn't let me sleep until I went through with it.

The prince-bishop let me kneel before him for quite some time before he spoke in a deep, cold voice. "Are you the girl who counter-feits currency? Are you the chit who ran away—stole a pistol and broke house arrest? Abducted a guest of ours from this place and took him no man may say where?"

I ought to have felt steady enough, kneeling at his feet, but the floor had gone all soft and floating. It was like being back on the river, on our raft. Distracted by this curious feeling, I did not answer.

The prince-bishop prompted me. "Well? Speak!"

I knew what I should do. I could not help Istvan or anyone else if I were mouldering in the palace dungeon. I ought to spring to my feet and answer back with spirit. I ought to counter the charges, refute them, debate my way to the door and depart, intent on my task.

Instead, the thought of mustering so much will exhausted me. I held my peace and kept my place. Indeed, it was all I could do to stay kneeling there. I wanted to lie down flat, stretch out my arms and legs, press my cheek to the cool floor and *sleep*.

The prince-bishop sounded far away. "I order you to answer me."

The floor pitched beneath me, as if our raft had found a snag. I lost my balance and tried to catch myself, to offer up some word of excuse. Too late. I could say nothing, do nothing, hear nothing. I could only sleep.

I am told that it was the prince-bishop himself who sent for Rigo. He had seen enough of me to realize, I learned, that no power short of sorcery could make me hold my tongue. Therefore sorcery was at work. Therefore Rigo was sent for. Rigo removed a spell of Dalet's—this time as easily as I might have removed my earrings. The spell was explained to me after I awoke, yawning and ravenous, sticky eyed, head aching with too much sleep.

How Dalet cast a spell on me, Rigo was not sure. He suspected my helping still the maddened horse might have had something to do with it. But she had infected me with a kind of sleeping sickness, one that dulled wits, diminished desire, and dampened anger. This had done its work so that I had not even been aware of my changed state.

By the time I was in my right senses again, Istvan had been gone five days and Julian a night longer. I came near losing patience at this news. Anything might have happened in that time. Any fate at all might have befallen both or either of them and none of us ever the wiser.

I tried to explain as much to Amyas when he brought me fresh clothing.

"I'm glad you're awake again," he told me, "but don't you think it's time you give up playing truant and started to pay attention to your own family?"

"Meaning you? Very well. How are you, Amyas?"

"Oh, wake up all the way and think for once. You could be in a dungeon this minute, but for Rigo."

Clearly Amyas wanted me to be as agitated as he was. I tried to distract him from the possibilities for drama in hope it would calm him. "Yes, I hear he pleased the prince-bishop. And you seem in good favor with Rigo, Tig tells me. So what scheme have you in hand, brother? An apprenticeship in the arts magical? Going to take service with Rigo, are you?"

"Don't change the subject. At this rate you'll finish attainted for treason. What possessed you to break house arrest?"

"What possessed you to tell Istvan about pistols?"

Amyas frowned. "Istvan? Oh, Fisher. That's right, I did, didn't I?"

"That's right, you did. If I'm to be accused of thievery on top of everything else, you are an accessory yourself, may I remind you. It was pure folly—he might have blown his head off."

"And you such an expert when it comes to firearms too. What became of it, anyway? Did Ludovic take it away from him?"

"It's in my pack. Or it was. Perhaps they've confiscated it."

Amyas emerged from a swift rummage through my things, which had been left in a heap at the foot of my untidy bed. "No, here it is.

Good balance, this. Here—" He turned swiftly and came back to me, where I was watching him from the edge of the bed. "You've changed the subject again. Stop doing that."

"Well, you talk then. Tell me the news. How's Father?"

"Father is worried half to death. He spent all his time watching over you. Then, once Rigo broke the spell, he went back to trying to persuade the prince bishop to let us all go home. The prince-bishop won't permit it. The whole city is in an uproar. Dispatches keep coming in from Ardres—rumor says every message is worse than the one before. Red Ned has hired an army of mercenaries." Amyas paused for my reaction, remembered he couldn't trust me not to interrupt with something he considered beside the point, and continued. "Word is that he used sorcery to raise the old king from the dead to lead his army. They will ride on the city and demand our surrender."

"What old king is that? The one snoozing upstairs?" This was not a respectful way to refer to King Corin, who had been near his dotage as long as I could remember, but I was only talking to Amyas.

"You know very well what old king—Julian the Fourth—your precious Julian the Good. He's come home. Water is turning to wine, loaves to fishes, ewes are bearing twin lambs—the signs are unmistakable."

"Milk," I said. "The water turns to milk."

Amyas paid no attention. "The prince-bishop doesn't like it. He's mustering the royal army. Supplying them will take a long time. And meanwhile, every day more of the countryside turns to Red Ned's banner—well, that is, to the old king's banner. No one thinks much of Red Ned. They march for King Julian."

"Poor Julian." I found my shoes and put them on. The river hadn't done them any good. "Any news of Istvan?"

"Nothing. No one knows how long until Red Ned attacks the city. Everyone fears a siege. Bread costs more by the hour."

"Have we heard anything from Neven?"

"Last word we had was Mother's reply to the letter Father sent after you ran away, saying that you hadn't turned up yet. They're all right."

"Have you been to Madame Carriera's?"

"They're all right too."

"I don't know when I'm going to get out of here, so will you do me a favor? Will you go round to Giltspur Street and ask Saskia to come see me? If she can't, ask her if she's ever heard of a treatise Maspero wrote about crafting the siege medal. It's about alchemy. Ask Madame Carriera, if you can."

"Why? What does it matter what your old Maspero did with his siege medal when we may be under siege ourselves?"

"I need to know about a book Maspero wrote. I've never heard of it, but Saskia or Madame Carriera may know it. Amyas, please. Promise me you'll help."

Amyas sighed. "I promise."

"Thank you." I kissed his cheek. "You're a good brother. Thank you for the clean clothes. Go away now, so I can put them on."

"Don't forget to wash."

"I won't." I couldn't be impatient with him. I needed his help. "You'll go to Giltspur Street now?"

"Yes, all right. I'm going."

My next visitor was Ludovic Nallaneen. I'd wanted to see him, and I didn't know who best to send for him, so this pleased me. By the time he arrived I had made good use of the soap and cold water and felt ready to receive visitors. Ludovic, though clean enough, did not look as well as I felt. There were smudges of weariness beneath his eyes, and he was in need of a shave.

"Good morning, Ludo. How are you?"

"Fine. You look better."

I sat on the cot and patted the blanket beside me. "Come sit down. You look as if you could use the rest."

Judging from his expression, it seemed as if Ludovic thought so too. "Not now. There isn't time. The prince-bishop wishes to see you."

"Again?"

"You're in your right senses now. He wants to speak with you."

"Oh. Is that all? Why did he send you?"

Ludovic gathered his patience in such a visible way that I knew he must be exhausted. Only under great strain did he ever betray the effort it cost him to be serene at all times. "He had plenty of people he could have sent. I happened to be given the task because I asked for it. I didn't want some innocent ordered into the lioness's lair."

I looked around me. "Is this my lair? I thought it was my cell."

"You've never been imprisoned if you think this is a cell."

"Not a jail cell. A nun's cell. I am shut away from the world, aren't I?"

"Unfortunately, no. Come along."

I rose and shook out my skirts. "How do I look?"

"Like Antigone set to wrestle Creon, best two falls out of three."

All false admiration, I sighed. "Oh, you're so well educated, Captain."

"And you painters are so ignorant. If Maspero had painted any classical subjects, you'd be much better off."

"Who won, Antigone or Creon?"

"In the short term, Creon did."

"And in the long term?"

"Difficult to say." Ludovic opened the door and swept me before him. "Probably Creon."

"That's the trouble with the classics."

"That's the trouble with life. Don't blame the Greeks and Romans. It's not their fault life is unfair."

Ludovic kept me talking until we reached the prince-bishop's presence chamber. My memories of the place silenced me as Ludovic escorted me through the door and fell back to stand at attention a few paces behind me.

The prince-bishop was seated in a chair, reading something. He glanced up as I stood before him. Then he went back to his reading without acknowledging me.

I kept my shoulders back and tried not to think of the way the chess squares of the floor had dipped under me last time. It was a rainy day, and the light coming through the windows was pearly and soft. Incense was burning somewhere nearby, half cedar and half cypress.

The prince-bishop looked up. "Rigo has studied everyone who was there the night that Dalet stole away your traveling companion. Of the whole company, only you were strongly affected. Rigo's theory is that whatever spell Dalet cast on the horses contaminated you while you held Istvan's horse. Rigo tells me that some enchantments leave traces that linger after the spell is broken. He used an example from the arts, perhaps you are familiar with the idea? When an artist alters a work, on occasion the earlier brush strokes show through. One may guess at the artist's original intent from such traces."

"Such traces are called pentimenti. They can cause a lot of trouble. But if you use the right pigments—"

"Yes, *pentimento,* that's the term. Rigo thinks he may be able to learn more of Dalet's intentions by studying the traces of her spell. You are to help him in his studies." The prince-bishop went back to his reading.

"How, Your Grace? If you please, how am I to help him?"

"Rigo is to study you." The prince-bishop looked past me to Ludovic. "Show her to his workshop, Captain."

Ludovic's hand was gentle on my shoulder. I shrugged it away. "Your Grace, I am very grateful to you for allowing Rigo to break the spell for me. But we have more to study than that. If Dalet stole the king's siege medal and used it to work her enchantment, shouldn't we learn all we can about the methods Maspero used to craft the medal? He wrote a treatise about it. A whole treatise I never even heard of before . . ."

The prince-bishop was staring at Ludovic in a meaningful way. Ludovic's grasp on my elbow was unyielding. I let him pull me toward the door, but I kept on talking, trying to explain the siege medal, the alchemical theory, the blood.

When the door was shut behind us, Ludovic allowed himself the luxury of shaking me. He did it gently enough, and I was nearly out of breath anyway, so I fell silent.

"Will you for once leave Maspero out of things?"

"But I can't. He's right in the middle of it."

"Just spare me. Spare my ears the sound of his name. Humor me. I'll take you to Rigo, and you can explain it all to him."

"Yes, of course," I said. "I was going to anyway."

I had imagined that a man of Rigo's standing would have had a room worthy of him. In this assumption, I was mistaken. Rigo's private chamber was small, too small for the task with which the prince-bishop had entrusted him. It was near the kitchens too, a feature that might be a benefit at times. In this instance, however, Rigo had moved the scene of his research somewhere quieter, somewhere more spacious, somewhere far from the heart of the palace.

With Tig at my heels, I followed Rigo and Ludovic down passage after passage, down stair after flight of stair, into the depths of the palace and beyond. I had thought, on my departure from the palace with Istvan, that I had been shown the secret heart of the place. I was misled. Rigo had begun his work in one of the palace cisterns.

"This is mud." I slipped and caught myself. "Isn't it?" Whatever it was, I didn't want to have any more to do with it than absolutely necessary.

"Simple mud. It settles out of the rainwater when the cisterns fill and are left undisturbed." Ludovic offered me his arm. I accepted it gratefully.

"We're in the highest level. Despite the unseasonable amount of rain we've had, we're perfectly safe here." He stopped and held his lantern higher. "Here we are."

I looked around. The chamber was vast, made entirely of stone, from the floor, thinly carpeted with mud, to the vaulted ceiling thirty feet overhead. It contained several long tables, pushed end to end, and thirty wrought-iron torch holders, clustered in a ring like a thicket of spindly trees. Rigo didn't bother to light any of the torches, just held his lantern over his head so that the shadows jumped and danced. "It's cold," I said.

Rigo smiled. "It only seems cold in comparison with the summer's heat. Here we are in the very heart of the earth. Heat and cold mean nothing here."

They meant something to me. "A brazier of coals would improve things a bit. It hasn't been much of a summer for heat."

"We are free of distractions here. The world is at a remove. This can only aid my work."

"Warmth would aid your work. You'll get chilblains down here."

"What is a physical inconvenience in comparison with the task before me?"

"You'll never be free of distractions if that's your attitude toward chilblains. For another thing, the damp is bad for books." I had noticed that the central table was stacked a foot high with books and papers.

"I'll send someone down with a brazier," said Ludovic. He looked around. "One should be safe enough. Don't ask for more. It would be a shame to smother yourself down here. Will you be all right?"

"Of course," said Rigo and I together.

"Stay with her," Ludovic told Tig, and took his leave.

Tig kept silent, arms folded across his chest, expression profoundly unimpressed.

"Where should we start?" I asked.

"Stand over there." Rigo directed me to a spot in the center of the ring of torch holders. With great care and the aid of a triangular device made of brass, he arranged the iron torchères around me. "That's good. Stay there just a moment longer." He marked my position with a lavish dusting of chalk. "You may help me mark the rest of the ring." He gave me a handful of powdered chalk and sent me off in the opposite direction around the circle of torch holders. Dutifully, I marked positions. The mud swallowed up the chalk at once, but despite that, a lighter ring remained visible. "We're well grounded in the earth. That's a great help. It isn't always easy to manage."

"It wouldn't be hard outdoors."

"Working outdoors renders one vulnerable to all manner of difficulties. One may be well grounded in the earth, but what is there to defend one from the air?"

I was puzzled. "Does one need to be defended from the air?"

"Each element plays a part. We are well situated here, shielded from the air, close to the water, though not too close, and well grounded."

"Is that why you didn't want a brazier? Because of the fire? Are you're using some theory based on the elements? Are you familiar with the works of Maspero?"

"One brazier can do no harm," Rigo conceded. "I ought to have asked Captain Nallaneen to send down a chair as well. Or at the very least, a bench. One can't sit in the mud, after all."

"Of course not. Are you familiar with the works of Gil Maspero?"

"Maspero?" Rigo blinked at me. "You have something you wish to tell me, don't you? Does it concern the works of this Maspero?"

"Maspero cast the medal that Dalet used in her spell to conjure up Julian. Julian said Maspero used his blood in the casting, and he said the royal archive had a copy of his treatise. I never heard of it. A whole treatise I never even heard of. If Maspero used some kind of alchemical theory in his work, the book could be vital."

Rigo echoed me thoughtfully. "A whole treatise you never even heard of. I take it you are familiar with the body of Maspero's work?"

"I have studied all I could."

"Perhaps you would be interested in a visit to the royal archives?"

"Is the treatise still there?"

"I have no idea. I think several of Maspero's works are there. The treatise you speak of may be among them. Even if it isn't, I always enjoy a visit to the royal archives."

"Surely you may visit there whenever you wish?"

"Of course. It's one of the great benefits of my work. Unfortunately I don't have time to visit there as often as I wish. You've provided us with an excellent reason. While we look in the archives, the servants can bring us a few chairs. I like a good straight-backed chair."

FOURTEEN

(In which I am sent to the library.)

Rigo led us back up into the palace. While I was getting the worst of the mud off my shoes, a messenger arrived from the prince-bishop.

Rigo studied the message. "Unfortunate. May I make you my emissary to the archives? Ask the archivist for the volumes you see fit. I will come when I can be spared and we will study the works of Maspero together." He borrowed my silverpoint crayon and scrawled an authorization on the back of the message from the prince-bishop. "That should do."

In my previous visits to the archives, I knew that I had not seen all there was to be seen. I had seen all I was interested in seeing, namely the cabinet in which the artworks of Maspero had been collected. I knew there were at least two adjoining chambers that contained the most select treasures of the royal library. Dimly, I understood that there were even more books kept nearby. Yet I never understood the extent of the royal archives or the nature of the treasures contained there, until I presented Rigo's message to the archivist.

Daniel, the archivist, a gentle-seeming fellow in a suit of rumpled gray, read the message twice. He did not look more than once at me, and Tig, at my elbow, might as well have been invisible. With a disapproving sniff, he turned and walked away from us.

I followed, nipping in front of Daniel as he opened the door, so that I could thank him for his courtesy. He said nothing as he led the way along a corridor. Through the doors that were open, I could see rooms full of light, where there were tables and chairs and shelves of books. Some of the doors were firmly shut, and I was sorely tempted to investigate, but the archivist was too brisk. Tig kept right on my heels, and I could tell from the way he looked around that the place interested him too.

Down the corridor we went. We came to a flight of spiral steps. Daniel led us clattering down. One flight below, another corridor duplicated the one we'd begun with. Just as many doors, just as many windows, and the light was nearly as good. Down another level, halfway along the corridor, and he led us into one of the rooms. This was smaller than I had supposed the ones above to be, and the light was dimmed considerably by the trees outside. I hadn't realized that there were trees in the palace, though I knew there were gardens here and there within the walls.

Daniel consulted the slip of paper again. With great deliberation, he took a book down from a shelf and set it at the table nearest the best window. Then he looked at Tig and me very gravely. "Take your time," he said, and moved a chair to block the door where he sat to watch us.

"Rigo needs all of Maspero's works," I said. I'd said it before. "He was quite explicit."

"I'll bring you the next when you've finished with this one," Daniel replied.

I was supposed to wait for Rigo. But then, I was to ask for Maspero's work to study with him. Daniel didn't intend to obey me. No doubt he would be more amenable to Rigo's direct order. Meanwhile, it could do no harm to examine the book I'd been brought. I should at least ascertain that it really had something to do with Maspero and his works.

Warily, I moved to the table and examined the book Daniel had selected. It was a thick volume bound in worn brown leather and looked well made and well used. There was nothing on the spine or the front cover to hint at title or author. I wiped my fingers on my bodice and opened the book.

Within, in a sprawling hand, the flyleaf proclaimed: *Nihil sine gaudeo. Maspero me fecit.* I made a strangled noise.

Tig obligingly thumped me between the shoulder blades. "Are you all right? What does it say?"

"Stop that. I'm fine. It says 'Nothing without pleasure. Maspero made me.' "

Tig looked impatient. "Maspero made you what?"

"Maspero made this book." My hands shaking as much as my voice, I turned the pages with care. The sprawled writing ran throughout, interrupted at intervals with diagrams and sketches, some marginal drawings no larger than my thumbnail. "It is. It's his notebook." I opened the book wide and pressed my face close to the pages, sniffing hard. "It smells like him." That was pure fancy on my part, but the smell of old paper and old leather was underlaid with something else, the faintest suggestion of sandalwood and sulfur. That scent made the artist seem more real to me than any of the printed treatises I'd read ever had. "*Nihil sine gaudeo* was his motto."

"It might have been his motto, but it doesn't mean 'nothing without pleasure,' " said Daniel. "It doesn't mean anything. Your fellow was certainly no scholar. *Gaudium,* or joy, would be the correct form after *sine. Gaudeo* would be a verbal form, 'I rejoice.' *Voluptas* or *delectatio* are better translations for pleasure. If that's the sort of pleasure you mean." He raised his eyebrows and waited for my reply.

"Er. You're right." Reluctantly, I conceded the point. "Maspero wasn't a scholar." I remembered what Istvan had said about Maspero working for pints of stout. "He did enjoy the pleasures of life."

Daniel relented slightly. "Perhaps *arbitrium* would be better. It's a good translation for pleasure in the sense of 'whim' or 'preference.' *Voluptas* in particular refers primarily to sensual pleasures. Eating and drinking, as well as the more obvious pleasures. Not the sort of thing one adopts as one's motto."

"No, perhaps not." Privately I wondered if that might not have been precisely the sort of motto Maspero had in mind.

Paging carefully through the text, I found a marginal sketch of a salamander, perfect to the gloss on its skin, done with seven quick strokes of the pen. "It's wonderful."

"You aren't going to kiss the pages or anything, are you?" Tig asked. My interest in the book seemed to revolt him more than anything I'd done yet.

I reassured him while I seated myself, reluctant to look away from the pages even for a moment. Even a casual glance revealed treasures. I found a diagram that could be nothing but the elevation for the Mathias Bridge, with notations I could not read no matter how I squinted and turned the page this way and that.

"What are you going to do with it, then?"

I blinked up at him. "Why, read it, of course."

Tig measured the thickness of the book with a glance, then measured me. "Now?"

"Of course now."

"All of it?"

"Of course."

"Won't it take a long time? It's all askew, that writing."

"That's all right, I'm used to it. I've read his inscriptions before." I did not mention that my experience of Maspero's inscriptions usually consisted simply of the words *Anno domini* followed by the year and *Aetatis suae* followed by an arabic numeral. In his portraits, Maspero limited himself to the year and the sitter's age. Given his tenuous grasp of Latin, perhaps it didn't matter if I could read the words or not.

"There are three more volumes," Daniel said. "I haven't eaten yet."

I turned back to the first page. Absently, I said, "Well, go and eat, then."

"I am forbidden to leave anyone alone here. It is my duty to guard the books. Even so, we have trouble with pilfering. I hoped that might be why the prince-bishop sent you here. We've reported the theft to the authorities."

"Hmm. Don't go, then." The interlaced lines of Maspero's casual hand was very difficult to decipher. Luckily the light was good. "You'll see I'm no thief."

"I haven't eaten yet either," Tig said loudly. He was standing in the best of the light so I looked up to ask him to move. Somehow, Daniel had come round to stand beside him, and they were both looking at me as if I had done something wrong.

"Well? What is it?"

They wouldn't answer me, just looked at each other and shook their heads gently.

"I don't suppose there's such a thing as a footstool here anywhere?" I asked.

"You could come back later with a footstool. You'd be far more comfortable." Daniel's concern surprised me. "I go off duty at four. Any time after that would be excellent."

"If you would stop interrupting and let me get on with my work, I could read more quickly. Tig, do you think you could find your way out of here without getting lost?"

Tig didn't bother to answer. The quirk of his lips made it clear that even to ask was to insult him.

"Go get some bread and cheese for the three of us then. And some wine." I handed money over. "I have my notebook with me, but not pen and ink, so fetch that as well."

"No ink in the archives," Daniel warned.

"I can't take my notes in silverpoint. That's all I have with me."

"No ink."

"Tell Rigo that I need to take notes. Bring me what he sends. And a lamp. This will take time."

"You won't need a lamp. You have to leave when I go off duty at four."

"Bring a lamp anyway. The light's not so good here."

Tig looked resigned. "You want a footstool too?"

"I'll make do without one. You'll have enough to carry. Oh, come to think of it, you don't need to bring wine after all. If there's a rule against ink, there's sure to be one against wine."

"There's one against food too," said Daniel, but he said it under his breath so I pretended not to hear.

"Get on with you," I said, and went back to work.

The notebook was the only work of Maspero's that Daniel would give me. When Rigo arrived, he would command the rest. My time alone with the notebook was limited. I read.

Maspero spelled things the way they sound. Sometimes he transposed letters or left them out. Other times, whole words were missing. Such mishaps seemed more frequent when he was in a hurry. Fortunately, it was easy to tell from his handwriting when he was in a hurry. The stately interlace of his formal hand yielded to a flurry of crotchets and hangers, the calligraphic equivalent of a troop of cavalry, pennants flying in neat ranks, startled into disorderly flight. Once my eye grew accustomed to the gait of his writing, I could follow it, albeit at a slow jog. Even more fortunately, he kept his excursions into Latin to a minimum.

Maspero's first royal commission was from the queen. It was for a man's ring set with a piece of jasper. That gave me a lurch of the stomach. There was a sketch of the original design. A little farther on, I found a revised design. The fiddly bits had been discarded. What was left was elegant simplicity. I wondered if the revision had been his own idea or Queen Andred's. If I had been given the leisure, it would have been pleasant work to try to find out.

The lurch of my stomach spurred me on, no leisure granted. The ring reminded me of Istvan, and Istvan reminded me of Julian. I counted up the days and hours since Dalet had stolen them from me and I worked all the harder. Ruthlessly, I scanned the pages of Maspero's notebook and untangled every mysterious bit of penmanship I could. Some resisted me, the way knots in thread resist me when I try to sew. I copied out passages I thought might prove helpful. I made rough sketches of the illustrations Maspero had done to catch his thoughts and keep them on the page.

Now and then I have done things that have made people unhappy. Any normal person must admit the same. I seldom mean to do so, and I am always sorry—almost always—yet that mends nothing. The harm has been done. Some of those unhappy people have wished me unhappiness. Their wishes came true in most elegant fashion during those days in the royal library. I was tortured superbly, for through his work on the page I was given exactly what I once wanted most in the world, that is, time alone to explore some of the workings of Maspero's mind. Yet I was not allowed to linger. No, quite the reverse. I was forced to canter through pages and pages, notebook after notebook, discarding treasures of knowledge in search of his alchemical chimera. One by one, I worked my way through the archives' collection of Maspero's work.

When Daniel understood my reverence for the work of Gil Maspero, his mistrust of me and his disapproval of Maspero's Latin grammar turned to active cooperation. When I tugged at a lock of my hair over a reference to crows in an oak tree, he was the one who reminded me of the sketch near the end of the first notebook, in which some of the birds were clearly crows, although those flying away were even more clearly doves. When my notes drifted here and there around the room, he was the one who retrieved the loose pages and put them in some sort of order at my elbow.

Three days passed in this way. Late on the third afternoon, Daniel took the volume I gave him and returned from the stacks empty-handed.

"I'm sorry. That's the last. There are no more holdings by or about Maspero in the archive." Daniel looked around at the clutter of objects I'd brought in to help in my studies. "I suppose I could help you and Tig pack all this up."

I was stung. "You still haven't brought me the treatise on alchemy. Maspero wrote about casting the siege medal. We know there's a copy in the archive. Bring it."

"I can't bring you what we don't have. The treatise on alchemy was stolen. We reported the theft to the authorities. Remember?"

"You told me you had to watch me read because there was a problem with pilfering. You never said anything about the treatise on alchemy. If you knew it was stolen, why didn't you say?"

"Please don't raise your voice. You didn't ask for the treatise on alchemy. You asked for Maspero's works. I've brought you all we have."

"One by one. Rigo's orders were perfectly plain. You were to bring me all Maspero's books. Why didn't you say something when I showed you Rigo's order? The time I've . . ." Honesty silenced me. I couldn't claim I'd wasted a moment. However, it had never been part of my plan to read everything *but* the treatise on alchemy. "Oh, never mind. Come with me." I took him by the arm.

Daniel resisted. "What are you doing? What do you want?"

"Rigo will wish to hear your explanation. We're going to see him."

Rigo was in his cistern. He admitted the three of us, for Tig accompanied me as usual, to the high-ceilinged space. It was no longer nearly empty. There was a chair and a footstool at one end of the long row of tables. The mud on the floor had been so marked with circles of chalk that the ring of candelabra seemed to be bordered in lace. In the center of the ring rested a small, squat casting furnace similar to the one Madame Carriera used in her workshop.

"What's that doing here?" I crossed to it and investigated. Thanks to an elaborate effort at venting with lead pipe and terra-cotta tiles, it was even in working order. "Are you going to cast something?"

"You know how to use such a device, I'm told," said Rigo. "You've been trained in this craft."

"I've been trained, yes. What are you going to do with it?"

"We're going to recast something. The preparations are nearly done. You've been very forbearing. I hope to begin work tomorrow. Please be patient until then."

"You can't start until you've seen Maspero's work. You never visited the archives, so I had to come here. Daniel says that the treatise on alchemy has been stolen."

"The treatise? What treatise? Ah, Maspero's treatise."

"Yes. The theft has been reported to the authorities, but there's nothing else to be done. The book is gone."

Rigo looked thoughtful. "Stolen? A pity. A great pity. You've looked for it yourself?"

"Daniel won't let me."

"Ah." Rigo went to his worktable. Eventually he found a sheet of paper, dipped his pen in the inkwell, and wrote. "Here's your authorization. You may search the archives until I summon you. Conditions should be favorable tomorrow morning. Be prepared. In the meantime, perhaps you will be able to busy yourself with the search."

Daniel spoke firmly. "I beg your pardon for the intrusion, Magister. The archives have been searched. Thoroughly. The treatise has been stolen. Other books too. The theft was reported and a complaint lodged against the thief."

"You know who stole it?"

"Of course we know who stole it. How could anyone come and go without our knowing it?"

"Why didn't you stop them?" I demanded.

"We would have, had we known. As it happens, we didn't know until soon afterward. The authorities have the full report."

"What authorities would you be referring to?" Rigo asked.

"The prince-bishop's administrator. We directed the report to him. That's why I hoped at first that the message Hail brought from His Grace meant that he'd chosen to interest himself in the problem."

"Oh. Unfortunately, that was not the case." Rigo seemed resigned. "Perhaps you wish to tell me the report's conclusions?"

"The treatise was among a number of works stolen by one of the archivists. A trainee, so to speak." For some reason, Daniel looked at me. "She was a countrified creature, for all that she was born and raised in Aravis. Her name is Betula Ansel, but she was always called Bet. She was very enthusiastic about the archives. We were all shocked to learn what she'd done."

"What, besides fail to return a few borrowed books in a timely way, had she done?" asked Rigo.

Daniel looked shocked. "She stole books, Magister. Irreplaceable books, the only known copies. She took them for her own exclusive use. Had she stolen the same weight in gold, she would have done less damage to the public good. What greater wrong could she have done?"

"Are you sure it was her doing?" I thought of Gabriel and his threats toward me. "Perhaps there was a misunderstanding."

Daniel shook his head. "It was Bet. After five years in the archive, she had discovered that she was not to be among those selected for further training and responsibility. Her work in the archive was sound enough. She would have been welcome to continue it her life long. But her interests were limited. Advancement in the archive requires a more general enthusiasm. In her disappointment and pique, she stole the books and ran away. We know she left the city by the Shene gate on the seventh of January. We've heard nothing of her since."

"What were these limited interests of hers?" Rigo asked. "Anything unusual? Anything . . . abstruse?"

"Bet's interests were strictly confined to what benefited her. Her concern for general knowledge and the importance of enlightening others was nonexistent."

"Presumably, she was interested in alchemy, then? If she took Maspero's treatise. And what other books?"

"The report to the prince-bishop contained the full list. I can remember only a few. Boethius on the consolation of philosophy, Pico della Mirandola on the nature of the soul, and Michael Scot on the sun and the moon."

"An intriguing selection. All unique to the royal collection? A pity. I'm familiar with the book on the soul. I regret not taking more detailed notes the last time I read it. Can you describe this errant librarian?"

"A full description is in the report sent to the prince-bishop." Daniel sighed and surrendered. "Betula Ansel is an unmarried woman between twenty-five and thirty years of age, slender, of middling height, with red hair and green eyes."

"She should be hard to miss," said Rigo. "Not many match that description."

"It doesn't do her justice," said Daniel. "She is a shrew. She looks daggers and speaks venom. The only thing worse than her frown is her smile. Her voice is too sweet, like poisoned music."

"Harder still to ignore in a crowd. I will have a word with the prince-bishop," said Rigo.

I realized that Tig was looking at me hard. I kept myself from asking *What?* aloud. He lifted one eyebrow and stared at me harder. I frowned. Rigo noticed and asked, "Is there some difficulty?"

"No, nothing," I said hastily.

"I think your assistant has something he wishes to say." Rigo regarded Tig benignly.

Such an affront startled Tig out of his customary silence. "I'm not her assistant. And I don't wish to say anything. Only, it was Candlemas when Red Ned of Ardres hired that sorceress. And she's red haired, same as he is."

Like the touch of a cold hand, the memory of Dalet's voice came back to me. Poisoned music? "You think Dalet and Bet are the same person?"

"Betula Ansel is pretending to be a sorceress?" Daniel looked thoughtful. "I suppose she'd be convincing in the part."

I rounded on him. "It isn't a play. Dalet has the power. She has only to open her hand and say the right words to make you do her bidding. I didn't even notice her doing something to me."

That seemed to amuse Rigo for some reason. After a moment, he said, "I'll go to the prince-bishop's clerks myself. I want the entire list of the books Betula Ansel stole."

"Something in those books gave her the ability to pass herself off as a wizard?" Daniel looked bemused. "Of course, in some parts of the world the mere ability to read is considered magical."

"It's Maspero's treatise. Whatever else she found, it's Maspero's work that gave her the power to . . ." I broke off, having remembered belatedly that the return of Istvan and Julian ought not be known in the world at large. Rivers running milk were one thing, frank testimony from an eyewitness like me quite another. ". . . to ally herself with Edward of Ardres."

"Whatever she called herself originally, Dalet is a powerful woman. In allying herself with Edward of Ardres, she has gained strength, powerful arms and legs to carry out her wishes. What has Edward gained?" asked Rigo.

"Eyes and ears," said Tig. "That witch woman sees it all and hears it all. The wind whispers to her when she wants to know something."

"Someone to frighten the children with when they go to bed at night, apparently," said Daniel.

"Someone to blame things on," said Rigo. "Suppose all Edward's schemes come to pass, whatever they might be. If he succeeds, he can blame any excesses on Dalet and say that he will make sure there are no such frights in store for innocent people if we will just let him do as he wishes."

"But doesn't Dalet realize that?" Daniel asked. "She must know that he could use her as easily as she uses him."

"No one could use her as easily as she uses other people," I said.

"I thank you for bringing me this information," Rigo said to Daniel. "It is tempting to equate your missing librarian with Tig's witch woman. Whoever Dalet is, our hypothesis changes nothing. Our work continues. Please continue to sustain Hail's researches in the royal archive."

Daniel nodded and turned to escort me away.

"It does change things," I began. The link between Maspero's work and Dalet's power over Julian was the siege medal. Any attempt to counter that power had to involve Maspero's work. Daniel's touch on my sleeve disrupted my argument. "Let me go. I'm not finished."

Daniel dropped his hand. He looked apologetically at Rigo. I interpreted his expression, and belated comprehension angered me. "Pardon me. I mistook you for an archivist. In fact you are a nanny. Are we late returning to the nursery?" I turned to Rigo. "You never intended to join me in the archives, did you? You only sent me there to keep me quiet. I've told you all I can about Maspero, and you refuse to hear me. The treatise on alchemy is crucial. I don't care if Dalet used to call herself Betula or Mary Magdalene. It's Maspero that matters."

"Maspero, Maspero. Enough of Maspero!" said Rigo. "You may return to the archive if you wish. The preparations are taking longer than I'd hoped. I won't need you until tomorrow at the earliest, perhaps the day after. Go now, quietly. I'll send for you."

"Why won't you listen? Why won't anyone listen? Maspero is the key. What preparations can you be making without studying what Maspero did?"

"If you refuse to follow my instructions, I'm afraid the prince-bishop will demand sterner measures. It's not as though you haven't given him reason."

"You don't listen—"

Rigo turned to Tig. "Fetch the guards. Confine her to her quarters. I must know where to find her when I need her, and in this humor there's no telling what she'll do."

"Will you listen . . ."

But no one listened. Tig and the other guards escorted me to the room where I'd wakened from Dalet's spell. There they locked me in and left me to shout or to be silent as I pleased.

FIFTEEN

(In which I look out the window.)

My room had a window. It had a door, which was locked except when my meals were brought; four walls, none of which yielded to a secret passage; a floor; and a ceiling. The furniture consisted of a cot with clean bedding, a three-legged stool, a candlestick, and a slop bucket. I knew I could attempt escape at any time, for I was permitted to keep the clothes and other articles I'd traveled with, which included Istvan's pistol and ammunition. Unfortunately, the guards visited me two by two with my meals. At best, I could shoot only one. I didn't want to shoot anyone at all. Shooting Dalet had been unavoidable, but I didn't want to repeat the experience, least of all with Tig or someone like him.

So I did not attempt escape. Instead, I looked out the window. It was a small window, and rather far from the floor for comfort, but if I stood on the stool, I could lean on the sill and crane forward. The view was worth the slight inconvenience. If I looked straight down, a sheer drop to the courtyard below, I could see a scrap of gravel walkway bordered by ramparts. Below that, I looked down on the crooked streets of the northern quarter of Aravis, where the city wall curves within the greater arc of the river Lida. That view was not so different from the one Saskia loved best. Beyond the river the hills gathered to conceal the Lida from me. I had walked and ridden along that river. It seemed impossibly long ago that I had first fled the city. The streets of the city seemed impossibly far away. I was pent up alone, unable to help Istvan or Julian or even myself.

I had the pistol. I had the stool. Even the candlestick could have been useful. What I lacked was the will to escape my captivity. I knew that Maspero was the key to everything, and I knew that Rigo disregarded his importance. But I had read everything of Maspero's that I could have shared with Rigo. Nothing I had read would convince Rigo of Maspero's importance unless Maspero's importance was already apparent to Rigo. So why escape? Where could I go? What could I do to aid my friends?

Thus the guards came and went in safety for two full days while I could muster no more resolve than to look out the window and think.

On the morning of the third day, I was permitted a visitor. Madame Carriera arrived when my breakfast did. There was a guard with us, but she ignored him.

"Saskia informs me that you are working here for the moment." Madame Carriera looked around my cell, crossed to the window, and looked out. "A pleasant prospect."

"I asked Saskia about Maspero—"

"Yes, yes." Madame Carriera seemed impatient. "I'm afraid Saskia is far too busy working to spare the time to visit. I only came to be sure you were decently housed. And to return the book you loaned me." She handed me a slim volume and turned away. At the door, she paused. "I took great care of it. I know you would wish me to. Keep up your studies." With that, she was gone. The guard closed the door, and the bolt scraped into place.

I was left alone with my bowl of porridge and the book. I ignored the porridge, for I had never loaned a book to Madame Carriera. The book she'd given me was one I'd never seen before.

I opened it with care. The volume was, in its purpose, the same as the notebooks of Maspero, but the handwriting on the pages was legible and measured. The sketches and notes were the work of Madame Carriera, done when she was an apprentice. I turned the pages, marveling, until I found the motive for the loan.

Madame Carriera, in the days of her apprenticeship, had studied the works of Gil Maspero. As well as sketching his masterpieces, she had taken notes on his writings. She had studied the treatise on alchemy.

"M.'s line is good but not his sense of color. M.'s work merely decorative," she had observed at one point. At another, "No depth." All the same, she had copied out whole paragraphs of the treatise.

The prime matter, Maspero believed, was the clay of which all things were made, the clay we are born into, the clay we leave behind us when we die. What interested Maspero was the life within the clay and the methods by which the particular life of a subject might be caught and set down in a likeness. Maspero's interest in capturing the life of a subject went far beyond mere portraiture. It was his belief that the proper technique could catch the essence of the subject and infuse an object, mere matter until the hand of an artist went to work, to create an emblem. That emblem would contain in miniature the spirit that animated the original. The artist could symbolize his model. His work would live as long as the work of art survived, capturing within it something vital of the model, long after the model had died.

How this process took place was not expressed in words but in pictures. There was the salamander again, in even fewer lines than Maspero had used. There was the tree with the crows turning into doves, in a silverpoint sketch. There was the design for the obverse of the siege medal, the city of Aravis triumphant, pennons flying from every tower, all battlements secure, the Lida flowing in a neat arc, orderly as a moat.

I turned the page, expecting the profile of King Julian. Instead there was the floor plan of the Chapel of St. Mary's by the south gate. After that, for the rest of the volume, came working sketches of the Madonna in the chapel there. Even in her youth, Madame Carriera had been a great admirer of the work of Andrea Mantegna of Padua.

I pored over Madame Carriera's pages again and again. I studied all the notes she'd made, scrutinized all the drawings. Maspero's alchemical notions seemed more easily expressed in images than in words. Given his problems with Latin grammar, the images were probably more reliable than words. The only solid conclusion I came to was the melancholy one that color had been the nearest thing Maspero had to a weakness. I wondered what it said of me that it took me so long to notice.

At last I put the notebook carefully away and returned to the window. Madame Carriera had been right about that too. It was a pleasant prospect.

The city wall rises and falls as it circles the city. Fortifications thicken the wall at intervals. There are sound principles of engineering behind those forms. The rise and fall of the ramparts is as orderly, though more graceful.

From outside the gates, the city seems all force, all solidity. From within, the crooked streets of the city seem bounded by the wall, straight and tight as a hoop round a barrel. From above, the rise and fall of the ramparts was a dance, a pattern of protection.

Though I could see only a portion of the wall, the curve of its arc held the whole implicit. To see one part of the wall was to deduce what the rest of the pattern had to be.

I am still ashamed it took me days of gazing out the window before I looked past my own thoughts and saw the world beyond. Three days of thinking about myself and my troubles instead of thinking about the problem at hand.

I was remembering St. Istvan's at Dalager, wondering what I could have done differently. I was thinking of the talk I'd had with Julian, the slow walk we'd taken down the nave and along the aisles of the church cut deep into the stone of the hillside, the search for the votive crown.

Maspero me fecit, the notebook had said. Maspero had made the votive crown, the jasper ring, the siege medal. Maspero had also designed the fortifications of the city. That rise and fall of masonry, that pattern of protection, could also say, *Maspero me fecit*.

Belatedly, I saw the world beyond. Remembering the time at Dalager, I looked out at the curve of the river, the curve of the city wall within. Belatedly, I looked at the wall and saw the curve of the votive crown. At last I looked and saw what was spread out below me. The

rise and fall of the crown, the rise and fall of the ramparts: alike,
Maspero had made them. The circle of the walls was the circlet of the
crown. What Julian had dedicated to St. Istvan was no mere emblem
of his rule, it was his own city, the symbol of his realm. Maspero had
made them alike.

I asked for more candles, and they brought them. It wasn't the best
sort of wax for my purpose, but it was better than nothing. The frus-
trations of working it helped me pass the time. On the fifth morning
of my captivity, I welcomed my second visitor with the arrival of breakfast. Ludovic Nallaneen came to see me.

"Good morning. You're making quite a habit of this," I said. A
guard observed us from the door as we greeted one another with de-
corum.

"At least I know where to find you when you're under lock and
key. Madame Carriera sent me to borrow your book, if you're not busy
with it."

"By all means borrow it. I recommend it." I glanced at the wreckage
of my efforts with the candles. "In return, all I really want is some
decent wax. Would you ask her for me? I want to make a model."

"I did wonder." Ludo studied the ruined candles with open curiosity. "I thought you might be trying to eat them."

"I want to make a model of the votive crown Maspero made for
St. Istvan's at Dalager. Rigo doesn't want to hear me talk about Maspero
any longer. I'm going to have to find another way to explain what
Maspero did."

Ludo looked resigned. "The girl who cried Maspero."

"So if it's not too much to ask, I'd like the modeling wax. About
a pound and a half should be plenty."

"Very well. Amyas and your father asked me to tell you that your
family is fine. So are Saskia and the rest. Do you have any messages
for them?"

I stared at him for a moment. "You make it sound as if I'm at
death's door."

"It isn't usually the happiest of circumstances, being confined to the palace."

"Rigo wants my help with his ritual. It can't take much longer, whatever he's planning."

"The preparations are complete. He's waiting for the new moon. Three more days."

"Then I'm all the more eager for the modeling wax. Give Father my love and tell the others I miss them. But bring me the wax."

"I'll see what I can do."

"I'll pay you for it now." I took out my earrings and offered them to him.

Ludo took them and tucked them carefully away. "It hadn't occurred to me that you might try to bribe someone with these. I'll return them to you someday. In the meantime, be patient and try to behave yourself. That's all I'm asking. Try." He left with Madame Carriera's notebook and I was alone again, with nothing to do but wish for a larger breakfast.

That night my dinner tray held a bowl of soup and a pound and a half of modeling wax. I finished the soup and started to make a proper model of the crown. The next morning there was no breakfast at all, only water. Rigo had given orders, I was informed. In preparation for the ritual, I was to fast. I was also to memorize some lines of gibberish. The text of the ritual had been written out in full. My lines were mercifully few.

I knew Rigo would not wish to hear my theory of Maspero's work. Better than a lecture on rampart design would be a model of the votive crown. I learned what the wax would do and what it wouldn't. The need for compromise became a challenge in itself. I used my eyes and my hands. In the end, the time ran faster than I realized.

Three hours before the ritual was to begin, I was escorted to the baths, where women coached my ritual responses as they helped me clean myself and then dress in robes of sackcloth. I was ready with an hour to spare. I wondered if they'd expected me to put up a fight.

Instead, I was so peaceable they took me back to my room and locked me in. I was glad of the extra time. I had finished the model, but every time I looked at it I thought of a new refinement.

I was still working on the wax crown when the summons came to attend Rigo in his improvised workroom. I wrapped the delicate model in a cloth and carried it with me. In addition to my allotted two guards, Tig accompanied me. I was glad to see him.

"The prince-bishop will be there for the ceremony," Tig said. "Rigo had better keep it short or that furnace will suffocate someone. It isn't meant for such a place."

One of my guards turned back frowning. "Hush, now." Tig was silent the rest of the way.

Rigo's cistern was warm. The furnace had dried out the mud on the floor. Many feet had trodden that crisp mud into dust, which had sifted into the air of the great chamber. It was hard to breathe freely there. For the first time I was uncomfortably aware of the mass of masonry above us. The palace seemed to brood over our heads. So disconcerting was the sense of dry heat in such a place, I felt restive standing there. To cover my uneasiness, I folded back the cloth to reveal my wax model. "I must show you something," I began. "Careful, this is delicate."

"We're ready to begin," said Rigo. He stood beside the prince-bishop in the center of the ring. Except for the guards, the three of us were alone.

Three days fasting had done nothing for my disposition. "I'm not ready. You haven't told me what you're doing."

"You've learned the ritual," Rigo said. "You're word perfect in your lines."

"You haven't told me what the ritual does."

The prince-bishop took the wax model from me and set it with care on the worktable. "Your role is simple. We must recast the siege medal. What power Dalet wields over Julian, either for her own benefit or that of Edward of Ardres, is linked to that. We know this, for it was the medal that called Julian back. It was stolen from among Julian's remains by one of the brothers at the abbey. His whereabouts are unknown. I fear it was his body that Dalet called Julian into. Something similar appears to have befallen the thief who despoiled Queen Andred's tomb. Dalet used the ring to call Istvan back into the thief's body."

I blinked at him. "How do you know that?"

"I've been asking questions. Those who serve me have been finding the answers. You are here to help us put the questions and the answers together to benefit Julian." The prince-bishop returned to the circle marked on the floor. "We require your help in the actual casting."

"But Maspero—"

"You are the artist I am concerned with. No one but you." The prince-bishop was firm.

"You want me to destroy Maspero's work to no purpose."

"Maspero's work has been used against you and every other citizen of the empire. It has been used against nature itself. The only way to set this necromancy right is to destroy that which links Julian to his enslavers. Julian's blood links him to the medal. To free him, the medal must be recast."

"Dalet has the medal that was cast with Julian's blood. We can't recast that one."

"Rigo's art is greater by far than that of Dalet's. She may keep the medal. Rigo will melt her spell with a greater spell of his own."

"Even if he could, it wouldn't help. Julian is linked to the medal, but there's more on the medal than the image of Julian. Look at the other side—look at Aravis. It isn't just Julian's blood that's the link. It's Julian himself. Maspero cast Julian and the city together."

"The arrangements have been made," the prince-bishop declared. "You play your part. Rigo plays his. The work is vital. The moon won't wait."

"Begin," said Rigo.

The air prickled with dry heat. The silence pressed in on me. Breathing became an effort. I remembered Tig's warning about the furnace, and for a moment I feared that we were all about to be suffocated. Then I realized the prince-bishop and Rigo were breathing easily enough. My difficulty was all my own.

Resigned, I hitched up the belt—the women at the baths had called it a cincture—of my sackcloth costume. If its draperies were anything to go by, the art of magic was a sedentary one. I just hoped I wouldn't brush too close to the forge and find myself bursting into flame.

I walked to the worktable. My breath came more easily as my resistance diminished. The tools were there, spread out before me. Among them was a bronze siege medal. My own medal was beside it, along with the clay mold prepared for the recasting. Rigo had added signs to the rim of the mold, symbols I could not read.

I took up the medal Maspero had made. More valuable by far than the bronze that made it, the medal was Aravis itself on one side, Julian himself on the other.

Rigo was chanting. The air in the chamber thickened, not just with heat and dryness this time but with a sense of shared purpose, of impatience.

I slid the medal into the crucible. The crucible into the cradle that bore it safely into the heart of the furnace. Slowly, what Maspero had made returned to molten bronze.

Did bronze have a memory? I thought it did. One could not cast and recast it indefinitely. What Maspero had bound, the furnace had set free. What could be made of it now was in Rigo's hands.

I tried my best. Concentration was the keystone of Rigo's ritual. My attention was to be focused on the mold. I prepared it, closed my eyes, and waited for Rigo to intone the lines I was to respond to. On that cue, I would begin the pouring. Molten bronze would, with luck, again take the shape of the siege medal.

Someone far away was knocking on a door. Stubbornly, steadily, the knocking went on. An intermittent thud, as of a booted foot kicking the door, joined the knocking.

Concentration. I squeezed my eyes more tightly closed, let out my breath, and drew another deep lungful. Rigo chanted on unperturbed. Perhaps he didn't hear the disturbance.

The knocking continued. Voices, some muffled, some not, joined the racket. The knocking and kicking stopped, but the voices increased in volume. A new knock, closer, turned into a thunder of blows on the door to the chamber. Protests, more kicking, and I had a sudden icy certainty that I recognized the voice.

"Here," said Istvan. He stepped past the guards into the chamber. In his hands he held the votive crown I had last seen hanging among the offerings at St. Istvan's in Dalager. As he held out the crown, I looked hard into his eyes. Whatever had befallen since I saw him last, nothing good had happened, nothing happy. He had fresh scars at wrist and jaw and temple, more punishment than any man still living should have suffered. Even under his chin, where a garrote might slice, there was a livid scar, a stark necklace. "Take it." He pressed the offering into my hands.

I took it clumsily. "What's this for?"

"Julian told me to bring it here. His link to the medal can't be severed. It can only be overruled by a stronger tie. You must forge a link to the city for him."

I held up the votive crown. "This city."

"Yes."

"Does Dalet know?"

"He can hide nothing from her."

"Time is passing," Rigo reminded us. "We cannot wait for next dark of the moon. You must complete the recasting. Finish this ritual, and then I will study the matter and construct a new ritual for the crown."

"Time is passing," I said. I couldn't spare a hand to adjust the belt again. "The furnace won't stay hot forever. We can't wait to work out a second ritual. I'm changing this one."

"These arrangements are carefully planned. I made all the calculations," Rigo protested.

"I'm sorry. Sometimes an artist has to wipe off the charcoal and do her own under-drawing." I put the votive crown down beside the wax crown on my worktable. My belt slid perilously, but I caught it in time, yanked it tight and tied a fresh knot, then tugged briskly at the bunched fabric until I felt less likely to trip over my own hem. I rolled the sleeves back out of my way once and for all, then lifted the votive crown to my eye level. It gleamed in the lamplight, its delicate lines an echo of the familiar line of the city walls.

Rigo broke my concentration with a touch on my wrist. Despite the heat in the chamber, his hand chilled me. "This is not for you to decide. I forbid you to change the ritual."

I looked at him, and Rigo's eyes held mine. I could not look away. I heard the muted chime of steel as Istvan's great sword left its scabbard, and then the blade was poised between Rigo and me.

Istvan's voice was deep and cold. "It is the king's command."

Rigo let me go. I focused on the sword Istvan held. All the heat of the casting furnace could not warm that steel. Rigo stepped back. Istvan put the sword away, and I was free.

Here was the votive crown, all Aravis, here in my hands. Here too was the work of Maspero, here in my hands. And here in my hands, held safely in the light, lay what was dearest to King Julian's heart. The heart of his kingdom, the keystone of the Lidian empire, the city of Aravis.

I set to work.

Sixteen

(In which I finish.)

Rigo resumed his chant. I wasn't listening with my full attention. I don't think I missed any cues. He seemed to be improvising, temporizing to allow my work to go forward before he moved to the next stage in the ritual.

I had to call for more materials, but my orders were obeyed with speed and accuracy. It took time to make the clay mold for the crown, more time still to allow it to dry. Still Rigo chanted, softly but steadily, as if by keeping his ritual going, he could hold his place in time. Hours passed.

Somewhere the moon set and rose again.

The votive crown was gold over base metal. I decreed that four ounces of bronze be added—lest Maspero's siege medal had been melted down in vain. I slid my own siege medal into the crucible. How could I hesitate to sacrifice my own work when I had to be so prodigal with Maspero's? When the time was right, I set the votive crown into the crucible. Let it all blend, I thought, base metal and noble, crows and doves alike.

Maspero symbolized fire with his salamander. His birds represented the element of air. The neat arc of the Lida represented water. The element of earth was present in the city of Aravis, captured in the shape of the votive crown. In recasting the votive crown, we remade the link between the city and Julian.

In a husking whisper, Rigo chanted his ritual. I recognized a cue.

As if no more than a moment had passed, I said my few words and the rite went on. I poured the molten metal and the rite went on.

The mold held, and the blazing sun of the metal began to fade from golden to orange to red to a sullen pulsing darkness. In a murmur, Rigo's ritual continued.

Somewhere time was passing, but it seemed to hang motionless around us, caught by Rigo's art and slowed until it seemed not to move at all. Only the gradual death of the fire in the furnace promised us that our work would come eventually to an end. The casting cooled as the furnace did.

Would I cool, I wondered? When I was as old as Rigo and the prince-bishop, would I be moving toward the grave? Would that darkness approach as inexorably as the darkness that had swallowed the brightness of my molten metal? What lay beyond the darkness? I hoped for peaceful rest. May my eternal repose be unmolested by wayward librarians turned necromancer.

Rest seemed impossible. I could hardly remember my last sleep. More remote still was the memory of my last meal. I was glad I had no more of the ritual to do than stand at my worktable and wait for the casting to cool. It was all I was good for.

Our great work cooled at last. The mold came away reluctantly. Within lay the new crown, dull in comparison with the original. I finished the piece, burnishing it here and there, taking pains despite the palpable impatience of Rigo and the prince-bishop. I was well pleased with my labors. All pride, I set my mark upon the new crown. *Hail Rosamer me fecit,* that mark meant. *Hail Rosamer made me.* When I could do no more, I set the crown forth on the worktable.

"There," I said. "That's all I can do."

Rigo took up the crown and crossed the intricate circle he'd made in the center of the room to present it to the prince-bishop. The final portion of the ritual was nearly inaudible, so hoarse had he grown. At last he stood motionless, eyes closed, arms at his side. "It is finished," he murmured.

The prickling warmth of the room abated slightly. As if a door had opened somewhere, the currents of air shifted, and every light in the room wavered. Then the lights steadied. The prince-bishop held the crown to his chest and allowed himself to smile at me. "Well done."

I managed to smile back. "Yes."

"Not before time." He glanced at Rigo, as if for permission, and then stepped outside the chalk circle. As he left the chamber, his retinue fell into step behind him.

Rigo watched him go. Without a word he set about cleaning up the mess we had made of the place during the ritual.

Gathering up my tools, I started to help. It was the perfect task for me in that moment. My mind raced even as my body protested any effort. I could not be still, yet in my fatigue any but the simplest chore was beyond me. Weariness made me clumsy, my eyes burned with strain, and still my thoughts chased themselves tirelessly. I had destroyed work from Maspero's own hand, work of surpassing merit. Yet from that work I had created something new.

Maspero's crown, modeled after Julian's city, had remade itself through my hands. Scalding metal had run easily for me, as easily as water runs cold and clear in a brook. The art in the work had seemed to move with equal ease, the way a fish darts along a brook, mindful of the currents but free within the world of the stream.

I had done all I could to make the work whole and sound and worthy. As sometimes happens, something compensatory had occurred in that timeless space of creation, and the act of making changed something in me. I was not the same person after Rigo's ritual as before. Not quite the same, for I could never forget the joy I took at the skill in my hands, the leap of art in the work, the soundness and the worthiness, the meaning of it all.

This was what I was for, the way a spoon is made for soup. I was made to make such things and I would never be whole without such work to do.

Hail Rosamer me fecit, said my mark. *Hail Rosamer made me.* Yet it held true the other way too, *I made Hail Rosamer.* The crown created me as much as I created it. How could I look on that crown and doubt that I had something to offer the world?

"Did the spell work?" I asked Rigo. "I had to change things. Could you keep up with me?"

Rigo smiled. "It was a pleasant challenge. I enjoy playing music much the same way. My flute and yours changed off melody and counterpoint, but we worked together harmoniously."

"When will you know if the spell works?"

"I know it works because we were able to complete the ritual. Ceremonies of this kind are interrupted most unpleasantly when they fail."

"When will you know Julian is free?"

"Time will tell." Rigo touched my arm and gestured.

I realized that Ludovic Nallaneen was beckoning me from the door. It was time to leave. I gathered my things and joined him. I didn't know where we were going, but Ludo seemed to. I smiled at Rigo. I smiled at Ludovic and Tig. "Did you see it?" I asked. "Did you see what I made?"

"Yes," said Ludovic. He took my tools away from me and carried them himself. "Tig, fetch the things from her room. Take them to Giltspur Street. If you see Amyas or her father, tell them she'll be there soon." Ludovic helped me up the steps. Flight after flight of steps. How could there be so many steps in the world?

"I'm hungry." Obediently I climbed more steps. "I want strawberries."

"Strawberries would be nice," agreed Ludovic. "Only nine months until they're back in season. Would you like something in the meantime?"

"Ginger biscuits. From Dalager." I kept climbing steps. "Don't we ever get to go down? My back hurts."

"Nearly there." Ludovic guided me through a door. After that the way was flat, or nearly. Mercifully we encountered hardly another step as he led the way along corridor after corridor.

The maze of hallways reminded me of Istvan's escape from the palace. "Where's Istvan?"

Ludovic sounded grim. "I don't know. He's probably keeping an eye on the prince-bishop. Don't worry. He knows where to find us if he wants us."

"The prince-bishop?"

"Him too."

I trudged after Ludovic. "Where are we, anyway?"

"Almost there."

"That's not very helpful. This palace is bigger than it looks."

Ludovic and I rounded a corner. Before us was a door to the outside. The guard, who wore a gray cloak over a green tabard, waved us past. We stepped forth into a kitchen garden.

The late afternoon light made me close my eyes hard for a moment. "What time is it?"

"Nearly six. Don't worry. Not long to supper."

Orderly rows of root vegetables barred me from the temptation of the pear trees espaliered along the stone wall. I let Ludovic hurry me along without attempting to purloin a single fruit for myself. Even a carrot would have tempted me, but I was obedient.

Beyond the garden was another guard, this one in a different uniform. He too let us go unhindered. Through that door was the courtyard leading to the main gate. The guards there displayed no interest in us at all. We walked unchallenged into a side street. I wondered if every regiment of guards knew Ludovic or if he had simply arranged bribes in advance.

"Are you rich?" I asked, as we turned off the Esplanade. My bones still ached, but the freedom of the streets lifted my spirits. Relief made me light-headed. "Or merely famous?"

"Me? I am poor but honest. The usual state of affairs, until next quarter's wages are paid. Why?"

I was patient. "The guards let us go. Did you bribe them? Or did they know you? But some of them had the regular palace uniforms on. So they couldn't all be from your regiment." I thought it over. "Even if they all knew you, it doesn't mean they'd do what you wanted."

"God knows you seldom do." Ludovic grinned at me.

"You're happy. What are you so happy about?"

"It's good to be safely out of the palace." Ludovic's dark stubble made his smile seem the more brilliant by contrast. "You're right. Some of the guards knew me. Some of them did what I wanted despite that. The rest I bribed. And it worked. You're out of custody." He gestured grandly, and I realized we were in Giltspur Street. "You're home."

So brief a time I'd been away from Madame Carriera's workshop, to hold so much change. I gawked about me as we entered. Had the ceiling always been so low? Were the stairs to Madame Carriera's salon always so steep?

Had it always been so crowded? Piers and Saskia each had me by a sleeve. Tig was there, and I could see Amyas grinning over Papa's shoulder. I'd been gone longer than I realized. Piers had grown taller. Saskia wore her hair up. Papa looked so thin. Even Amyas seemed different, larger and more capable.

The salon was as elegant as ever, spotless and spacious. Yet to me it seemed as airless and hot as Rigo's workroom. I caught myself swaying and squared my shoulders.

"Give her something to eat," called Ludovic. "She must be hollow by this time."

I looked around for him. "Where's Istvan?"

Ludovic frowned. "I was wondering the same thing. Make them feed you something and get a bit of sleep. I'll see what I can find out."

An elegant hand fell on Ludovic's shoulder. Madame Carriera turned him toward her. Though she wore the clothes she painted in, she was as immaculate as ever. "A word in your ear, young man," she said. Her displeasure was plain.

"It's not his fault," I said. "I know I shouldn't be here. But he took me away from the palace, and where else could I go?"

Madame Carriera looked fierce. "You asked him to bring you here? After you ran away without a word?"

I shook my head. "I'm sorry. I was wrong." Words caught in my throat. The effort required to explain myself was too great. What explanation was there, after all? I had abandoned my studies. I had ignored her teaching. I had destroyed the work of a master. All my weariness came down upon me. The room no longer seemed uncomfortably warm. I felt cold and sick.

"At least you had the decency to return my notebook," said Madame Carriera. "It helped, then?"

"The crown is the city," I meant to say. The words stuck in my dry throat. Instead, I said, "The king is the city."

"I brought her here," said Ludovic. "The responsibility is mine."

"Under my roof, all the responsibilities are mine," said Madame Carriera. "Don't make me regret it." She looked around the crowded room. "Any of you." Her eye fell on Piers. "There's soup in the kitchen. Go heat it up. Water it down, there'll be plenty to go around. Hail should have hers thin in any event. If she eats too much at once, she'll only make herself sick. Now, Hail, sit down and tell us everything."

"Thank you." It wasn't enough to say, but it was all I could find words for. I shook my head. Carefully I sat down on the bench Amyas brought me. "Thank you all." My voice wobbled and my eyes stung.

"Come on," said Saskia. "Out with it."

I shook my head.

My father sat on the bench and put his arm around me. "She's had enough."

I leaned into his warmth. The chill within me retreated, replaced by the silent reassurance of his touch. My head was heavy, so I put it on his shoulder. I was asleep before the soup came.

When I woke, it took me a few minutes to realize where I was. My bed was comfortable, warm, and clean. The ceiling was freshly plastered, ornamented in each corner with a neatly frescoed emblem representing the seasons. From my pillow, I could see the tumbled fruits of autumn directly overhead. It reminded me I was hungry. There was something else I needed to recall. I couldn't remember what.

I realized I was in Madame Carriera's house, in the garret room I had shared with Saskia. I looked around. Yes, judging from the neat array of personal effects, Saskia was still in residence. At a guess, she'd done the fresco. It was in her style.

From the angle of the light through the fly-blown windows, I guessed it was midday. All my things were on the floor at the foot of my bed, an unsightly tumble of possessions.

Clumsy with too much sleep, I washed and dressed, took care of the basics. I was eager to make my way to the kitchen and find something to eat. And then—what then? There was something else I had to do. I couldn't remember what, but it was sure to come back to me. Distracting myself with food would encourage the evasive thought to come forth and make itself known.

In the kitchen, I found bread and cheese. While I was slicing the cheese, I scowled with the effort of recollection. There was somewhere else I ought to be. Never mind. Food was the first imperative. I sat down with my slabs of pale cheese and dark bread and fell to.

"Awake at last," said Saskia. She came through the kitchen on her way to the scullery carrying an armload of beets. "There's soup left if you want some."

The bread and cheese went quickly. I found the soup and ladled myself a bowl. No beets in it, I was glad to see. "I thought you'd be off on your own by this time. Hasn't your masterpiece been accepted by the guild yet?"

Saskia dropped the beets at my feet and deposited a bucket of water beside them. "Scrub those. For that, I should make you do it without a brush."

"For what?"

"For asking me that, as if I'm no better than Gabriel, going off and setting up in competition. You know very well that I've been accepted, but there's no way I can leave Madame Carriera with only one apprentice. There's more work than Piers and I can manage as it is, even with your brother to help us grind pigment."

"Amyas helps?"

"He's not bad." Saskia pulled up a stool and sat down where she could study me intently. She seemed satisfied with what she saw. "It's good you're back, though."

I finished my soup and helped myself to another bowl. "It's good to be back."

"I have work to do." Saskia rose and shook out her skirts briskly. "Wash up the dishes when you're finished, don't forget."

"Did you do the fresco?"

"The four seasons? I did."

"Excellent work."

"Yes, I know." Saskia looked pleased with herself. "I made Piers take down the old plaster for me. He had so much practice doing the other room, he didn't even protest."

"What did you base the emblems on?"

Saskia beamed at me. "Nothing but pure genius. I am a member of the guild now, remember."

"So grand you've become."

"Don't you forget it. And don't forget those beets." Saskia went up to the workroom and left me alone.

I helped myself to one more bowl of soup while I tried to concentrate on what I was forgetting. Something was eluding me. Something I needed to do. Or somewhere I needed to go. Something . . .

I put the bowl down half empty. Somewhere else. I needed to be somewhere else. I went out the back door, leaving the beets.

The city seemed strange to me. I walked the tangle of streets, looking for signs of the harvest season. I found few. The dealers' stalls were sparse. What goods were for sale were oddly expensive. Where I had once known a city of crowded markets and wide-flung windows, I found grim scarcity and windows shuttered. To make the streets seem bleaker still, a fine rain, little more than a mist, began to fall.

I walked in the direction of the Shene gate. There was somewhere I should be, but I could not remember where or why. It felt odd to be out alone. I'd been on my own when I walked home along the Lida, convinced I was fleeing from the law. Since I'd encountered Istvan under the bridge, I'd been in company, never entirely alone. At least, never alone and free to go where I wished. My liberty intoxicated me. I walked faster.

By the time I reached the Shene gate, I was breathing fast with excitement. My cheeks were warm. I had found where I needed to be. I had realized what I needed to do.

There were soldiers before the gate. Recruiting officers were addressing the knot of bystanders there. As they spoke, young men came forward, occasionally in pairs but most often alone, and enlisted. The prince-bishop's army required men for the campaign against Edward of Ardres. A mighty army would march forth from Aravis and conquer Red Ned once and for all. His threat would be ended before the leaves were off the trees.

More young men were arriving all the time. They all looked as excited as I felt, though the men who had already enlisted were looking a little puzzled about what there was to be so excited about.

I watched and listened avidly. This was what I had to do. I had to go north with the army. This grand force of fighting men would put paid to Red Ned once and for all. Aravis would be safe then. Before I came forward to join them, though, I needed to prepare. I needed my things. Sturdier shoes, something to eat. My notebook.

In haste, I turned back toward Madame Carriera's. The effort required to leave the recruiters at Shene gate was great. It was like walking on ice, to make myself move in any other direction. But I couldn't go to war without my notebook.

SEVENTEEN

(In which I go to war.)

When I returned to Madame Carriera's house for my things, I discovered I had been missed. Saskia was waiting for me at the door. She followed me up the steps, wanting to know where I'd been. At the landing outside Madame Carriera's salon, Ludovic Nallaneen intercepted me. I yielded to his entreaty, and we went into the salon to talk.

"Where did you go? What have you been doing?" Ludo asked.

"I walked down to the Shene gate," I told him and Saskia. "The army is gathering there."

"Don't I know it," said Ludo. "The prince-bishop is enlisting recruits. It isn't a particularly safe place for an unaccompanied woman. Nor man, for that matter."

"You left the beets," Saskia reminded me. "That doesn't surprise me, but you might have washed up the dishes you used."

"I'm sorry. I forgot."

Saskia did not seem interested in my penitence. "You might have told me you were going out."

"I didn't plan it. I had to go. I knew I had to go somewhere. But I couldn't remember where."

"You could have told me before you left."

"You weren't there."

Saskia looked cross. "Neither were you."

"I'm sorry." I turned back to the stair. "I only came back to get my things."

Ludo put his hand on my arm and left it there. "No, wait a moment. Sit down." He steered me to a bench. "Where are you going?"

I looked up at him. It made my neck hurt. "I need my notebook. And my other things. And I need to go back to the Shene gate."

"What for?"

"The recruiting officers are there."

Ludo's dark eyes narrowed. "They aren't recruiting artists. I hope you don't plan to enlist."

"No. Not formally. I'm not a soldier."

"No. We agree on something. That's good." Ludo sat beside me, his arm over my shoulders. Saskia stood between us and the door looking vigilant. "Now, Hail. Why do you want to go to the Shene gate?"

I searched for an explanation. I wasn't successful. I knew the urgency of my wish to rejoin the soldiers, but I couldn't explain it. "Well, to join the army. I have to go with them."

"Ah. Why?"

"To fight for the prince-bishop?" It didn't sound convincing, even to me. "To fight for Aravis?"

"You?" Saskia looked worried. "Hail?"

Ludo was looking worried too. "Where did you get that idea?"

I couldn't put my feelings into words. "I don't know. I just have to. I woke up knowing there was something I have to do. It took me a while to realize what it was."

"Has she ever had this notion before?" Ludo asked Saskia.

Saskia shook her head, frowning. "Never. She was a bit odd when I talked to her in the kitchen. She didn't say much."

"She didn't?" Ludo felt my forehead. "Hail, do you feel ill?" To Saskia, he added, "Her clothes are damp."

"It's raining." I drew away from him indignantly. "No, I don't feel ill. I feel fine. But I have to get my notebook." I started for the door.

Saskia stopped me. "Hail, don't go."

"Hail—"

There was a note in Ludo's voice that made me turn and stare. "What's the matter?"

Ludo said, "I've spoken with Istvan. He's spoken to the prince-bishop. Rigo gave the crown you cast to the prince-bishop. Together they've begun another ritual. Rigo's spell should free Julian from Dalet's power. So they are using the crown to call Julian to them in Aravis."

"The crown is the city," I said. "That makes sense."

"The call doesn't seem confined to Julian. Citizens began volunteering for the prince-bishop's army. They want to enlist to help the prince-bishop fight to protect Aravis. They can't explain why."

"Dear heaven," said Saskia. "Is that where you got the idea?"

At first, I didn't answer. I searched my memory of waking. The urgency I felt had been there from that moment, running beneath my thoughts. If it wasn't my idea from the beginning, I had made it my own. "I cast the crown. Rigo cast the spell. I might have some link to it."

"Judging from your behavior," said Ludo, "you do."

"If the spell Rigo cast worked, Julian should be free of Dalet's spell. Won't he come to Aravis as soon as he can?" asked Saskia.

Ludo said, "Istvan doesn't believe the prince-bishop wants Julian in Aravis."

"Well, if the prince-bishop is using the crown to call Julian, why does he need an army?" asked Saskia. "Why can't he wait until Julian comes to get the crown?"

"What if Julian brings Red Ned's army with him?" countered Ludo. "They won't want him wandering off all on his own."

"It's Julian's crown, not the prince-bishop's," I said. "We'll take it to him."

Ludo sighed. "That's what Istvan says."

"Good. Then it's settled. I'll just go pack my things and be right back."

*   *   *

It was far from settled. There were many arguments about my plans. I won them all. My trump card was the link I felt to Rigo's call. I did not try to emphasize my reaction to the call of the recruiting, but I didn't need to. My symptoms were few but clear. It was painful for me to ignore the call of the spell Rigo was casting.

At last even my father yielded. He granted permission for me to travel under Ludo's protection. My preparations were made and my plans approved. I was going forth with Istvan and the prince-bishop and Rigo and Ludo. Together we were going to free Julian from his captivity and put paid to Dalet and Red Ned of Ardres.

Tig was given his new orders. Ludo reassigned him to accompany me. We even had the same horses we'd arrived with. Tig was not happy.

Madame Carriera was resigned to my departure. She did not try to change my mind. Amyas and Piers agreed that I was going on a grand adventure. Saskia refused to speak to me.

Early the next morning, with great pomp and panoply, the prince-bishop blessed us. It was a lengthy business, but we all felt the better for it. Holy soldiers, there's a strange notion. But that's how we felt as the Shene gate opened and the prince-bishop led his army forth. Rigo rode beside him, the crown gleaming on the pommel of his saddle. Istvan rode beside Rigo.

I was luggage. No matter how I protested, no matter who I argued with, no matter how long, I was relegated to the supply train. The support required by an army is vast and various. I had my possessions, my horse, and Tig, who grumbled all the while. We took up position among the dust and noise of the rear guard. The extremely rear guard.

I had just enough sense to know that I was not going to enjoy much about our journey, but nevertheless my heart was light as we began. The urgency was still running under my thoughts, steady and relentless. The relief of responding to it, of doing something about it in the world made me feel light-headed as well as lighthearted.

My packing had been a matter of hot debate back at Madame Carriera's house, for I had recovered the pistol I carried for Istvan. Amyas had proved an unexpected ally in this. Thanks to him, I had an ample supply of powder and shot to go with it, along with an odd assortment of rags and oils I was supposed to use when cleaning it. Amyas insisted that I clean it after every target practice. Amyas insisted that I practice shooting frequently. Ludo promised to supervise me strictly. I consented to this notion, mainly because the idea of conducting target practice on my own sounded like a good way to hurt my ears and get into trouble at the same time.

I also possessed sufficient food and clothing for a reasonable journey and carried a document bearing Ludo's sign and seal, for all the good that would do anyone, entitling me to indent for provisions from the army's supplies, such as they were.

Best of all, I had the prince-bishop's permission to accompany the Lidian army. Nothing in writing, nothing so overt. But he had inclined his head graciously in my direction at the valedictory service, and if I allowed myself to draw conclusions from the gracious little gesture he made, he even blessed my horse particularly.

So we rode away from the city of Aravis, and I was off on my travels again. Though I had been on the road before, the way north along the river seemed strange to me. The year was turning as it should. The days were growing shorter, the nights cooler, the air more crisp, the sun less strong. There was haze over the hills in the mornings. There was dew in the long grass.

Some fields had been sown, had grown lush, and were ready to reap. Yet no one had ventured forth to bring in the crop. Some fields, closer to the debatable lands near Ardres, showed signs that the land had been tilled, yet the crop had never gone in to the earth. Some fields lay fallow. This untenanted state of the land was clearly, cruelly wrong. That no one dared to bring in the food they would need for the year ahead, that single fact compelled belief in the power wielded by Edward of Ardres.

"What will they eat?" I asked. "How will they come through the winter?"

"Red Ned won't go hungry. He means to king it in Aravis," someone answered.

"What about the farmers?" I asked.

"The dead don't eat much," someone else called back, earning screeches of laughter. The luggage train was not the most polite part of the prince-bishop's army.

I didn't mind the rude company. Tig's disapproval of me, something I'd grown accustomed to and missed when it was not in evidence, grew dilute when compared with his disapproval of our traveling companions.

We were accompanied by the boys, nominally responsible for the safe transport of luggage but really there principally for their employers, the knights, to kick and complain to; the whores, responsible for the usual duties; and the cooks, responsible for the well-being of our entire venture. I found it startlingly like my early days in Madame Carriera's atelier. As soon as I resumed my habit of checking all my bedding for unwelcome surprises, and guarding everything I possessed against pilfering, I quite enjoyed myself.

In such an assembly, my passage was so well secured that I could spare attention from my riding. My notebook open on the pommel of my saddle, I used the time well. It provoked some comment at first, but soon enough my companions grew accustomed to my work.

"Going to draw my portrait, eh?" one of the prostitutes asked. "Have you seen my best side?"

With a rude gesture, Tig discouraged her attempt to share her best side with us all.

"I am a mere apprentice," I explained. "How better to practice my art than to make a few rough figure studies of what I see around me?"

"Well, you're in the right place when it comes to figures. But why do you think you'll have any call to draw the likes of us?" the woman countered.

I considered what an excellent model for Mary Magdalene she would make, but it was time for diplomacy. "You've heard of the procession of the Magi. The Three Kings came bearing gifts. Who is to say their luggage train did not much resemble ours?"

"God help them if it did," someone called. "This is more like the flight into Egypt."

"The road to Damascus," someone else offered.

I would never have guessed my companions could be so inventive. Eventually they tired of offering me suggestions, and soon my notebook drew no comment. I was free to study them, and I made good use of the opportunity.

In the workroom you may pose a model all day and half the night if the model has the stamina, but there is nothing like the figure in motion. That's how the body really works. No better practice for an artist, and I had dozens of models to choose from, all working for free.

Our progress was swift, for the prince-bishop had provisioned us generously. We rode day into night each evening, then made camp and rested our stock and ourselves. Before first light each morning we rose, brushed the dew from ourselves, washed as well as we could, snatched breakfast, and clattered our luggage back together. By the time the sky grew bright in the east, we were on our way again, screeching with laughter and groaning with blisters.

I saw little of Ludovic. He had his duties to perform, and he trusted Tig to keep an eye on me. Istvan rode the length of our cavalcade several times a day, as if to round up any stragglers. From time to time he rode beside me, though he said almost nothing. My notebook didn't seem to bother him. I was glad of that. I'd have been hard-pressed to explain why so many of the studies I did were of him. Rigo and the prince-bishop, I saw only from afar.

As we drew near to Ardres, the land grew more barren. The noise of our passage seemed louder than before, perhaps because there was little else to make a sound. Only the wind traveled across the deserted fields. Tig said less than ever, but he knew the way things should have been. The look in his face spoke more clearly than words of the depth of the wrong done the land.

Near the milestone that marked the border, Istvan rode ahead. By the time the vanguard reached the border, orders had come back to us. We were to make camp at the crossroad.

That was a long night, the last night on the road to Ardres. The weather had turned warm during the day and even after sundown it did not cool. There was no wind at all. The air was warm as fresh milk, and the sparks from our fires sailed high in the calm darkness until they were lost among the colder fire of the stars overhead.

Our fires blazed bravely. Food and drink were plentiful. There was laughter, music, and even a little dancing. All the same, the hours crawled past. As the sky above us swallowed up the sparks, the empty night around us seemed to swallow up our merriment, and hunger for more. We laughed too hard, too long at every joke. Our well-being had to be overdone to be felt at all. We ate too much and drank too much and tried our best not to think at all.

Ludo joined us for a time. I watched him in the firelight as he listened to the determinedly cheerful talk all around him. My notebook open on my knee, I kept my eyes settled on him as my hand moved slowly across the page. It was a challenge to catch his expression as he listened, a perfect balance between readiness to act and utter fatigue.

When he saw what I was doing, Ludo came to sit beside me. After a leisurely look, he closed the book gently on my hand. I opened it and resumed my work.

"Must you?"

"It's just a study. Ignore me. It's better if it doesn't look posed."

"Why don't you ignore me? In fact, why don't you ignore us all? Let it go. No need to busy yourself recording all this for posterity."

His air of indifference nettled me. "I'm not recording it for posterity. Posterity may go hang itself for all I care. I am merely practicing my craft."

"No one need practice all the time."

"That's not what I hear from Madame Carriera."

"And you pay such heed to her teaching."

I turned the page and began to get down Ludo's new expression. The notebook annoyed him, but the conversation didn't. I had hardly caught the line of his mouth and jaw when he took my charcoal away. Indignant, I reached for it, and he caught my hand.

"Aren't you going to ask me why I'm here?"

"You came to talk, didn't you?"

"Hail, there are a hundred things I ought to be doing instead of sitting here."

Contrary to popular opinion, I can take a hint. "Why are you here, Ludo?" I asked obediently.

"I'm glad you asked." Ludo brought out my earrings. As he held them out toward me, the hoops blazed in the firelight, reminding me of the dying gleam of the crown as the cast metal cooled. "I thought I should return these to you."

I accepted the earrings eagerly. Once I'd put them on, I felt more my old self than I had in a week. My smile and thanks seemed to cheer him. Ludo handed me back my charcoal, and I started on the new turn of his expression.

Ludo rolled his eyes. "Must you keep scribbling?"

"Yes. I've had enough to eat, and I've heard most of these jokes before. What else is there to do? Besides, what else am I good at?"

"Do you only do things you're good at?"

I caught back my honest answer, which would have been, *Yes, of course. What else?* and studied Ludo with sudden doubt. Was he flirting with me? Here? Now? Hadn't he noticed my raucous companions? A closer look reassured me. Simple mockery, no more. "Don't you?" I countered.

"Obviously I do all sorts of things I'm not good at."

"Oh." That was not what I'd expected him to say. Belatedly it occurred to me that a half share of the mockery in Ludo's expression was reserved for himself.

He took my hand in his, held it up to the light, and turned it this way and that. "Is this your only god, Hail? Do you care for nothing but art? You seem to think of nothing else. Lord knows you speak of nothing else."

I met his mockery squarely. "The Lord knows He gave me a gift. It is my duty to use it."

"Need that consume every waking moment?"

"I've allowed myself a few distractions. Istvan and Julian, for example. If I'd paid proper heed to Madame Carriera, I would never have copied the medal. That's what started me on this path. Better if I had kept to my studies."

"Perhaps." He examined my palm more closely. "What if you lost this hand, lost your skill with it. What would you care for then?"

"If I lost my sight, do you mean? My sense of touch? Every way there is to act on my skill? If I lost it all, I think I would care for all the things I care for now, provided I had used all I could of my gift for as long as I possessed the power to use it. If I had set it aside, left it until later to learn my craft, I think I would care for nothing in the world." I had given this topic some thought when I thought I was going to be punished for attacking Gabriel, and again when I faced Madame Carriera's lecture when I returned to Giltspur Street.

"You're too profound for me tonight." He let me go and gave me back the charcoal. "I won't keep you from your divine crusade any longer. Get back to work at once."

I caught the mocking twist of his mouth, and as he saw it on the page, the mockery blossomed into bitter laughter. I laughed back at him. "Are you visiting from fire to fire until you bring cheer to the entire encampment? Good thing you saved us for last. Tig can be final proof of your skill."

Tig kept poking the fire, ignoring me studiously. A glance over at him sobered Ludo.

"You mustn't joke tomorrow, Hail. If Tig tells you something, take heed and do as he says."

"Of course. You would break my neck otherwise."

Ludovic was very serious. "You do as Tig says. It is his duty, as surely as you have decided it is your own duty to set down every detail in your sacred notebook."

I considered the matter carefully and nodded. "What happens tomorrow?"

"We must let the scouts tell us that. If we lure Red Ned out to meet us here, there will be a fight. If he has the wit God gave him, he remains in his fortress and we will venture as close as we dare. Either way, there will be a fight. It may be tomorrow. It may take longer. Days, perhaps. Even if it does, you listen to Tig."

"Of course."

"Easily said. Mind you do it."

"I said I would."

Satisfied, he rose. A few more pleasantries around our fireside and Ludo left us. I put my notebook away and curled up to watch the fire. My eyes burned, and I closed them and let the chatter and the laughter drift past. The sense of the words scattered, and I rested in the ring of light.

I thought the heat of the fire woke me, but it was the heat of the night. I pushed up on one elbow and rubbed my face. I'd been sweating, and my skin felt sticky. The fire had gone to embers, and overhead the stars were gone. A heavy overcast had rolled in. In the east there was a sullen flicker of distant lightning. Nothing stirred the air. The unseasonable warmth made it hard to breathe. I was not the only one awake, but no one spoke. The silence and stillness felt utterly wrong.

"What is it?" I whispered to Tig.

He croaked softly back, "Change in the weather. It must be almost sunrise by now."

I studied the sky again. The lowering cloud made it impossible to guess the hour. It felt like midnight to me.

Tig started gathering up his things. "It's going to rain."

I helped him fold his blanket, and he helped me with mine. It was all too strange, the heat, the darkness, Tig being cooperative. I rubbed the back of my neck. It felt the same as ever, only warmer and damper than usual. No chill foreboding, no presentiment of danger. Just sweat.

All around us in the dark, people slowly began packing up. The fire was stirred back to life, and by its light we worked as quickly as we could. Hardly anyone spoke.

Tig checked my packing. "Is the pistol loaded?"

"I never had a chance to practice with it."

"Is it loaded? No? Let me load it for you."

"I can do it."

"Good for you. Let me." Tig checked the pistol over and loaded it far faster than I could have. When he was satisfied with it, he wrapped it back up in the oilskin and handed it to me. "There. All but the powder in the pan. But be careful. And once it starts raining, you leave it alone, right? Won't do you any good then. Mind you, don't let your powder get wet either."

He went on scolding softly as I put it all gingerly away.

The horses were restless, which made it difficult to saddle up. Tig scolded them too, but gently. "It's the weather, that's all. They smell it coming."

Truth to tell, I was beginning to think that I could smell something coming too. There was a different scent in the heavy air. It was a cold smell, like moss and wet stone. Like a river, perhaps, but a river no sun had ever shone upon.

"Are you getting a cold or something?" Tig asked me.

"Smell that? What is it?"

Tig sniffed. "Horse."

"No, more than that."

"Horse manure."

The breeze rose until not even Tig could pretend he didn't notice it. The horses stirred fretfully and tried to turn their rumps into the wind. All the folk around us murmured and grumbled. After the closeness of the warm night air, the wind out of Ardres seemed icy. There was an edge to the chill air that reminded me of the damp stone of the church at Dalager, but this smelled of age unsweetened by incense or devotion. This was ancient, cold, and strange.

First with a single drop, then a scatter, then in a cold curtain, the rain set in. The churned earth of the horse lines turned to mud. After a quarter of an hour, it was hard to remember a time when it had not been raining. It was a large, determined sort of rain that seeped in everywhere. I blinked and brushed at my eyes again and again, trying to keep my vision clear, but the rain overwhelmed me and I gave up. I would be wet, my things would be wet, and Tig would disapprove of me greatly, forever and ever, world without end, amen.

At last came the order to mount and ride. We were, as ever, to bring up the rear, keeping close for our own protection, yet not so close that we interfered with army maneuvers. We kept up as best we could, while the prince-bishop's army proceeded, step by treacherous step, toward Ardres.

Eighteen

(In which I retreat.)

There was a battle that day. At sunrise the rain stopped and we saw the army of the enemy ranged against us. The cannon were deployed on the best ground available, but it was not a favorable place. Nor was it a favorable time, as the ground was sodden with rain and the river already unseasonably high. We were all too likely, should the battle go against us, to be backed to the riverbank and driven into the opponents at our flank. I understood little of this at the time, but one does not hear ballads and reminiscences for as many years as I have without grasping a few essentials.

At the time, I was merely glad it had stopped raining and pleased that the sun seemed to be rising on a clear day. It was exciting to be among the crowd, to see the ranks and order of the enemy ranged against us. The excitement ran along beneath my pulse, part of that steady urgency that had accompanied me so long.

"There's Red Ned," Tig said. We had a poor vantage from our position at the extreme rear, but Tig knew where to look and what to look for. "Just by the royal standard."

I found the figure Tig intended. He was one of a knot of men near the foot of the standard bearing the banner of the kings of Lidia. There was no definition of heraldry that permitted such a breach of manners, but the intent to link Edward of Ardres's army to King Julian's antique authority was unmistakable. I craned my neck until it ached. "Where's the king?"

"There beside that bitch Dalet. She's riding a milk white mare."

I followed Tig's scorn to the pair of horsemen nearest the standard. The white horse was caparisoned, no other word for it, down to what looked to be bells on the bridle. Its rider, done up in a regal style gone at least a century out of fashion, was Dalet. Beside her, on a black horse, rode Julian. He was in practical clothing, with the only fanciful touch a tabard bearing what looked to be his heraldic arms. If the spell Rigo worked with the crown affected him, he didn't show it. He sat his horse easily and seemed to keep his attention on what was immediately before him. I could not see that he ever seemed to look up, or around, still less to scan the throng around him.

The sun rose higher and higher while the armies made their dispositions. Orders were bawled to drop us back farther and still farther.

My neck ached, and I felt sticky and vile as my clothes went slowly from wet to clammy to all but dried. I began to wish I hadn't come or that the whole day were over and all disposed, for good or even for ill. I tried to get out my notebook, but Tig snarled at me to pay attention. Though I obeyed him, I could not help but snarl back. "Are we to wait here all day long?"

"No one asked you to come."

The battle started while we were squabbling. I've heard the songs. Seven days and seven nights the eagles battled. Rot. The battle lasted half a day. After that there were skirmishes, little more than running fights, that lasted three days at most.

Tig and I were on a little rise, the rest of the camp followers around us. I could tell the armies apart as long as the columns were drawn up in order. When the men advanced and met to skirmish, the columns melted into chaos. I could not tell, even with banners, who fought whom, let alone who was winning.

I had to watch. If I let myself look away, I felt guilty for wishing to escape. Tig was right. No one asked me to come. To watch, even if I flinched and cried while I did so, was my duty.

By the end of the first hour, it was clear to my companions that the prince-bishop's gunners were hopelessly mired. It was a question of losing as slowly as possible. Victory was not an option. The land was against us. To retreat was all that could be hoped.

Our withdrawal was not utter chaos. So busy was I, obeying Tig's orders, I did not even have time to be afraid. Only after a long while, when I was well along the way to exhaustion, did our pace slacken and our retreat cease.

"We can stop now," Tig told me. "Dismount and see to the horses."

"With what?" I felt like bursting into tears.

"Do the best you can. As soon as they've cooled off a bit, let them have a drink."

We were beside the river again, that infernal river that had hemmed in our forces for so long. With difficulty, because my arms were weary and the horses were uneasy, I led Tig's horse and mine into the water. We stood up to our knees in the chill current. The horses drank, and I stared into the water. It was dark brown, quite opaque even before we churned our way in. Perfectly usual color for river water at that time of year, yet I knew something was wrong with it.

I was slow to realize that the drumbeat I'd carried with me was gone at last. There was nothing in its place but the knowledge that where I now felt emptiness something had once buoyed me up. The cold flow of the river pushed at my legs. The horses tugged me gently forward as they drank. I stood fast against the current, yielded but little to the horses, and as I stood there I realized with slow horror that the burnt umber of the water held not merely mud but blood.

Awareness of the horror rose until it filled me, filled my mouth with the taste of blood, my nose with the smell of blood. The horses took no notice and I drew back, revolted by them.

"Hail?" Tig called to me from very far away, but I was already scrambling to get clear of the horses, clawing at the muddy bank of the river, scraping my knees to regain solid ground. If he said anything more I did not hear it. I only lurched to my feet and ran, panting and mindless, back the way we had come.

*   *   *

I came to my senses slowly. For a long time all I knew was that I was cold. I ached in some places and was numb in the rest. Hearing came next. There was a fire somewhere nearby. No heat from it but I could hear the occasional crackle. I smelled horses. Mud. Shit. Not just horse shit either. People.

My mouth was dry, metallic tasting. I swallowed painfully and opened my eyes. I could see the sky. It was ultramarine, the color of the Madonna's mantle. After sunset or before sunrise. I couldn't decide. It occurred to me eventually that I could wait and see which. Or I could do something. So I tried to sit up. No. Settled for rolling onto my side. That hurt. It would hurt more, I realized, if the numbness ever left my bound arms and legs.

No one had noticed that I was awake. I decided that was just as well. For a moment I wondered if I ought to pretend I was still dead to the world, at least until I had some idea of what had happened. I could remember the smell of blood, but the rest of my recollection was blurred. I had run for a long time, driven along like a sheep. All night? I thought the sky was growing lighter.

Someone kicked the sole of my foot. I couldn't help reacting. Someone stepped into my range of vision, and I realized it was Dalet. Even in the poor light, the costume she was wearing was more striking at close range. It wasn't just old-fashioned. It verged on the biblical. She even wore a wimple to cover her hair and throat. It was faultlessly white, and the crown that held it in place was familiar. It was the one I'd made for Rigo. For the king.

"Almost ready," Dalet said, though not to me.

My mouth tasted terrible, so I spat. It didn't come out right, my mouth was too dry, but the intent was clear enough.

Dalet kicked me again. "I could put you back to sleep if I wanted to. It's better this way." She walked around me sprinkling what looked like white sand as she went. The mud should have made that sand disappear at once, but it didn't. The sand lay like a white ribbon against the rich brown mud.

"Let me go." I said it, first louder and louder, then softer and softer as my voice returned and then left again. I was so frightened I didn't even stop when she laughed at me. "You bitch," I finished, but by that time I was audible only to myself.

She was going to do something to me, and I knew what. Like an extra lurch in every beat of my pulse came the certainty that she was going to call back the dead, and this time it was my body that would provide her a receptacle.

Gold has no memory. The words came back to me, and I would have sworn aloud if I'd been able. Instead I swore inside my mind, bloody great oaths of rage against Maspero. Without him, none of this would have happened. None of it.

My mind tangled itself in *none of it* for a while. After I thought it over and over a few dozen times, I began to realize that my wits were not the sharpest.

Dalet began to laugh. In an annoying little singsong, she said, "I know what you're thinking."

I found I could speak after all. "Who?" If Maspero was right, and suddenly I found myself hoping he was, I'd never know. It would all be over for me by the time she called back the soul that would reshape me into something else utterly. *"Who?"*

Dalet's amusement reminded me that she liked to turn into owls. I bit back the desire to repeat myself further. She held up a woman's wedding ring. Perhaps our thoughts were linked, or perhaps I read the answer in her satisfaction.

Queen Andred. I thought of Maspero's gisant. I had never seen it. I would never see it now. In a way, I would become it.

It pleased Dalet to answer my question. "Only to please Julian. To advise Edward. To obey me." She continued with her preparations. "She was old when she died. So she'll come back old. But she was wise. She knew how the world works."

I saw the medal Dalet wore. The siege medal, the real one, which Maspero had forged for Julian. My copy was lost, merged into the metal of the crown that I had reforged for Rigo and the prince-bishop. Our army scattered, our battle lost, at last it occurred to me to wonder what had become of the prince-bishop. How had she come by the coronet?

Dalet finished her ring of sand. I rolled back to look up at the sky. Sunrise was not far off. She didn't seem to be in any hurry. Against the deep blue I could just make out shapes moving overhead. Birds? Perhaps not.

Strange the way the memory works. I heard myself praying aloud. It wasn't mere repetition of comforting words, either. This was real prayer, the burning kind, sincere as a child's, eager to strike a bargain.

"Stop that." Dalet looked as if she wanted to kick me, but she didn't cross the sand to do it. If she did something to stop me speaking, it didn't work. The words kept bubbling out of me like water from a spring. "Be quiet."

I tried to keep my eyes on the sky behind the birds. Or whatever they were. If I were to be cast out of my body to wander with those lost things, it would happen no matter what. Passionate prayer wouldn't hurt my chances.

Dalet looked cross. "I can't stand that noise." She made a rude gesture in my direction, and my voice dried to nothing again. I kept on shaping the words of my prayer despite my silence.

Dalet began her necromantic ritual. It sounded like a nasal drone to me, but I could feel, under my leaping heartbeats, the power there within her.

It was a ritual of order and severity. I sensed the shape of it coming and going all around me, and I could sense Dalet's power, like a thunderstorm gathering, behind the shape of the ritual. It would be like sinking into the mud, once the power closed in on me. I would know nothing more than the eternal coldness of the earth.

My prayers faded away, not merely from my lips but from my thoughts as well. It was all a lie. Even if it was truth for some, there was no truth in it for me. Why should there be? My sins were too numerous to count. I was as bad as any sinner had ever been, and worse than that, I was silly. The vanity, the absolute laughable vanity of it, of trying to make what I could feel, what I could think, into something that had value.

My mortification burned until I was half glad of the chill mud beneath me. I hoped gold had no memory. I knew mud had no memory. I was counting on it. I welcomed the oblivion to come. Let the earth swallow me.

The last sin in my long litany: despair. It weighed me down, pressed me into the earth. Dalet was calling the queen, calling Andred the Fair back into the world she had known so well.

From a distance, I heard. But I didn't care. I felt nothing. I could do nothing. My whole life, I had done nothing. Or worse than nothing—I had tried to do something and I had failed. Every work of mine was marred, every single thing that I had put my hand to. Except the circle I had chalked on Madame Carriera's floor.

What was Adam before the creation? Dust. The dust we all return to. What was there, that day in Madame Carriera's house, but her stone floor, her bit of chalk and my bit of dust, my hand? Something more was there too, but what? The voice that bade me draw? The idea of a circle? The need to make the mark, to divide the world into order and disorder, dark and light?

No matter what it was, no matter where it came from, that which made creation necessary was in the world before I was, and it would remain in the world after I left. No matter if my ears were stopped, someone else would hear it. Another circle would be drawn, perfection from the dust.

But my ears were not stopped yet. The world was far away, but I was in it still. I opened my eyes, and the sky was there, deep above me. There was no breeze. No clouds. Only the dark flecks that wheeled and soared against the blue.

My heart beat in my ears, steady as the tempo of Dalet's incantation. I could feel the power of that incantation weighing upon me. Part of the power was from the siege medal. Part of the power was from the coronet I'd made out of Maspero's votive crown. It was not just the blood that had been employed in Maspero's casting that made her magic strong. It was the power of his invention, his idea, his design. My work was weak by comparison, a pale copy of his, a mere thread of gold in the base metal that replaced the citadel he'd crafted. But my work was mine. Part of Dalet's power derived from the crown she had stolen—the crown that bore my mark.

It was easy to think in circles, lying there looking up. The wheeling shapes circled us. Dalet's voice circled me. I thought with longing of the mindless ease with which I'd achieved that chalk circle the first day. One day I would know so much of my art that I could forget it all and draw again, close the ring in perfection. The thought came to me with such gentleness that I could not tell from where it came, within me or without. It came, and I could not tell if was realization or resolution. *I will make something.*

I felt the cold again. The mud was my bed. The sky was all the blanket I had. The sun cleared the horizon, and I prayed.

The words of Dalet's incantation rode the tempo she set, deliberately slow and growing slower. The hammer of my heartbeat in my ears grew as I prayed. As I felt the cold anew, shivering racked me. The tempo faltered, not just in my ears but in the outer world. Dalet drew more deeply on the sources she had mastered, yet her incantation grew uneven in tone and measure. Her voice wavered. Her concentration intensified. As she drew on her sources, the power wavered, shivered. She steadied it and went on.

Dalet had called me, using the power of my work, and drawn me to her. I had left the horses at the river's edge and followed her summons, step by step, the rest of the day and all night long.

I had left the horses at the river's edge, but Tig had not. He had followed me doggedly until nightfall and picked up the trail again, now with the horses rested, at the earliest opportunity.

I saw him slip near. I remembered the fight with Istvan on the night the king returned. Tig could not fight like Istvan. I knew that he could never overcome her. If she had sentries posted, he had eluded them, well and good. But Dalet was even stronger now, and she would no longer need to flee.

Tig glanced about, then looked to his left. My range of vision was limited. I could not see what or who he was watching. Yet something in his posture warned me that he was waiting for a signal. For no reason in the world, I was sure that the signal was to be from Ludovic.

Bad enough Tig was stalking Dalet. The unreasoning fear that Ludovic was with him made my heart jerk and my throat tighten. Whoever it was, it was bad enough. Let it not be Ludo.

Dalet's chant faltered, resumed at an increased pace, then wavered and stopped. She looked around, not impatient at the interruption, merely curious. She saw whoever Tig was watching and she smiled. "Time enough," she said. "I'll finish . . ."

Tig shot her in the back with my pistol.

She fell without a word.

I strained to look. When I saw Ludovic join Tig in his wary inspection of the body, I relaxed back into my mud. Overhead the sky was clear blue. Nothing wheeling any more.

Tig untied me. At first I was as useless as if I were still bound. Cold and caked with mud, I was helpless. With a combination of scolding and what sounded to me like clucking, Tig helped me to my feet and propped me there.

If ever I complained at traveling with the luggage, the luggage was well revenged. To be borne away to safety was my only desire.

This desire was not fulfilled. Far from it. Tig urged me over to the mortal remains of that bitch Dalet. Without any consideration whatsoever, he urged me to remove the crown. Once I had pawed it aside, he covered it with a cloth and tied it in a bundle.

"Orders," he told me.

At Tig's insistence, I climbed up into the saddle of a horse held ready for me by another soldier, one of half a dozen attending us. As my head cleared, I looked around and realized that Ludovic Nallaneen was not with us. The figure to which Tig had shown such deference turned out to be Istvan, who was looking more battered than I'd ever seen him. He carried Ludo's sword, its blade too foul to sheathe. The harvest that blade had reaped was all around us, men of Dalet's escort, slain.

Tig followed my addled look with ease. "No one stays to fight him any longer."

"They stayed," I said. I meant Dalet's men. My voice was very small, but it was mine again.

"She made them." Tig tied the bundled crown to my saddle and mounted his own horse.

I looked back as Tig took my reins. Dalet, forbidding still, lay prone in the mud, attended even there by her escort. "Shouldn't we do something? Bury her?"

"She's dead. That will have to do. Bad luck to touch her, even."

"You made me touch her."

"Only to get back what she stole. You had the right to get it back. Anyway, if there is bad luck for you, Rigo will set you right."

"Where is he?"

"Back with the captain. The prince-bishop is dead. Killed. The army has scattered. We're headed back to the captain, if we can get there. Rigo will use the crown to free the king."

"Dalet's dead. Won't that free him?"

"Not from Red Ned. Not without help."

"I thought Ludo was with you. I couldn't see very well." Truth to tell, though my vision had cleared, my wits were still scattered. I hung on and let Tig lead me. The world folded in until it consisted of nothing more than coldness and the aches in my back, my neck, and my knees. The mud dried into a crust that weighed me down like armor. I wanted to be clean and dry and warm in my own bed in Giltspur Street, or better yet back home in Neven, or even just to be allowed to sit on the ground and be still for one clear moment, without fear for myself or my friends.

Istvan swept us with him, swept us on. We had slain Dalet, Red Ned's necromancer, but we did not exult in our victory. We rode hard in desperate silence, as if we were fleeing trouble instead of riding toward safety, if one could find any in a remnant of a battered army.

I cried a little, sniveling to myself as I jolted along. No one noticed. After my eyes grew sticky and my nose stopped up, my sobs trailed away. What was there to cry over, after all? An ache or two and a trifling weariness? I was alive. Not buried in mud. Merely covered with it.

NINETEEN

(In which I keep vigil.)

I expected, as much as I expected anything given how little I understood of what little Tig explained, that we would travel to where Ludovic and the others waited for us, and once there, we would stop. I was cheered by the thought of stopping, sustained by it. The dearest wish of my heart was to get off my horse, even if I had to fall off it like a sack of turnips, and land once more in the mud.

We did not stop, just as Ludovic and his men had not been waiting for us. They had been on the move, and we continued our travels as we met, merged, and formed a larger group.

I looked up from the pommel of my saddle and realized Ludovic was riding beside me. I blinked at him, and said as clearly as I could, "Where are we?"

"Nearly to the Folliard Bridge. We've got to beat them there, or they'll cross the river before us."

"Oh."

"It's going to be close. We've had to fight as we run. Fortunately Istvan's with us now, and none of the troops we cross paths with want to risk engaging him. Lucky for us. There are so many sides fighting now, it's hard to tell who is for us and who is against us."

"Oh."

Ludovic took pity on me. "The king is dead."

I thought of Julian as I'd seen him last, dressed in battle gear, a puppet in Dalet's keeping. My thoughts must have shown in my face, despite the mud.

"No," Ludovic said, "The real king. Corin. That's what we're fighting over now. Red Ned has as much right as anyone to the throne now the king is finally dead and the prince-bishop has been killed."

"Julian's not dead?"

"No. Though for all I know, he can't die, any more than Istvan can."

Ludovic rode beside me in silence until a signal came from the vanguard that he was needed. Before he spurred ahead, he said, "Don't look so tragic. We won't keep this pace much longer. We'll have to stop soon." At my look of piteous gratitude, all he did was smile and add, "To rest the horses."

We did stop eventually, and Ludovic spoke true, it was to rest the horses. Once they were watered, we climbed a grassy ridge and let them graze, unsaddled, in a picket line along the shoulder of the hill. Sentinels kept watch. The countryside stretched out below us seemed empty, nearly peaceful.

While I lay staring up into the sky, head pillowed on my saddle, wondering if I would live out the day, Tig joined me. "They want to see you."

"I'm right here."

"They want to talk to you."

"Send them over."

"You're to come with me."

I made a noise. It wasn't very rude, because I couldn't spare much energy to put into it, but it got the idea across.

"I'll give them the message."

When Tig left me alone, I looked at the sky again. We were halfway through a fine day. There were large white clouds sailing across the blue, the puffy kind shaped like beehives. Back home in Neven, they say bees come from Paradise. If you are a very good person, when you die, the bees come to take your soul with them to Paradise, so you can't get lost. I wondered if I would be a good enough person, by the time I died, for the bees to bother about. I didn't think so. In truth, the thought of more traveling, even to Paradise, made me feel tired. So I closed my eyes and let the clouds sail on without me.

The horses must have been given an unusually long rest, for the sun was well down the sky by the time Tig woke me. "Captain says you're to drink this." He handed over a small unstoppered flask.

I sat up and sniffed at it warily. Whiskey. Good whiskey. I drained the flask and handed it back. "Thanks. Now how about helping me up?"

Leverage is a marvelous thing. I made it. In the process I noticed that Tig's face was still marked by his sleep. Faint on the skin was the imprint left by the fold of his sleeve where he'd rested cheek on arm. "Got some rest yourself, I see." He rubbed his face briskly when he realized what I meant. I tried to brush some of the debris off my clothing but gave up. The mud was dry now. As I moved, the stiffened fabric made a faint sound, not a rustle, yet not quite a scrape either. I picked up the crown in its dirty cloth and tucked it under my arm.

Ludovic said, "Finally," when I joined him. He was with Istvan, and while I'd been asleep others must have joined us, for there were many more in our party than I remembered. One of the men stood at Ludovic's elbow, staring at me. It took me a long affronted moment to realize that the man was Rigo, dressed most soldierly and nearly as muddy as I.

"Hello," I said.

"You have the crown?" Rigo held out his hands impatiently.

I looked at him with wonderment. Weary he was, clearly. Disturbed by matters I could not hope to comprehend. Yet no greeting? No acknowledgment at all? "Tig must have told you already."

"He did. Give it here."

I marveled, seeing that urgency, that they hadn't taken it from me

while I slept. Yet perhaps they couldn't. Perhaps there was more to
Tig's wild talk of bad luck than I knew. "What do you want it for?"

"To free the king, of course. There's no time to explain fully."

"Look, I made it. Right? And I took it back from Dalet when Tig
wouldn't touch it. If we are in such a hurry, why didn't you just take
it?"

Visibly strained by the patience he forced into his voice and expression, Rigo said, "It must be given freely."

"I didn't exactly get it that way. Will that make a difference? What
are you going to do?"

"Dalet used trinkets to bind Julian to her will. Her will is no more.
Still, Julian is linked to her."

"What will you do with the crown if I give it up? How can you
loose a bond Dalet forged?"

"First we must free Julian from Edward of Ardres. Using the bond,
I shall call Julian to us."

I looked around. "Who is us?"

"We are," said Ludovic, as if I were deaf. I nearly was deafened,
the way he said it.

"Are we going to be enough to fight off Red Ned? He isn't just
going to let Julian leave."

Istvan said, "We're enough."

I waited for Rigo to say something, and when he didn't, I prompted
him. "What will you do when Julian is safe? Will you recast the crown
again?"

Rigo shook his head. "We'll get him back first, and then we'll see."

"Will we?" I turned to Istvan. If anyone held Julian's welfare more
dearly than his own, it was Istvan. "You believe them?"

"I believe that we must free Julian from Red Ned. We have the
high ground here. We can do it."

For the first time I realized that our hill commanded the rolling
landscape in every direction. We were not very high, but we were most
excellently strategic.

"And then? When Julian is free of Red Ned, will he be free of
Dalet? Of Ludovic? Of any of us?"

"If he were free of everyone but me, I would be well content," said Istvan. "Courage, child. Give Rigo your crown."

I obeyed.

On a sunlit afternoon, with no artifice, and only his own skill and my handiwork to aid him, Rigo set to work crafting his enchantment. We stood in a ring around him, as silent and as motionless as we could manage, while he cast his spell in place of Dalet's. The sun moved down the sky and our shadows had grown long before Rigo finished. When he did, there was a space of pure stillness, filled only by the sound of the breeze in the high grass. Then Tig pointed, and we all turned to look. Riders on the horizon.

"Here they come," said Istvan, and he smiled.

There weren't very many of them. They weren't trying to restrain the king. They rode with him, it seemed, and when he lifted a hand and drew rein, they drew rein with him.

I could feel the tenor of Rigo's spell alter and intensify. He used Dalet's magic to beckon Julian. "But he's coming," I found myself protesting. "He's right there. We can just give him the crown. You needn't make him come kneel at your feet." I looked hard at Rigo. The spell was clear to me now, the nature of the call he used. I could read the intention as I had felt the urgency in the recruiting spell.

No mere urging, this. Rigo compelled Julian to come, summoned him with the coronet I'd made to help free him from Dalet's sway. The act of creation had altered something inside me so that I could understand the use to which Rigo put it.

In the name of every good cause ever thought of, Rigo was using my work to force the king to join us. I'd made it, and Rigo had turned it over to the prince-bishop, for the help of his army. Dalet took it from the prince-bishop, added it to her magpie collection of jewelry and talismans, and used it to increase her own power. Used my work.

I'd taken it back from Dalet and rendered it up to Rigo willingly, and here he was, summoning Julian back to some fresh bondage. "That's not what it's for," I said. "It's supposed to free him."

Rigo ignored me, but Ludovic answered. "Free him from what?

From life? It can't be done. Dalet improved on her spell after Istvan. Istvan can be distracted by the damage when he's hurt, even if he can't die. But Julian is invulnerable. Nothing hurts him. He can't be allowed to fall into enemy hands. The wit of Ulysses and the strength of Achilles, with more wisdom than Zeus himself. He's our true king."

I regarded Ludovic with wonder. "But Julian is real. And they don't look much like enemies right now." The men with the king had made a protective little knot at his heels and were eying us nervously. "Are you worried that Red Ned will come and catch us all?"

"That would be worth a few worries," Ludovic admitted, "but all reports suggest he's headed toward Aravis instead."

"Why are we here, then? Why aren't we on our way to Aravis?"

"The city can defend itself. We need the king. Whoever has Julian, the empire will follow."

"Whoever has Aravis, the empire will follow. Aravis is the empire," I said.

"Aravis will keep. First we need Julian."

"He's right there. Give him the crown yourself."

"He must come to us."

"He isn't coming any closer." If Julian could feel the spell as I could, I didn't blame him. It pounded behind my eyes like a headache. Whatever Rigo's spell had started out to be, it had dwindled to this simple monotonous call.

"Give it time."

I realized Istvan was at my side. He was not pleased. "Enough." He put out his hand to Rigo, but the spell kept him off. "Stop it."

With deep indignation, I realized he was talking to me. "I'm not doing anything."

"Stop it."

This time I understood him. I reached for Rigo, and there was nothing to prevent me. I took the crown away from him as if it were a toy. "This isn't yours," I reminded him. As I stepped back, the cessation of the spell was wonderful, silence after long senseless noise.

Istvan drew me back, slipped between me and their protests. "Saddle two horses," he told me.

I put my hand through the crown, ran it up my arm to hold it securely. When I turned, Tig was there, three horses saddled.

"I'm going with you."

I smiled at him. "Ludovic won't like that."

"No."

Istvan backed toward us. Tig put me in the saddle and held Istvan's horse while he mounted. He was on his own horse before Ludovic had finished countering his old orders.

Rigo was standing, empty-handed, in the dwindling circle of his spell. I could feel the remnants of it dissipating, through the fading tingle on my arm. He lifted his hands as I looked back. I blinked at the open joy in his expression. No anger there, only joy at the end of that monotonous call. I had freed someone already, it seemed.

I lifted my hand to bid him farewell and felt the weight of the crown shift against me. Arm crooked and held carefully to my side, I rode with Tig and Istvan to join Julian.

Julian's men obeyed him and let us through. "They're coming," Istvan warned, as we joined Julian. "We should go."

"We should." Julian held out his hands to accept the coronet from me. There was no ceremony in it. The weight of the crown seemed to hold a living warmth, as if it went eagerly to its owner. Julian set it on his own head and something eased as he straightened in his saddle.

This close, I could see that Ludovic had been wrong. Julian was not invulnerable. The harm he'd taken on his way to this moment was not physical, though his battered clothes and gear told of a considerable struggle. But in his eyes was old pain as well as fresh, and I knew that whatever Dalet had done with her spell, the price of his physical safety was exacted in less tangible ways.

"Time to go," said Julian.

Istvan nodded. The pair of them ignored the rest of us, and when they rode, we followed without orders, Tig and I at their heels and the ragtag band of men accompanying the king after us. After us came Ludovic and his men, I assumed. We made a brave procession. I wondered, as we turned north of east, away from the direction of Aravis, where on earth we were going.

*　　　*　　　*

We rode the sun down, and by dusk we'd reached the Folliard Bridge. The river held the day longer than the hills around us did, and its surface gave back the light of the autumn sky. Istvan led us down to the water, drew rein, and dismounted. "Here," he said, and dropped to sit cross-legged near the spot where I had found him first. "Just here."

Julian joined him. The rest of us drew back. Even back with the others, I could feel the stirring of expectation, see it in the way they sat. They were waiting.

"Getting dark. Best see to the horses." There was nothing else to do. I helped Tig and the others as we settled in for the night. In the camp we made there was firelight and soft conversation, even laughter. In the darkness beside the river, there was only silence as Istvan and Julian kept their vigil.

In time the moon rose, saffron pale, not far past the full. The shadows deepened.

If Ludovic, Rigo, and the rest had started after us, they had not come so far. We were a little knot of travelers, alone between the river and our picket lines, clustered by our fire, waiting for the light.

I did as Tig did, and kept my back to the fire. It was easy to look out into the night, to keep my night vision clear, as easy as ignoring the soft murmurs of someone else's conversation. I didn't want to talk. I didn't want to listen. I wanted to fix the scene in my memory, beyond all chance of misremembrance. Just so, the moon on the water. Just so, the darkness and deeper darkness beneath the arches of the bridge.

This was how I would paint Julian crowned. Not the way I'd handed the crown across to him, as prosaic as passing a ginger biscuit. A nightscape, with only the light of the moon to show the scene. A few men at arms, not spruce warriors, but real soldiers, well battered by the work they'd done on the king's behalf, holding torches. Perhaps someone would hold a candle, shielding the flame from the breeze with his hand. I could see exactly how I'd paint that hand, with the candle's flame not shown, yet the light burning at the edges of his hand, his frayed cuff, illuminating the wonder in his face as he watched the crowning of the true king.

Istvan would crown him, I decided. No, better that he should offer the crown, let Julian crown himself as he had done. The truth, above all.

Time seemed to withdraw. Stars rolled their slow way west, and the moon walked among them. We were waiting for Istvan and Julian, and they were waiting for something we could not guess.

I blinked into the darkness and spun myself promises of the picture I would paint. It would be a fit companion piece for Miriamne's adoration. My masterpiece. Mine.

There were stars in the water. I realized the moon had gone. Set already? No light in the east to hint at morning coming. Our little fire had burned past embers to ash. There were only stars, filling the sky above us, reflected in the water before us.

I never saw such stars. Never so many, never so large, with the Milky Way spanning the vault over us like another river, a remnant of light that required true darkness to appreciate. More and yet more, the longer I looked. It came to me that I was seeing many more stars reflected in the river.

The river was rising. There was the edge, where the reflected sky gave way to perfect darkness, hardly eight feet from where I sat. Where the water's edge had been, water moved, the silent river coming to meet the trees behind us.

I could still see Istvan and Julian, standing now. They were side by side, knee-deep in the water. Only the coronet the king wore gave back the starlight. All the rest was shadow.

I saw the gleam of the crown change as Julian turned his head. He had glanced at us, huddled in wondering silence on the shore. But then, as I stared, eyes burning to see better, he went back to gazing upstream. Waiting.

I looked north. I could, if I dared, find a better point of vantage from the bridge. But I dared not walk on that span, not that night. What Julian and Istvan could wait to see, I would abide.

Perfect silence in the night, even the sounds of the river hushed for the occasion. I could smell autumn: dried grass, the woods behind us, the lingering tang of the wood smoke from our fire, and mud. The chill of the night lay on my skin, burning the tip of my nose and my fingers' ends with cold, the way I'd imagined my painted candle flame would edge that hand with light.

The breeze picked up. It was out of the north, and with it came the sound of leaves rustling, as if a forest came down to us, unseen. I could smell the wind. I could nearly taste it.

With that sound and that scent as herald, the little ship sailed from beneath the central arch of the Folliard Bridge. It had a sail that gave back the starlight, pale, but no color to it, and as we watched, the set of the sail changed, and the ship angled toward us.

But not toward us, Tig and me and the rest, huddled awestruck in the mud. Toward Julian and Istvan, waiting as the river came inching higher, over their boot tops, over their knees. Or else they were moving out, into the current, and the water climbed as they went deeper.

No one visible at the helm, but the little ship came about, a hesitation against the current, no more. With a commonplace sound, the crumple of stiff fabric, the sail dropped, and in that strange starlight we could see a woman aboard.

She was an old woman, but she held herself straight. She wore a crown set with gems, no faceted sparklers, but large deep jewels, flattened and polished like enamels, burning with color. She handled the lines and cables with ease, and her hands were very white as she held them out to welcome Julian and Istvan.

"Andred," said Julian, and he let Istvan lift him a little so that she could reach down and help him clamber aboard.

It was most unkingly, that clambering, but Julian came aboard, and together he and Andred reached down for Istvan.

Istvan hesitated, then unbuckled the sheath of Ludovic's two-handed sword. Sword and scabbard in hand, he turned back to shore, looking for someone to take it from him.

I rose and came forward, in reverent silence. The water came half-way up my thighs as I waded out to him. It was only water, pure common river, despite the stars. Istvan gave Ludovic's sword to me, and I held it to my breast. It was heavy, but it was not dead weight. Such was the balance of the weapon, it seemed to have its own kind of life, and it seemed to welcome my arms around it as I waded back to shore.

No word of thanks from Istvan, no farewell. He turned from me without a word, all his attention on Andred and Julian. Istvan put his hands up, one to each, and when they drew him in, he came as a bird comes to the branch it has chosen. With ease, he folded himself aboard, and I saw his arms go round them both.

The river was still rising and the leaves were still rustling as the pale sail ran up the mast again. They jibbed, not gracefully, and caught the wind. They sailed away and left us there with only the wind and the water and the light of the stars to comfort us where we huddled on the shore.

In the morning there was nothing to see, only the bridge and above the waterline a wide margin of pungent mud that hadn't been there the day before.

There was little to say. No amount of arguing would change the river. Only time would dry the mud. And the stars, I felt sure, would never burn that way again.

Dalet had summoned three people back to life. The third had been late arriving and had borne the others back with her. That was all.

TWENTY

(In which I conclude my travels.)

Ludovic and his men, Rigo with them, joined us at the river as the sun was rising. Our fire had burned low and our spirits with it. Only Tig was awake to welcome them as they surrounded our makeshift camp.

At Tig's prodding, I rose and limped forward to meet Ludo. I held the two-handed sword high in my arms, as carefully as I would hold a baby. I did not wish to let the sword belt slip and trail in the mud. Tig stayed close behind me, one pace to the left and one behind.

In silence, Ludovic dismounted and took the sword and scabbard from me. He held it lovingly, drew the sword to check its condition, then ran it safely into its sheath again. With ease, he put the belt and harness on and shrugged the sword into its familiar position, hilt over his shoulder. "I thank you. And now, I'm almost afraid to ask. Where's Julian? Where's Istvan?"

"The old queen came and took them away," said Tig, before I could find an answer. "She sailed away with them."

"What old queen?" demanded Ludo.

I put my hand on his sleeve. "Queen Andred. Dalet had called her back, but Tig killed Dalet before Andred arrived. She took the long way, I expect."

"She came because she wanted to," said Tig. "They were glad to go with her."

"Where did they go?"

"Downriver and away in the darkness. There's no following the way they went," I told Ludo.

"You've gone mad. Someone dropped a net and came away with Istvan and the king in their catch, while you stood there and let them. Red Ned is on his way to Aravis, and there's no one left to stop him."

"There's everyone in Aravis." I ticked off fingers. "There's whoever is going to succeed the old king. There's whoever is going to succeed the prince-bishop. There's the troops still stationed in the city. There's you and all these people you seem to have with you. When did you get the guns back?"

"Artillery, Hail. That's artillery. They've been on the high road, trying not to mire themselves any more than necessary. We picked them up yesterday. That's what slowed us down so you could get away. All these mythical people of yours seem very comforting in the abstract, but in truth, I don't think anyone left in the city is going to do anything without orders. And whoever is succeeding whom, they don't know who they are yet. So they can't issue orders. Am I making myself clear? No one in Aravis can be depended upon for anything."

"Well then, they won't be opening the gates just because Red Ned tells them to, will they?"

"You can't count on that. Who's left to hold the city, after all?" demanded Ludo.

"Everyone but us, really. All the guilds. No merchant worth his salt is going to give Red Ned a chance to do the year's inventory."

"All he has to do is wait them out."

"How, Ludo? They don't have this year's harvest in Ardres. He can raid for supplies, I suppose, but the city is sure to be able to hold out longer than he can."

Ludovic sighed. "If he takes the city, we still have Rigo. He might be able to help, I suppose."

"No," said Rigo. "I won't. I did what I had to on the prince-bishop's orders. I won't risk angering the wardens again. What's left is for you and your men to do. If Edward of Ardres has any of Dalet's work left to use, I will do my best to help. But the rest is mere use of force. I won't help you with that."

Ludovic looked harried. "Oh, hell. We'll bring the artillery on as fast as we can, but the city may have fallen by the time we get there. If it rains again, we'll be later still."

It didn't rain. The guns kept up with us perfectly well, and by the time we reached the city, the gates were still firmly closed against the raiders who were besieging Aravis.

On our way to Aravis, we met other remnants of the prince-bishop's army. The military hierarchy reasserted itself. Ludovic became a mere captain again, one officer of many.

Red Ned turned to meet our forces with relief. He couldn't have held his troops for long. They were too hungry to resist foraging for supplies.

I didn't see anything of the battle that broke the siege, for I was left back with the luggage again, without even Tig to keep an eye on me. It didn't matter. I'd seen too much fighting. It was bad enough having to listen to the roar of the guns, knowing the damage the fight inflicted.

Waiting with the baggage train suited me. I was tired. I'd been caught between the mud and the stars for too long. I didn't even want my notebook. I was tired of storing up the details of the world. It was time to sit in one place and let those details form a whole. I wanted to be clean in a clean place, where I could be left alone to work on my painting: Istvan and Andred and Julian, by firelight, by candlelight, and by starlight.

I was alone in the throng of camp followers, and that was fine with me. The way I felt, I'd be alone forever, even if I spent the rest of my life in a crowd.

By sundown, the day was won. Red Ned died under his battle standard, just after the best of his men died there too. The artillery ceased. In the silence afterward, there was a distant roaring, like the tide coming in, and all along the walls of the city we could see people shouting their approval. We were welcomed as heroes.

That didn't mean they opened the gates, however. The good folk of Aravis were much too sensible to welcome in an armed throng, however heroically we'd defended the city from Red Ned. After all, Aravis hadn't needed much defending. The siege had lasted scarcely two days.

After a long night of sending messages back and forth, the city and the army came to terms. In the morning they opened one gate for us, and we were welcomed home, quite harmlessly, to the city. It was a little like Twelfth Night revels, marching back in through the Shene gate. By the time I came through, most of the crowd had dispersed. There was still a holiday air about the streets and a festive degree of litter strewn about.

It was odd, walking in Giltspur Street with nowhere to go and nothing to do. I was on my own at last, not even Tig to shadow me. Alone, with no one and nothing to stop me doing whatever I pleased.

I knocked at the door of Madame Carriera's house. The persuasion of the mind has very little influence on the heart, and none at all on the pit of the stomach. As I knocked, my heart ached as if I had run five miles. My stomach twisted. My spirits rose and fell like waves on the river.

Saskia let me in. Her welcome was friendly, but I was distracted by my dread of the interview to come. "I must see Madame Carriera. If she will permit it."

Saskia was bewildered. "What about your father? What about Amyas? They'll be so happy you're back safe."

"I must speak to Madame Carriera first."

"Very well. Wait here."

After what seemed like a long time, Saskia brought me to Madame Carriera's salon. After another wait, Madame Carriera came down in a sweep of stiff black skirts. "Have you come to apologize? Or to beg me to take you back?"

My heart dived deeper than I had ever known it to go. I hadn't realized how much I'd hoped for a welcome, even as I'd braced myself for rejection. Dismay took all my stratagems away, and only honesty remained. "Madame Carriera," I said, as I sank down before her on the well-scrubbed floor, "I am here, if you permit, to resume my studies. Will you teach me to be an artist?"

Madame Carriera stopped frowning, seated herself, and waved me to a chair opposite her. "Oh, get up, girl. This isn't a masque, so stop playacting. Why should I take you back? You've done nothing but inconvenience me."

I sat carefully on the edge of the chair. It was highly polished lacquer, spindly and old, and felt as if it would fold under me like a trap. "I don't know why you should. But I'll work hard. I won't run away again."

"It's easy to promise now. What will you say when some new distraction catches your fancy? You gave up your career for the last one. And you must know, you had some promise."

Had. I felt my heart freeze at the word. Past tense. Was it all gone for ever? Half tasted, never enjoyed? I told myself sternly that nothing had changed. I had nothing to lose by persisting. "At Twelfth Night, when the mummers come masquing house to house, do you answer the door? Or do you let the laughter go past? Do you let the music fade away down the street and never think of following it?"

I had to blink then, but it was already too late. Fat tears splashed down and stained my bodice. I cleared my throat and pretended I didn't notice. I knew if I said one more word, my voice would start to shake. And I couldn't think of one more word to say. So I closed my lips tight and tried to steady my breathing. A particularly large teardrop slid off the tip of my nose and made a mark on the arm of my chair. I rubbed at the lacquer with my sleeve and only succeeded in smudging the finish.

Madame Carriera sighed deeply. "This was the sort of thing I dreaded when I took you on. I thought there would be household breakage and stubbed toes. I was right. You are an annoying creature. But you are not wholly without merit. Do you think I'd let someone else have the credit if you prove successful? Not likely." She rose, smoothed her skirts, and studied me gravely for a long minute. "Blow your nose, child. I think we understand each other better than I thought. After all, I always let the mummers in."

I finished my studies four years later. My masterpiece, *When the King Comes Home*, was accepted by the guild, and I was welcomed to their ranks. In the fifty years since, I have quarreled with them many times, but it was good to be welcomed properly to the fellowship first. I remember with pride and pleasure my first dinner at the guild hall, where I fell out with Gabriel over the proper way to bind a hog bristle brush.

Gabriel died a rich man ten years later, knocked down a flight of stairs in a drunken argument over the terms of a commission.

Saskia entered the guild soon after my return to Madame Carriera's workshop. Her career flourished, and she trained her apprentices wisely and well.

Piers not only made a success of himself in Aravis, he traveled to Vienna and Rome and eventually settled in Venice, where his artistic gifts and hard work earned all the accolades due him.

Tig never spoke of that night we spent by the Folliard Bridge, the night Andred came for Julian and Istvan. I have spoken of it with Ludo. He had spent more time than I with Istvan. He listened harder and had the wit to ask more questions. Together we puzzled over the events surrounding Julian's return.

If Maspero's alchemy worked upon his art to put his theories into practice, perhaps that is why the ring recovered from Andred's grave could summon Istvan back. Certainly that is why the siege medal cast with his blood could summon Julian back. But why did Andred's wedding ring, which Maspero had no hand in making, serve to summon Andred back?

More than that, Andred was buried with all the proper rites. She should have been safe from any necromancy. Yet she returned at Dalet's command. Unless Dalet did not command. Perhaps Andred's return was spurred by Julian's plight. Perhaps she came to rescue Julian and Istvan as Julian once came to rescue Istvan and Andred.

With Madame Carriera's permission, I offered my help to Daniel in the hunt for Maspero's missing works. The archivists made inquiries in Ardres, but what little might have been left behind by Dalet was lost in the ruin of Red Ned's defeat. Whatever wisdom Maspero might have recorded has been lost for good.

My brother Amyas settled in Aravis. It was easier for my father to have someone in the city to manage our wool transactions. Amyas soon established that the demand for earth of cullen warranted a steady trade, which we were well able to supply from Neven. Saskia married him, which was another source of pride and pleasure to me, and of course to Amyas as well.

I have an atelier of my own, students even, though it drives me mad when a student ignores my advice. This should not be, as I hardly ever took any advice myself, but I can't help it.

I have been happy to work as much as I can and to stay out of trouble, but it grows harder by the year. The church never did name a successor to the prince-bishop, and there was no clear heir to the throne of Lidia. Aravis remained strong, but the outlying regions fell away. Haydock, Cenedwine, and Galazon broke away. Soon there was nothing to show there had ever been an empire except the size of the taxes we pay.

Aravis itself is strong, but the cost of its strength has been some of its beauty. No longer do we have a rivalry of patrons who vie to commission new art and sponsor fresh entertainments. Now we have mend and make do, somber clothes, and long faces. The world's all ocher and no orpiment.

Sometimes I think I should travel, see what's beyond Aravis. Go to Vienna, perhaps. Then I think, no. I have traveled quite enough, walked plenty of miles, ridden too hard, and been rained on far too often. What I am, I carry with me. Things would look no different in Vienna if I went there with a discontented heart.

Let the young take a turn, not that they seem inclined to do much but complain and put their noses in other people's business. No life in them, I sometimes think. They seem to have no ideas. We had more ideas than we knew what to do with.

I intend to live in Aravis and will probably die here too. My brothers invite me home to Neven, but they seem glad when I decline. My nephews or nieces come, singly and in bunches, to stay with me. Now they have grown children of their own to make the journey. I always make sure they see a bit of the world while they visit, but Amyas has views of his own on that subject.

Ludovic's son came to see me once, a charming lad with a great look of the old boy about him. Once a month or so, someone from Tig's family pays a call, as if I'll wither away to nothing without their regular disapproval.

Life is short, as the wisdom of the ages has it, but fortunately art is long. I don't expect to understand much more of either than I already do. I was born with what wisdom I have, and the many years that I have lived served only to make the scantiness of that wisdom more evident. Though I do seem to do better than most people.

When my life is at an end and I am at heaven's gate, I hope to represent myself fairly. I don't expect a swarm of bees to lead me there. I have tried to do right as I've seen it, but in truth there are few of my sins I'd have done without. If honest repentance is required, St. Peter will turn me away. Fair enough.

If heaven is too much to ask, I will wander downward to the circle of hell appointed me. I hope the journey will be comfortable. No need for haste, as I have eternity to make my way. I intend to go slowly. As I make that last venture, I will keep watch. The way will be crowded with people, but I have a good eye for faces. I will look for Istvan, for Andred, and for Julian. They may be safely in heaven. I hope they are. All the same, I will watch for them, on the chance they've gone not to Paradise, but to a well-deserved Elysium.